HOLLYWOOD RAJ

THE RADFORD SAGA

CHARLES DENNIS

VINGSBO PRESS
LOS ANGELES

Also by Charles Dennis

BALM OF ANGELS
THE MAGIKER
GIVEN THE EVIDENCE
GIVEN THE CRIME
SHAR-LI
THE DEALMAKERS
BONFIRE
A DIVINE CASE OF MURDER
THE PERIWINKLE ASSAULT
THIS WAR IS CLOSED UNTIL SPRING
SOMEBODY JUST GRABBED ANNIE!
THE NEXT-TO-LAST TRAIN RIDE
STONED COLD SOLDIER

In memory of Christopher Plummer and Edward Hardwicke, whose cousin and father were charter members of the Hollywood Raj

Oh what a tangled web we weave,
When first we practise to deceive!

- Sir Walter Scott

FOREWORD

In the six years since this book was first published, the world has gone through some dramatic and frightening changes the present American public would never have thought possible.

Readers of the first edition were startled to discover the Hollywood studios in the 1930s submitted their movies to Los Angeles-based German consul, Georg Gyssling, for his review. The moguls dutifully followed Gyssling's censorship notes, and removed anything that might offend Hitler and the Nazi Party. This remorseless toadying was in fear of losing the lucrative German movie market. Seventy years later, history would repeat itself when the modern Hollywood studios removed any scenes that might offend the even larger Chinese market.

Ninety years ago, Sinclair Lewis wrote a cautionary novel called *It Can't Happen Here*. A hugely popular writer in the 1920s (*Elmer Gantry, Babbit,* and *Dodsworth*) and the first American author to win the Nobel Prize in Literature, Sinclair Lewis upset the apple cart of American complacency targeting middle-class values with his searing wit and graphic descriptions.

Seeing the global threat of fascism and the potential for an American dictator to take power and destroy democracy like Hitler did in Germany, he created Buzz Windrip, a populist politician, who becomes President of the United States. Windrip was inspired by Louisiana's rabble-rousing governor, Huey Long, who was planning a 1936 run for the presidency in the hopes of ousting Franklin Roosevelt. Long was assassinated in 1935 a few months before Lewis's novel was published.

MGM acquired the film rights to *It Can't Happen Here* for a hefty $200,000. Joe Breen, the antisemitic head of the Motion Picture Production Code, advised Louis B. Mayer that the movie would alienate the German and Italian governments and any future box office revenues. He told him to cancel the production. Mayer followed Breen's advice, bit the bullet, took a $200 K hit, and canceled plans for the movie.

Flash forward ninety years: Donald Trump – legitimately voted out of office in 2020 - inspired an insurrection urging his followers to storm the Capitol Building. It is a scene reminiscent of Kristellnacht. In other moves straight out of Hitler's playbook, Trump continues to hold mass rallies for the right-wing disenfranchised where he promotes The Big Lie – it was he who won the election and not Joe Biden. He mocks liberals, the handicapped and immigrants. He preaches his own version of racial purity, Make America Great Again. The country is torn apart.

It can't happen here? It is happening. Interestingly, the Trump presidency created a new interest in Sinclair Lewis's 90-year-old novel and *It Can't Happen Here* appeared on Amazon's list of bestsellers.

When I wrote *Hollywood Raj* six years ago, it was never meant to be a cautionary tale. It is being published once again not only as entertainment but as a warning that **it can happen here!** America, beware!

Charles Dennis
El Rancho Del Navitas
Shadow Hills, California
February 5, 2024

Table of Contents

THE MUSTACHE HAS TO GO

The winding mountain road was engulfed by an impenetrable fog. Despite almost zero visibility, the chauffeur behind the wheel of the Mercedes sped along the treacherous terrain as if he were competing in the Tour de France.

"I say," said Richard Ives-Curtis, who leaned forward from the back seat and tapped the man on the shoulder. "Do you think you might slow down a bit?" It was late September 1938. The Englishman had been traveling all day: by plane from London to Munich, then by train to Berchtesgaden. Contrary to ardent Nazi propaganda, the trains did not always run on time. Ives-Curtis's was two hours late. It was almost dark when he climbed into the waiting limousine for the last leg of his journey to Obersalzberg.

"*Ja, ja,*" replied the chauffeur. "*Berghof.*" The man's breath reeked of some local pilsener.

"Bloody hell!" Ives-Curtis spoke fluent German but dared not utter a word *auf deutsch* in the driver's presence. Instead, he stared out the window wondering just how close to the edge they were. There were no guard rails to prevent the vehicle tumbling hundreds of feet to a fiery finale. On such a foggy road as this, he had been captured twenty years earlier. Recaptured. How many times had Ives-Curtis escaped from the p.o.w. camp? And the disgruntled Krauts had brought him back every time.

"*Englischer?*" asked the chauffeur, interrupting his passenger's reverie.

"Yes." Ives-Curtis hastily translated. "*Ja.*"

"Chamberlain."

Dear God! Does he think I'm the Prime Minister? Is it possible the drunken lout's trying to assassinate me? Surely a bullet to the back of the head would be more affective and cost efficient than hurtling a Mercedes over the precipice.

The inebriated chauffeur turned around, flashed a smile displaying crooked, yellow teeth and pointed gleefully to the back seat.

"Chamberlain war dorten. Am letzte Woche."

Ah! The Prime Minister had been in the limo the previous week. Inaugurating his controversial shuttle diplomacy. Ives-Curtis, however, could display no knowledge of this to the drunken driver. Instead, the Englishman shrugged to convey an inability to understand a single word.

The wordless charade was interrupted by the Mercedes abruptly coming to a violent stop accompanied by an almost supernatural cry of pain from outside the vehicle. Ives-Curtis was thrown to the floor. When he managed to climb back onto the leather seat, he continued to hear the same horrific cries. For his part, the chauffeur was clutching the steering wheel and staring like a catatonic at the fog bound night.

"What happened?" asked Ives-Curtis. "What's going on?" He tapped the driver's shoulder, but the man said nothing in reply.

The chisel-featured, prematurely grey Englishman with piercing blue eyes emerged from the car and walked around to the front of the Mercedes. Under the beam of the headlamps, Ives-Curtis stared in shock at the sight of a three-hundred-pound wild boar with its tusks enmeshed in the grille work. The creature was writhing in agony and bleeding profusely all over the road. The Englishman darted back from the wounded beast. He remembered only too well a hunting incident from his youth when his Aunt Jessica's fiancé was fatally gored by a similarly wounded *wildschwein*. Ives-Curtis had an Enfield service revolver secreted in a hidden compartment of his suitcase. The local authorities, if they knew, might wonder why a supposedly innocuous writer for *British Homes and Gardens* was carrying a weapon so close to the residence of the German Reich's Chancellor.

"You there!" Ives-Curtis opened the driver door and rudely shook the still catatonic driver. "Have you got a gun?" He mimed firing with his thumb and forefinger. "Bang-bang."

"Bang-bang," repeated the driver, followed by hysterical giggling. Automobile fog lights came into view, followed by the tooting of a horn.

A Maybach Zeppelin advanced towards him, then came to a halt. Inside the vehicle, a voice called out in a pronounced Boston accent: "What seems to be the problem here?"

Ives-Curtis called back: "We've had an accident."

"Flat tire?" asked the unseen American.

"Wild boar. You wouldn't have a shotgun, would you?"

"No. Will a revolver do?"

"Splendidly."

"O'Malley, could you help the gentleman out?"

The driver door of the Maybach Zeppelin swung open. An Irish gorilla wearing a fedora and heavy woolen overcoat stepped out into the darkness brandishing a Smith and Wesson.

"Where might it be?" asked O'Malley in the thick cadences of County Mayo.

"If you follow me," said the Englishman, feeling like the chief floorwalker at Harrod's directing a customer towards the lift. Ives-Curtis pointed down at the boar still palpitating on the ground.

"Jeysus!" exclaimed O'Malley. "What do you think his Ma looked like?"

"These creatures are extremely unpredictable. It might be best if you don't—"

The Irish gorilla squatted down, stuck the barrel of the revolver in the boar's left eye and fired two shots. Having dispatched the creature, O'Malley stared at the grille of the Mercedes and pronounced: "He killed the car."

"I beg your pardon?"

"The fuckin car's had it."

Ives-Curtis had been so preoccupied with the unpredictable nature of the boar that he had failed to notice the entire front of the Mercedes had collapsed like an accordion. It was, indeed, as dead as the *wildschwein*.

"Where were you heading?" The American called out in the darkness from inside the car.

"The Berghof," replied Ives-Curtis.

"Fetch the gentleman's bags, O'Malley. We're all bound for the same destination. Come along, sir."

The Englishman climbed into the back of the Maybach Zepellin where he found himself seated next to a middle-aged man in horn-rimmed glasses with a rapidly receding hair line. "Never encountered a wild boar," said the American. "My son Jack would have loved to examine the carcass. But this isn't the most propitious moment. Don't want to keep our host waiting."

"You're Joseph Kennedy, aren't you?" asked Ives-Curtis, who recognized the newly appointed American Ambassador to the Court of St. James. "It's a great honor, Mr. Ambassador."

"My father would hate me for saying this," said Kennedy, "but I love you English. No one shows me any respect back in the States. Just an uppity Mick, who made good. Over here, I'm treated like royalty. And who might you be, sir?"

"Rupert Templeton," replied Ives-Curtis without blinking at the deceit. "On special assignment for *Home and Gardens* magazine. Pleasure to meet you. *Der Führer* has graciously permitted me to do an article on the Berghof."

"Gather he's got quite a spread," said Kennedy.

"The Reich's Chancellor designed it all himself. A modest little cottage when he first bought it. Now grown to outsize proportions. Rather like the Third Reich itself."

"Are you an admirer of Hitler, Mr. Templeton?"

"Oh, I have no personal politics," laughed Ives-Curtis. "Simply mad about architecture."

* * *

Having refreshed themselves and changed into formal dinner wear, the two travelers descended the stairs to a reception area that could easily have been mistaken for the lobby of a five-star hotel. Standing at the bottom of the staircase was a skeletal, shifty-looking man, whose head resembled that of a predatory insect. His military uniform seemed one size too big for his scrawny frame. The man clicked his heels together and introduced himself.

"*Herr Doktor* Josef Goebbels."

Ives-Curtis nodded politely. From his well-documented dossier, he knew the English-speaking, club-footed Dr. Goebbels was an intimate of Hitler's and would undoubtedly serve as the unofficial translator that evening. The Englishman also knew to steer clear of the skeletal man should he develop a ruptured appendix over dinner; Goebbels was a Doctor of Philosophy and a failed playwright. But his passion for theatre and films made him a natural choice to be the Third Reich's Minister of Propaganda.

"*Der Führer* is most pleased that you accepted his generous invitation, Herr Templeton. He is, how you say, a fan of your magazine and your articles, in particular. Are you pleased with your room? It has a magnificent view of the Alps, does it not? And the paintings? Are they not exquisite? *Der Führer* painted them himself. The world lost a gifted artist, but Germany found a great leader when Adolf Hitler went into politics."

Kennedy cleared his throat to remind Goebbels that he had billing over the unknown English magazine writer.

"I have not forgotten you, Herr Ambassador. One learned in the theatre to save the best for last. Frankly, I wish to have a private word with you." The propaganda minister snapped his fingers twice in the air. Two uniformed servants appeared, as if by magic. "Take Herr Templeton to the library, please. Grant him his every wish."

Walking with a pronounced limp, Goebbels took hold of Kennedy's arm and steered him down a wide carpeted corridor adorned on both sides with magnificent paintings by the Old Masters.

Kennedy nodded at the ornate framed canvasses and asked:

"Is this your boss's work, as well?"

Goebbels laughed like a hyena. "I was warned of your sense of humor, Herr Ambassador. No, no, no! That is a Rembrandt. A Titian. Rubens. Da Vinci. All liberated from the Jews."

"Liberated?"

"Does the word offend you?" challenged Goebbels.

"Not particularly. The world lost a helluva p.r. man when you went into politics, Doctor."

"It lost nothing. I am the world's *greatest* p.r. man. My market is the entire planet." Goebbels fanned his arms out to encompass the globe. "We have a great deal in common, you and I."

"Do we?"

"To begin with, we are both called Joseph. We are both family men. And we have both flirted with the arts."

"My involvement was strictly business, Doctor."

"Why so modest? RKO is a big film studio."

"A small, big film studio," corrected Kennedy. "I am no longer involved with the company."

"Not according to my researchers."

"Trust a p.r. man to redefine spies as 'researchers'. Shall we adjourn to dinner, Doctor? Mustn't keep the *Führer* waiting."

* * *

Although Ives-Curtis and Kennedy had already finished their first course, the Reich's Chancellor had yet to appear. Goebbels nattered on about British Prime Minister Neville Chamberlain's visit to the Berghof the previous week. How the *Führer* had traveled to Czechoslovakia to ease the Czechs into a peaceful acceptance of the German annexation of the disputed territories Hitler had renamed the Sudetenland.

"Why go to war? Did anyone complain when we annexed Austria?" asked Goebbels. "The Sudetenland was ours for centuries. The League of Nations took it away. If you lose your wallet on the street and I return it, you say *danke*. We don't come to blows. *Der Führer* made this crystal clear to Herr Chamberlain. Would America go to war for this, Herr Ambassador?"

Before Kennedy could reply, the Reich's Chancellor marched briskly into the dining room. Goebbels gestured for the visitors to stand up, shot his outstretched right arm into the air and shouted: *"Heil Hitler!"* Hitler returned the salute then signaled his guests to resume their seats. His attention turned to Ives-Curtis.

"I heard about your accident on the road, Herr Templeton. My deepest apologies. The driver has been disciplined."

"Oh, no! It wasn't his fault," said Ives-Curtis after waiting for Goebbels' unnecessary translation to end.

"The man was drunk. Such behavior is unacceptable. I don't drink. I don't smoke. I don't eat meat."

Neither Ives-Curtis nor Kennedy was enamored of vegetarian fare, but they beamed pleasantly when asked by their host how they had enjoyed the green and leafy dinner. Hitler daubed his lips with a napkin, directed his gaze on Kennedy and asked: "President Roosevelt is a Jew, yes?"

"No, he's not."

"He is a Jew," insisted Hitler. "The original family name was Rosenfeld."

"Not true."

"You dare contradict *der Führer*?" asked Goebbels.

"Shut up!" said Hitler, waiting for the humiliated Propaganda Minister to translate what he'd just said.

"Your researchers have made a mistake," said Kennedy drily.

"Researchers?" asked Ives-Curtis.

"A German euphemism for spies. Dr. Goebbels taught me that one before dinner."

Der Führer persisted: "Have you any evidence to the contrary, Herr Ambassador?"

"I've known President Roosevelt for years. I was in the import business with his son James. Franklin's a lot of things. But he's no kike. I can smell a Jew."

When Goebbels finished his translation, Hitler chuckled in his rat-a-tat-tat rhythm and asked: "Am I correct in assuming that you don't like Jews, Herr Ambassador?"

"A few individuals," replied Kennedy. "But as a race? No."

"Your great aviator, Charles Lindbergh, does not like them at all. Do many of your countrymen feel the same way?"

"Not so many as should," replied Kennedy. "My fellow countrymen love the movies. But the motion picture industry is controlled by Jews, who sell their biased dreams to the public."

"Georg Gyssling has done an admirable job," piped up Goebbels, the ultimate yes-man. Gyssling, the German Consul in Los Angeles, had been granted unprecedented content approval over all Hollywood films by the studio moguls and any possible anti-German sentiments that might be contained therein. "He is keeping the Jews in their place."

"I know what Gyssling is doing," snapped Hitler.

"Have you never married?" asked Kennedy.

"I am married to Germany," replied the Reich's Chancellor. "There is no time for another wife and children."

A Scottish terrier raced into the dining room at that moment and leapt up on Hitler's lap. He attempted half-heartedly to shoo the little dog away. "The dog is not mine," he explained to his guests with atypical embarrassment. "It belongs to my secretary."

As if on cue, an attractive woman in her late Twenties bustled into the room, scooped up the little dog and departed wordlessly. Ives-Curtis knew from his "researchers" that the secretary was Eva Braun, Hitler's longtime mistress. Married to Germany, indeed!

The Reich's Chancellor rose abruptly from the dining table, rubbed his hands together and announced: "*Ins Kino gehen!*"

Goebbels translated: "Movie time."

Hitler loved movies. Particularly those made in America. He was forever berating Goebbels about the inferior quality of German films. He demanded to know why the Third Reich could not make bigger and better films than the ones the Jews churned out in Hollywood. How could the savvy Minister of Propaganda explain that the best talents had all fled for their lives to America? *Der Führer* led the way to his private screening room. As they followed him, Kennedy leaned into the Englishman and remarked *soto voce:* "I like his style. Hitler's got the right attitude about the Jews. But the mustache has to go. He looks like Charlie Chaplin."

As Ives-Curtis and Kennedy settled into their overstuffed, leather club chairs, Goebbels told them in confidential tones: "We don't show any films made by Universal."

"I thought the ban had been lifted," replied Kennedy. "Didn't old Carl Laemmle make the cuts to *All Quiet* Gyssling asked for?" Consul Gyssling had submitted an extensive list of objectionable lines and shots in the Academy Award-winning adaptation of Eric Maria Remarque's harrowing World War I novel *All Quiet on the Western Front*.

"Yes," replied Goebbels. "Saved himself from a lawsuit at the same time. The film contained scurrilous lies about Germany. Now that Laemmle no longer runs the studio, the old Jew spends all his time 'rescuing' his relatives from the evil clutches of the Third Reich. Still more lies! But *der Führer* does not forgive or forget that quickly. Universal is still in the doghouse."

Hitler ignored the Propaganda Minister's chatter as he perused a typed list of names on a sheet resting on his knees. He crossed off some and made check marks next to others. Ives-Curtis wondered if the targeted ones were enemies of the Reich, destined to be executed at dawn. Was the inebriated chauffeur on that list?

Finally, Hitler looked up from the names and asked: "What is *Stand-In?*"

"A comedy, *mein Führer*. With Joan Blondell."

"Why don't we try that?" asked Hitler and handed the list of available motion pictures to Goebbels. "I like Joan Blondell. She looks like a Bavarian milk maid."

Goebbels bit his lower lip, cleared his throat, and spoke hesitantly: "It also stars Leslie Howard."

"No!" *Der Führer's* reply was positively venomous. "He is on the proscribed list. Are you totally demented, Goebbels?"

"What about *Dombey and Son?*" asked the Minister of Propaganda in a high-pitched voice. He feared *der Führer* might launch into an endless anti-Semitic tirade that would keep them up all night. "It's Dickens. You like Dickens. RKO. The Ambassador's old studio."

Hitler continued to fume like a petulant child for another two minutes, then asked suspiciously: "Who are the stars of this film?"

"Freddy Bartholomew and Osmond Radford." As a hopefully soothing coda, Goebbels offered up an item of trivia. "Radford was a German prisoner-of-war for two years."

Der Führer did not reply, but waved his hand to signify the film should start rolling.

As the opening credits appeared on the screen, Ives-Curtis leaned into Kennedy and whispered: "What was the problem with Leslie Howard?"

"Don't you know?" asked Kennedy. "Another goddam kike."

* * *

Dombey and Son was a mess. Truly awful. At the ripe age of thirteen, Freddy Bartholomew was a bit long in the tooth for the role of six-year-old Paul Dombey. RKO had forked out a small fortune to borrow Master Bartholomew from MGM. Which meant they couldn't blame the red ink on him. But who was going to be the fall guy? Eventually, they put the Indian sign on Sir Osmond Radford, a big West End and Broadway star, who'd never really made a dent in films.

All this ran through Ives-Curtis's mind as he lay in bed staring out at the Alps illuminated by the full moon. Poor Ozzie. He'd been his best mate during the Great War. They'd been prisoners together when their planes had been shot down over Germany.

Ives-Curtis was back on the mountain road again with the inebriated chauffeur. Then the crash.. Far more powerful than the first time. The Mercedes vibrated wildly, then raised violently off the ground. Ives-Curtis grabbed the door handle and leapt out of the automobile. The wild boar was crying out— enraged— struggling to get to its feet. How could it still be breathing after the impact? Have to finish it off, thought the Englishman. Have to destroy it.

His feet felt encased by cement as he attempted to reach the front of the Mercedes. The wild boar roared defiance and turned its attention on Ives-Curtis. It had transformed itself into some sort of mythological beast possessed of a human head. Hitler's head. Spewing hatred and evil. The Englishman reached for his gun, but his pockets were empty. He fled back inside the Mercedes and locked all the doors. Hitler began pounding on the window. Moments later, Joseph Kennedy stood beside him demanding that Ives-Curtis withdraw from the safety of the car. The two pounded on the window in tandem. It would only be a matter of seconds before the glass shattered and Ives-Curtis would be dragged out of the vehicle.

The inebriated driver turned around from the front seat. He pointed his thumb and index finger at the Englishman. "Bang-bang! Bang-bang!"

"Come out of there, Ives-Curtis!"

Ives-Curtis? How did they know his real name? Someone had betrayed him. Who? What did it matter now? In a few minutes he would be dead, never to see his unborn child.

Rapping on glass from the other passenger window. Ives-Curtis turned his head around. The scrawny Minister of Propaganda was grinning at him, dangling a leather purse from his fingers.

"We found your wallet!" said Goebbels. "Good news, yes?"

"Go away!"

"Dickie! Dickie!"

Who's that? An aviator in a Royal Flying Corps uniform walked towards the Mercedes brandishing a pistol. Someone was coming to the rescue. He wasn't going to die after all. The aviator seized Goebbels by the scruff of the neck and tossed him to the ground.

"Well, just don't sit there, Dickie. Move your bleedin' arse." The aviator removed his helmet and goggles. It was Ozzie. Dear, beloved, faithful Ozzie.

The other passenger window shattered at that moment and O'Malley's powerful hands reached in to grab hold of him.

Sir Richard Ives-Curtis awoke from his nightmare in a cold sweat, heart pounding through his chest. It wouldn't take a Joseph in Egypt to sort out the meaning of all that imagery. One thing was clear, however: the battle for the Greater Good was about to begin. Ives-Curtis would have to contact Osmond Radford immediately and make sure his old chum was on board.

GYPSIES AND SCALAWAGS

Hell is empty and all the devils are here. "What is that infernal racket?" Sir Osmond Radford shouted aloud. "Is there no concept of the Lord's Day— even in Beverly Hills?" The actor-knight rolled over in his four-poster bed hoping to seek solace from his beloved wife, but she was not there. "Hyacinth! Darling, where are you?" No response. Not a single human sound to be heard at Best of Times on that Sunday morning.

Radford swung his six-foot frame out of the bed, put on his slippers and dressing gown and trod gingerly towards the bay window looking out onto Tower Road. The sound of hammering and drilling from across the street stopped abruptly. Stumbling back to the bed, he peered myopically at the telephone on the bedside table. Where the devil had he put his spectacles? Like a blind man, he stubbed his fingers into the holes and dialed a familiar number. "Hugh?" He cleared his throat and spoke in the distinctive sandpaper voice that had driven women to distraction throughout the Teens and Twenties. "It's Ozzie. Could you possibly give me a lift to the match today ? … I think 1:30 will be fine… Alright, come earlier. But eat before you get here. Willi can never say no to you and, frankly, I can't afford to keep feeding you… Send Gwen to cooking school, damn it!" He replaced the receiver and walked into the magnificently tiled bathroom his wife had created for them. "I am a long way from Kent," Radford announced to his reflection in the mermaid encrusted mirror over the sink, arching his upside-down parentheses eyebrows. He stirred up the cream in his shaving mug. A few wrinkles, but he had earned them. The actor-knight, who was a prominent member of the expatriate British film colony known as the Hollywood Raj, patted his flat belly approvingly. He'd kept his figure and his looks. What he *had* lost was his career. As a former West End matinee idol, Radford had toured for several seasons as Percy Blakeney in *The Scarlet Pimpernel* and Sidney Carton in *A Tale of Two Cities*. Why the deuce hadn't Fox scheduled his screen test? If they didn't want him, why not say so? No, no, no. Do not think about *The Hound of the Baskervilles* today. Bad luck. Ha! Was there an actor, who wasn't superstitious?

He took a brush to his hair, slightly more salt than pepper. I am fifty years old, thought Radford, and I have lost my compass. I perform on the radio Saturday nights and unashamedly extoll the virtues of a breakfast cereal.

Taking long deep breaths, Radford entered the walk-in cedar closet. A small statue of an Indian goddess holding a lute in two of her four hands sat atop a chest of drawers. She was Saraswati, the goddess of speech and learning. Hyacinth had presented it to him for good luck years before. The actor-knight gently touched Saraswati's head, a ritual he performed every morning. *Tis, a far, far better thing I do, than I have ever done before.* The Sunday morning ritual had begun. He stepped into a pair of white flannel trousers, buttoned up his white cotton shirt, draped a white sweater across his shoulders, and knotted its arms at the throat. Another deep breath. Osmond Radford was now ready to play cricket. But first he needed a strong cup of coffee.

When he finally opened the bedroom door, two Harlequin Great Danes leapt up to their full height and mauled him adoringly. They had been waiting impatiently since dawn for their master to awaken.

"Yes, yes, yes," said Radford soothingly as the twin Dromios— one of Syracuse, the other Ephesus— followed him down the stairs. "I love you both, lads. But allow me to descend without breaking my neck."

The actor-knight walked into the sunken sitting room. The Sunday newspapers were spread out on the coffee table just the way he liked them. Sir Osmond sat down on the toile sofa and stared at the legendary Russell Flint portrait of Lady Radford hanging over the fireplace. The Great Danes sat devotedly in front of the hearth. What news on the Rialto, wondered Radford, picking up the Los Angeles Times. The front page announced Germany's annexation of the Sudetenland courtesy of Neville Chamberlain. In exchange, Hitler had vowed not to invade any more countries. The Herald said that the Third Reich was going to stamp all Jewish passports with the letter J.

"Good morning, Sir Osmond," said Wilhelmina 'Willi' Klarfeld, in a thick German accent. The Radfords' devoted cook and housekeeper was extremely tall— an inch or two more than her employer's six feet. "Here is your *Kaffee*." Willi stepped down into the sitting room carrying a tray laden with a pot of

hot coffee and a variety of fresh baked *Kuchen*. She had fled from Germany two years earlier and made her way to America via a circuitous route through the Panama Canal.

"*Danke schon*, Willi."

"Only English, please, Sir Osmond. How will I otherwise learn?"

"Where is everyone this morning?" Radford's long fingers performed a nervous adagio movement on his thighs.

"Lady Radford has early gone— *nein*— has gone early to Martin Kohlinger. Alec is … I don't know. Miss Flavia is rehearsing in the garden."

"Rehearsing for what?"

Willi raised an eyebrow and made a face to indicate 'What else?'

"Of course," replied Radford. "How foolish of me."

The hammering and drilling resumed across the street at even greater volume than before.

Radford massaged his temples with his fingertips and exclaimed: "Hell's bells! What is going on over there, Willi? Isn't there some sort of by-law restricting construction on Sundays?"

"The new neighbors. Two young men. They are attorneys."

"Indeed. Are we to assume they're erecting a courthouse?"

"They are being very nice. One is named Lowenthal. Speaks German. Who knows when a lawyer might be needed? *Ach*, I forgot. Mr. Laver phoned while you were asleep."

"Steve Laver? The publicist for my show?" Radford was sipping his coffee and munching on a slice of Willi's cinnamon *Streusel Kuchen*.

"*Ja, ja*. From CBS. Very nice man. He reminded— *nein, nein*— he said to remind you that the reporter is coming at noon."

"An interview on Sunday! I play cricket on Sunday. Hell's bells!"

The front door opened at that moment. Lady Hyacinth Radford entered the vestibule wearing an elegant Schiaparelli business suit with several bolts of imported Belgian fabric tucked under her arm. A protégé in London of legendary interior decorator, Syrie Maugham, the former Hyacinth Talbot had graduated to her own successful design business both in New York and Los Angeles. At 46, the chestnut-haired beauty looked remarkably as she had done when Russell Flint painted her almost thirty years earlier. The watercolor portrait had caused a sensation in 1911 when it was first exhibited in a gallery on Bond Street. The dazzling, vibrant work epitomized the Scots-born Flint's *oeuvre*. He adored beautiful women; his watercolors were almost continental in their sensuality.

He had depicted Hyacinth strolling barefoot in a garden, casually holding a straw hat at her side. Her face was serene, yet enigmatic. The young Osmond Radford froze in his tracks when he beheld Flint's masterpiece in the gallery window. That face! He fell in love instantly with the girl in the painting and vowed to marry her. But what was her name? How was he to find her? Fate brought them together a few weeks later at a garden party in Bloomsbury. So tongue-tied was Radford at meeting Hyacinth in the flesh, all he could do was offer her two comps to see him perform the role of the Caliph in *Kismet*. The play was the hottest ticket in the West End. Radford counted off the days until the beauteous Miss Talbot would take her seat in the stalls.

The young actor waited for her in his dressing room after the performance, but she never appeared. Radford was crestfallen. A week later, he received a handwritten letter on pink stationery. Miss Talbot apologized profusely for not attending and offered to reimburse him for the tickets. She would never have stood him up if it hadn't been a matter of the utmost importance. As a token of good will, she had sent him a small statue of Saraswati, the goddess of speech and learning. She hoped the goddess would bring him further luck and good fortune in his already thriving career.

Twenty-seven years and three children later, Sir Osmond Radford still felt his heart race every time his wife walked into a room.

"What's wrong, dearest?" asked Hyacinth, staring at his distraught expression. "Are you feverish? Perhaps Willi can make you some chamomile tea."

"Where have you been?"

"Discussing the designs for Martin Kohlinger's house. What a dear, sweet man! Lost his entire family escaping from Germany. We must invite him for dinner. Willi can prepare one of her marvelous— What is wrong, Ozzie?"

"A reporter is coming to interview me at mid-day." Radford removed a silver cigarette case from his inside pocket and lit up a Hignett, the brand he imported on a regular basis from England. He had smoked Players for years, but switched to Hignetts when they added his image to their popular series of cards depicting West End theatre stars.

"Is that today?" asked Hyacinth. "I'd quite forgotten. We should bring in some fresh flowers from the garden. Are you going to dress like that? Why not! It's the essence of you."

"But Sunday is my cricket day!"

"Yes, dearest. At two. The interview is at noon. The stars are in alignment."

"And still no word about the bloody screen test!" blurted Radford.

"Ohhh! That's what this is all about." Flavia took her husband's hands in hers. "We should do some yoga."

"I-I-I don't want to do yoga," he replied, ripping his hands loose from hers. "I want this day to be over. And tomorrow, as well."

"You're being silly."

"I don't expect you to understand, Hyacinth. I've been wandering in the desert for two years now. Longer. Since we left New York. I have lost my compass."

"What about *My Favorite Story*? It's a huge success, Ozzie. Every star in Hollywood has appeared on the show. You're a household name."

"It's radio! I read from a script. That's not really acting. You saw me play Sherlock on stage—"

"A dozen times, dearest," said Hyacinth. "You were divine."

"You're more thank kind – as always. It was the role of a lifetime. And the opportunity to immortalize that performance lies within my grasp. Years from now, our children's children will be able to see their grandfather play Sherlock Holmes. There will be a living record of my work. Even when I'm dead."

"Does it mean that much to you, dearest?"

"Yes!"

"Then I shall pray for you tonight." Hyacinth put down the bolts of cloth, went through the kitchen and out into the garden. She stopped in her tracks at the sight of her eldest child, Flavia, standing on the small outdoor stage, dressed in a great hoop skirt and pantaloons. When had she ceased to be the tomboy, whom Sir Osmond had dubbed the Pirate Queen? How had evolved into the chestnut-haired beauty, who now paced up and down the wooden stage. She was twirling a parasol and reciting in a thick Southern accent:

"Fiddle-dee-dee! War, war, war; this war talk's spoiling all the fun at every party this spring. I get so bored, I could scream."

"Excuse me," said Hyacinth, in mock serious tones. "I'm looking for my daughter and I can't seem to find her anywhere."

"It's me, Mummy!" said Flavia. "I'm preparing for *Gone with the Wind*. Did you really not know it was me?"

"Completely fooled. Your accent was perfect, Flavia. David Selznick would be a fool not to hire you for that part. Shall I have a word with Irene? She wants me to redo their bedroom. Not that David ever sleeps there."

"I want this part, Mummy. Cockfosters! I'm 26-years-old."

"Don't be rude, dear."

"Cockfosters is an Underground station, Mummy. On the Piccadilly line. Twenty-six is old for an actress in Hollywood. I just can't seem to move up the bloody ladder. One goes to all the right parties and trendy restaurants. We know everybody worth knowing. But I can't seem to get past these bit parts. I've lost my compass."

"Like father, like daughter. Perhaps the two of you should join forces and organize an expedition in the sitting room. Thespians! My father would have been appalled. He said actors were nothing but gypsies and scalawags. Why don't you ask Uncle Jasper to help? He knows David Selznick quite well."

"Knows and *owes*, Mummy. David is holding Uncle Jas's marker for five thousand dollars."

Flavia enjoyed a special bond with Jasper Radford, her father's older brother. Both were black sheep and reveled in that distinction. He always addressed his niece as Princess Flavia and affixed HRH to all correspondence. Jasper had the ability to make Flavia laugh until she was forced to seek refuge in the loo.

"Marker?" asked Hyacinth.

"An IOU."

"Does your father know?"

"He's been dodging Jas's calls all week."

"Oh, dear! That will doubtless result in Aunt Eunice camping out on our front door step with her begging bowl."

Willi called from the kitchen window: "Lady Radford! It is Miss Julia on the telephone. From Boston."

At 19-years-of-age, the flaxen-haired, blue-eyed Julia Radford was enjoying considerably more success than her older sister. Straight out of London's Royal Academy of Dramatic Arts, Julia had been cast as the ingénue in *The Conflicted Heart*, a metaphysical drama in blank verse that ran for six months in the West End. A neophyte Broadway producer, whose family made millions selling laxatives, brought *The Conflicted Heart* to America with three members of the original cast— including Julia Radford.

The play had rehearsed in New York for a month with several Broadway veterans replacing the rest of the original cast. When the show moved to Boston for a three-week run, it opened to tepid and bewildered reviews. The producer vowed to persevere and deliver the show to a more sophisticated New York audience.

Flavia followed her mother into the kitchen to speak with her baby sister, whom she adored.

"Hello, Ju-Ju! Have you taken Boston by storm?"

"Hello, Flaves. Are you playing Scarlett O'Hara?"

"Not yet. Only a matter of time. George Hurrell took some photos of me dressed as Scarlett and I sent them by courier to Selznick's office."

"George Hurrell?" boomed Radford from an extension phone in the library. "By courier? That must have cost a pretty packet."

"Hello, Daddy!" Julia adored her father. She, in turn, was the apple of his eye. "What news of Sherlock?"

"Careful, Ju-Ju," warned Flavia. "That has replaced the Scottish play as the name one dares not speak."

"Where's Alec? Isn't *Dawn Patrol* opening soon?" Their brother Alec had played a supporting role in a much-anticipated drama about British flying aces in the Great War.

"Alec went to Mexico."

"What!?!" exclaimed Hyacinth and Radford simultaneously.

"Hello, Mummy!" bubbled Julia.

"Hello, my sweet girl. I was going to book the Super Chief this week for your opening night in New York. Then two new jobs fell into my lap. Manna from heaven. I'm treating Daddy to airplane tickets and a suite at the Waldorf."

Radford paid no attention to the bantering of his wife and daughter. His mind was still preoccupied with his errant son. "What the devil is Alec doing in Mexico? We're playing cricket today. Aubrey's expecting him."

"I'll sub for him," said Flavia. "A woman can't play cricket!"

"Why ever not? Don't be so Victorian, Daddy! I've soloed a plane cross country, hunted moose in Montana and single-handedly caught a fifty-pound marlin off the coast of Baja."

"And gave your poor old father heart palpitations with each of those accomplishments. No, no, Pirate Queen. Can you imagine the imperial rocket that would emanate from Aubrey Smith if one even suggested the notion of a female standing in front of a wicket?"

"Hellooo, family!" said Julia. "This is my phone call. I'm paying for it. I need to speak with Daddy. Alone. Do you mind awfully, Mummy? It's about the theatre. That sort of talk bores you into the ground."

"Chat away, sweet girl. See you in New York!"

"Bye-bye, Ju-Ju! Love you to bits."

When she was certain her mother and sister were no longer on the line, Julia told her father: "We're not going to New York, Daddy. They posted the closing notice after last night's performance."

"Oh, Julia! I'm so sorry. You must be devastated."

"The reviews were dreadful and the audiences not much better. The laxative heir became culturally constipated, lost his nerve and decided to call it a day."

"Not a very nice day. Well, my darling, I shall wire you some money, with which you will buy yourself a first-class train ticket and come west. Your old room awaits you. As does your loving family."

"I don't want to come out there just yet, Daddy. Noel has a play opening in New York that needs an ingénue. And Orson Welles wants me to do *Rebecca* with him on the radio. Being part of the Mercury Theatre would be very prestigious. My career is on the stage, Daddy. Not as a movie starlet. You understand. Break the news gently to Mummy."

Radford hung up the receiver in the library, deeply disappointed that his youngest child would not be making her Broadway debut. He'd been looking forward to attending the opening night. But he also wondered why the show's abrupt closing didn't seem to bother her that much. And why wouldn't she want to seek comfort in her family? It must be a man. Oh, dear! With whom had she fallen in love?

SCARLET EVERY DAY

"Hello. Hello. Hello." The rapid-fire delivery of an English music hall performer could only mean one thing: Hugh Harcourt had arrived much earlier than expected. "Where are the Radfords?"

The actor-knight made a beeline from the library straight into the kitchen where he found a chubby, florid-faced man in cricket whites devouring a huge slice of Willi Klarfeld's cinnamon *Kuchen*. Hard to believe that Hugh Harcourt had once been a svelte leading man, fighting off a sea of adoring young women, who besieged numerous stage doors hoping for his autograph and other things. At 52, Harcourt smoked too much, drank too much and, ate too much.

"Wilhelmina, I absolutely forbid you to serve this man any more food," said Radford, with all the authority he could muster.

"*Ach*, Sir Osmond. It is Mr. Harcourt. He is being your best friend for years."

"Exactly!" said the ebullient Harcourt, reaching an arm around Willi's shoulder and giving the embarrassed German housekeeper a peck on the cheek. "Blimey! Had to go up on tiptoes for that. Well, Ozzie. Sobered up enough to pass muster with Old Aubrey?"

"You're certainly feeling your oats this morning, Hughie. Did you and Gwen have a romantic evening?"

"There was romance alright," replied Harcourt, dropping his voice to conspiratorial tones. "But not with my wife."

Willi abruptly excused herself, remembering the dinner menu she had to check with Hyacinth.

"Think she's ever had a tumble?" asked Harcourt, after the embarrassed German housekeeper had departed from the kitchen.

"You're an incorrigible satyr, Hughie."

"Not what you think, old man. Not by a long chalk. Dash it all, Ozzie. I'm in love."

"What?!? Not somebody's wife, I trust. Aubrey will chuck you off the team."

"She's not married." Harcourt's eyes lit up, and his voice was positively rhapsodic. "Her name's Toby Winslow. She's not English. A genuine American. From Brooklyn. She has an entire language of her own. And a body like the hood ornament on a Phantom IV. She's just twenty and she worships me. Can't keep our hands off each other. She's the cigarette girl at the Trocadero."

Radford took a few moments to absorb all the salient points. Finally, he said: "She's not English?"

The doorbell rang. Radford stared up at the wall clock like a condemned man on Death Row. "Hell's bells! Noon already. Come with me, Hugh. Your assistance is required."

Harcourt accompanied Radford to the front door. Standing on the doorstep was Steve Laver, an eager-beaver CBS publicist, accompanied by a horsy, buck-toothed Englishwoman in her late 30s, wearing fake pearls and a garish floral print dress. Radford was startled to see an unkempt, bespectacled photographer, armed with portrait camera and tripod, hovering behind the woman.

The twin Dromios raced in from the sitting room. Barking loudly, they leapt up on the startled visitors. Radford summoned Willi and instructed her to lock the Great Danes in the laundry room.

"Sir Osmond." Laver flashed his patented let's-be-friends smile, as he placed a hand behind the woman's back and eased her gently over the threshold. "This is Millicent Hedgerow. With *The News of the World*."

"Good news, I trust," said Radford.

"An honor and a privilege," said Millicent in plummy tones. She held out a limp-wristed hand, clearly aping a gesture she had seen members of the Royal Family perform in newsreels. "A great many people in England still remember you fondly, Sir Osmond."

"You're far too kind," purred Radford, taking her hand, but not kissing it.

"I'm Harold," said the photographer in a flat Illinois accent, after no one bothered to introduce him.

"Do come in." As Millicent, Harold, and Laver passed by him, Radford hissed in the publicist's ear: "There was no mention of photographs."

"It's a Sunday newspaper, Sir Osmond. Frankly, they're more interested in a family portrait than an interview."

"It's *not* a good time, Steve. I have a cricket match at two."

"Shouldn't take long. Harold's one of the best. We set this up a month ago… They sell a lot of corn flakes in England."

"And an awful lot of coffee in Brazil." Radford sighed in resignation, then turned to his guest. "Dear Miss Hedgehog—"

"Hedgerow." She corrected the actor without the slightest hint of offense. "Please, call me Millicent."

"Frightfully sorry. Please allow me to change into something more appropriate for the shoot. In the meantime, my friend, Hugh Harcourt, will attend your every need. Shan't be long." Taking the steps two at a time, Radford arrived on the upstairs landing where Hyacinth awaited him, a concerned look on her face.

"They want photographs! Steve never said anything about—"

Hyacinth interrupted him: "Alec is here."

"Where—? How did he—?"

"Up the back stairs. He was afraid of running into you. Please, Ozzie, be kind. He's had an accident or something."

"Hell's bells! What now?"

"He's in his room. I need to change into something more lady of the manor. What's she like? The reporter?"

"Put a bit between her teeth and she could win the Grand National." Hyacinth shook her head and tried to suppress a laugh.

"You are dreadful, Osmond. Probably why I fell in love with you. Feeling better now?"

"Like the captain of the Titanic just before he spotted the iceberg." He touched his wife's cheek fondly and knocked at the door of his son's room. When there was no response, he turned the knob and let himself in.

Alec Radford stood at the window staring out at the garden. At 23, the blonde-haired middle child was not as tall as his father, but quite good looking with the beefy body of a professional rugby player. He was also an expert horseman, which had gained him entree to Darryl Zanuck's polo-playing clique— until the young man's explosive temper resulted in his banishment from the Riviera Country Club and Fox studios. Alec's splendid seat on a horse afforded him steady employment as nameless (and, often, wordless) officers in the endless stream of historical epics the studios were grinding out.

He dreamt of movie stardom and desired to best his father in a world that the latter had failed to conquer."

"Why did Mother turn the garden over to that simpering little Jap? There's not a greener thumb in Southern California than mine."

"Turn around, please," said Radford, determined not to fall into a familiar pattern of conflict with his difficult son.

"Going to read me the riot act again, pater?"

"Why do you insist on calling me that? You know how much I dislike it."

"Isn't that how you addressed your father? Uncle Jasper told me that grandpapa insisted you call him—"

"Alec! Please, look at me."

Finally turning around, the young man revealed scratch marks all over his badly sun-burned face. Even from the other side of the room, Alec reeked of tequila.

"Good Lord! What happened?" asked Radford. "Automobile accident?"

"Not this time. No. These are souvenirs of a rather fiery señorita south of the border."

Radford sighed deeply and asked: "Should one be fearing any legal repercussions?"

"Not to worry, pater. Family honor's intact. Even if one's bank account is slightly depleted. Had to pay for the services of a rather slimy Tijuana *abagado*."

"Flavia!" Radford's voice was unusually loud and curt. His eldest child stuck her head in the door a second later.

"That was quick," snarled Alec. "Listening at the keyhole?"

Flavia stuck her tongue out at her younger brother,

"Get out your makeup box," said Radford. "Fix your brother's face as best you can. Put him in a blue blazer, pour a gallon of black coffee down his throat and have him report chop-chop to the garden."

* * *

Down in the sitting room, Hugh Harcourt was regaling Millicent Hedgerow, Steve Laver, and Harold the photographer with tales of his and Radford's youthful escapades while touring in Australia. All the while the faithful Willi served them coffee and *Kuchen*.

Radford sauntered into the sitting room wearing a grey pin-striped Savile Row suit. He was immediately questioned by Millicent Hedgerow.

"Do you think there'll be a war, Sir Osmond?" Her stenographer's pad was open, pencil poised for his response.

Taken aback momentarily by the unexpected political question, the knight responded diplomatically: "One hopes not."

"Are you on the side of appeasement?"

"One prefers to be on the sunny side of the street, if you follow."

"But as an Englishman, you must have some concerns about—"

Hyacinth sailed into the room at that moment. "Why don't we talk about my husband's radio show? That is why you're here? I'm Hyacinth Radford. Hello, Steve. So nice to see you again."

Millicent furrowed her brow, stared down at her notepad and posed another question: "You were decorated for heroism in 1918. If there is a war, will you serve again?"

"My first duty, as always, is to King and country. One hopes Hitler keeps his word about— "

"Does everyone have coffee?" interrupted Hyacinth. "Or perhaps you'd prefer tea, Miss Hedgerow?"

"I'm fine. Thank you, Lady Radford. Did you decorate this house?"

"Yes. We miss England terribly. I wanted it to feel as if it had been transformed from somewhere in Kent and plunked down ever so gently in Southern California."

"The house is called Best of Times," said Millicent. "That's from *A Tale of Two Cities*, isn't it? My mother said you were the best Sidney Carton she ever saw on stage. My grandmother, as well."

"Thank them for remembering me," said Radford. "They're far too kind."

"Why don't we snap that photo before it rains?" said Laver, hoping to lighten the moment.

"Does it *ever* rain in California?" asked Millicent.

Radford moved swiftly to the French windows, opened them, and said:

"With apologies to Lord Tennyson, come into the garden, Millicent."

The buck-toothed journalist, turned to Lady Radford and said: "He's quite witty, isn't he?"

Harold was setting up his camera on the far side of the swimming pool when Flavia strode into the garden. Wearing a pair of black bell-bottomed slacks and a flaming red silk blouse, she pushed her hair off her forehead and extended her other hand to Millicent: "I'm Flavia. Do forgive my keeping you all waiting. Promptness is a virtue I struggle with interminably."

"What a pretty blouse," said Millicent. "Red is very bold."

"Scarlet. I always wear something scarlet every day. For good luck."

When Millicent stared blankly, Flavia explained: "*Gone With The Wind.* I'm determined to play the lead."

"But you're English!"

"So is Leslie Howard. And he's playing Ashley Wilkes." Without pausing for breath, Flavia launched an emotional tirade in a thick Southern accent: *'Who are you to tell me I mustn't? You led me on, Ashley. You made me believe you wanted to marry me.'* Do forgive me, Millicent. I've memorized the entire novel. It's my Bible. As God is my witness, I'll kill myself if I don't get the part. Not really. I'll simply enter a convent."

"Goodness!" exclaimed Millicent. "You're certainly passionate about your work. Are you presently employed?"

"Just finished *Union Pacific.* For De Mille."

"The lead?"

Flavia tossed her hair back and laughed theatrically: "Heavens, no! Just another wanton woman. This time in the Old West. Belly up to the bar boys, what?"

Hyacinth, who was only just recovering from the shock of her daughter's impromptu Scarlett O'Hara impersonation, rushed over to join the women, and pleaded: "Please, don't write that! One doesn't want the public getting the wrong impression of our Flavia. Ah! There is my son. Resplendent in a blue blazer. Come over and meet Miss Hedgehog, darling."

"Hedgerow."

"Of course. This is Alec, our pride and joy. He went to Eton and Sandhurst."

"Briefly," growled Alec.

"And you're an actor as well?"

"Yes. Just finished starring in a film at Warner Brothers."

"Indeed?" Millicent began scribbling with her pencil.

"Actually," said Flavia. "It's a featured role."

"Bigger than yours," muttered Alec. "With Errol Flynn, Basil Rathbone and David Niven. You might mention that. We're all old chums. Play cricket together every Sunday."

"For which we mustn't be late," piped up Sir Osmond, who had resumed the nervous finger tapping adagio on his trousers.

The twin Dromios began howling pitifully from the laundry room. "Goodness!" exclaimed Millicent. "Sounds like *The Hound of the Baskervilles.*"

Radford gritted his teeth and resisted an overwhelming urge to throw the buck-toothed journalist into the swimming pool. Instead, he turned to the photographer and inquired: "Harold, are you ready for us?"

"Waiting for that cloud to pass," replied the photographer. "Aren't we all?" asked Radford in the most *sotto* of *voces*.

"Is that an amphitheater?" asked Millicent, noticing the tiny outdoor stage for the first time.

"Nothing so grand," replied Hyacinth. "My husband built it. He and the children often put on plays for their own amusement. I paint the backdrops."

"Do you perform for an audience?"

"Occasionally. Just members of the Raj."

"In India?" asked Millicent.

"No," laughed Hyacinth. "There are so many British subjects out here, that we have been dubbed 'the Hollywood Raj'. The most glamorous outpost of the Empire. My husband says it's a wonder anyone's left to act in the West End. Please, don't write that down. It makes him sound glib."

The buck-toothed Miss Hedgerow wasn't writing anything. Her attention was riveted on an ethereal young Japanese man in a linen suit and straw boater, who walked trancelike towards Lady Radford. Extending an upturned palm whilst tears streamed down his face, he resembled an actor in a silent film

"Ito!" exclaimed Hyacinth. "What's wrong?" She dashed over to the young Japanese man's side and waited for him to speak.

"A letter has just arrived from Japan," replied the young man in stilted English.

"Oh, Ito! I'm so sorry. Please, wait inside. We shan't be much longer."

Ito bowed gratefully and turned back towards the house. Hyacinth returned to a bewildered Millicent, who asked: "Who was that?"

"Our gardener. He's extremely sensitive."

MESMERIZED OR TERRIFIED

Alec sat in stony silence in the back seat of the battered Cadillac as it wended its way down Coldwater Canyon into the San Fernando Valley. Radford and Harcourt sat up front discussing the plight of England following the Munich Accord.

"Good thing I don't have any money over there," said Harcourt, turning east on Riverside Drive and heading towards Burbank. "Not that I have any over here."

"My brother wrote to me the other week—"

"Jasper? Why didn't he just ring you up?"

"Priam, my eldest brother. a proper country squire. Runs the family estate in Kent. Thinks this is all a lot of hoo-hah by the Fleet Street boys to sell more newspapers. Old Priam thinks we shouldn't meddle in foreign wars."

Alec broke his silence and said: "I'm studying German."

"What!?!" Radford turned around to glare at his son now decked out in his cricket whites.

"Germany's going to rule the world," said Alec. "Mark my words. And I don't want to be left behind sitting on the curb like some Mexican peon, who can't speak a word of English."

"Don't be an ass, Alec!"

"*You* speak German."

"A few phrases. I *was* a prisoner-of-war for three years."

"Better dust them off, pater. We'll all need the ability to communicate with the conquerors."

"No one's going to let Hitler conquer the world."

"Who's going to stop him?" challenged Alec. "Have you read *Mein Kampf*?"

"No. Have you?"

"Twice. Quite brilliant. It has insight, direction and purpose. Hitler dares to tell the truth. He says aloud what most people think but are afraid to admit." Radford buried his face in his hands, lifted his head and took a deep breath:

"I don't suggest you speak this way in front of Aubrey and the others."

"Really? You'd be surprised how many people feel as I do. Particularly my age. Hitler's put an end to the Depression in Germany. More than Franklin Delano Rosenfeld has achieved over here."

"Here we are!" boomed Harcourt, trying his best to diffuse the unpleasant mood as he steered his car into the entrance of Griffith Park. Radford *père et fils* climbed out of the Cadillac in hostile silence.

"Don't let him get to you, old boy" said Harcourt, wrapping a comradely arm around Radford's shoulder. "Probably just growing pains."

"Growing pains! At 23? No, Hughie, it's much more than that. I've tried everything to get close to him, but he insists on pushing me away. His behavior is positively anti-social. Snarling at the breakfast table. Picking fights at the drop of a hat. Why is he so bloody angry all the time? Why does Hyacinth continually make excuses for him?"

"Dash it all, Ozzie! She's his mother. She was there when you weren't."

"You mean the war? Was it my fault I was shot down and interned for three years? Do you think I-I-I liked being away from my family? All I dreamt of was coming home to them. When I finally did, Alec didn't talk to me for a week. Four-years-old and he already had a chip on his shoulder."

Boris Karloff and C. Aubrey Smith, both passionate cricketers, had arrived in Hollywood a decade earlier and were dismayed to discover that there were neither cricket grounds nor anyone interested in the game. With the advent of sound, more and more stage trained actors arrived in Los Angeles from all over the Empire. Aubrey promptly founded the Hollywood Cricket Club.

A legendary bowler, tall and imposing with shaggy sheepdog's eyebrows and a walrus mustache, Aubrey had been educated at Charterhouse and Cambridge. Whether on screen, where he commanded battalions in far flung outposts of the British Empire, or in life, where new boys from England had to present themselves to him for approval ("What school did you attend? Are you a batsman or a bowler?"), Aubrey Smith was the acknowledged leader of the Hollywood Raj.

"First innings will commence," shouted Aubrey. "Today's umpires will be Herbert Marshall, Ronald Colman, alternating with Cedric Hardwicke and Nigel Bruce. Don't come running to me with any protests. Ronnie? Bart? Willie? Cedric? Are you lads ready?"

"We are the court of last resort, Aubrey," replied Hardwicke, with a characteristic degree of irony.

"Jolly good! I shall captain one team, and Karloff the other."

"Is it any different than last week?" asked Colman.

"I say, Ronnie," warned Nigel "Willie" Bruce. "Better not let Aubrey hear you talking heresy."

Six years past his Biblical allotment, Aubrey Smith was in remarkable shape. He ate, breathed and slept cricket. In fact, he had a clause in all his contracts allowing him time off to return to England every year for the test matches at Lords. Clutching his bat in his large hands, Aubrey squinted in the direction of the opposite wicket where Hugh Harcourt held the ball in his hand. Despite his excessive weight, Harcourt was still a powerful bowler, whose unique spin drove batsmen to distraction.

Aubrey took a mighty swing at the ball, failed to connect, and almost knocked over the wicket behind him.

"Niven!" he bellowed.

David Niven had appeared with Aubrey the previous year in a highly successful film version of *The Prisoner of Zenda*. The relationship endured off-screen, and Niven, who had lost his own father during the Great War, worshipped Smith and was at the older man's beck and call.

"Yes, sir," said Niven, rushing over to the older actor, and snapping to attention.

"Do you have my spectacles?"

"I do, indeed."

Without a word, Aubrey opened his large palm. Niven whipped out the bifocals from his pocket and placed them gingerly in the older actor's hand.

"What the deuce!" exclaimed Aubrey, squinting towards the opposite wicket. "These are my reading spectacles, boy."

"Sorry, sir. That's what you gave me."

"Now, now, Aubrey," cooed Boris Karloff. "Don't blame it on your props." The next innings found Karloff's team up to bat. Radford and Harcourt stood in front of their respective wickets with Alec bowling directly behind his father. His first pitch all but struck Harcourt in the chest and the florid faced actor jumped aside just in time. He hastily put his bat back in the crease before Bart Marshall could call him out.

"I say, Ozzie!" shouted Harcourt. "Have a word with the lad, would you?

That was bloody close. Gwen's far too young to be a widow." Radford spoke over his shoulder: "A little less frenzied, Alec."

"You two *are* on the opposite side, pater. I'm out to win."

"Winning at cricket, Alec, doesn't justify homicide."

"Quite. Couldn't have said it better myself," said Nigel Bruce in his lovable, bumbling fashion.

Basil Rathbone, Niven and Aubrey stood on the sidelines watching the very public friction between father and son.

"Fierce bowler, young Radford," said Aubrey.

"Positively ferocious," said Niven. "On and off the pitch. What our American cousins call 'a pain-in-the-ass'. Don't you agree, Basil?"

Seemingly absorbed in the match as he ran his index finger along the side of his aquiline nose, the 45-year-old Rathbone was deep in thought about his prospects to escape typecasting as Hollywood's most popular villain. If only they liked his *Baskervilles* screen test. His wife, Ouida, assured him he was perfect casting for Sherlock Holmes. She'd even bought him a deer stalker cap and Meerschaum pipe for good luck.

"The boy's quite impossible," said Rathbone, in his deep sonorous voice. "Dreadful attitude. Rubbed Eddie Goulding the wrong way. I warned him repeatedly."

"Going to be a bit dodgy at the premiere next month," said Niven. "Someone should give the little blighter a heads up. But not Mrs. Niven's boy. Kill the messenger and all that tosh."

"Not a profession for the faint of heart," said Rathbone.

"Cricket?" asked Aubrey.

"No," replied Rathbone. "Acting."

"Ah!"

After several more innings, the cricketers retired to the verandah of the pavilion where Ouida Rathbone, one of the Raj's most socially active and aggressive wives, was pouring out champagne to the thirsty players. She was known as 'Ouida the Organ Grinder' because of her constantly cranking things up for her husband's benefit.

Radford walked over to Leslie Howard, newly returned from London where his film version of *Pygmalion* was enjoying great success.

"How are things back home? Is war on everyone's mind?"

"Not enough," replied Howard, taking out his pipe and stuffing it with tobacco. The blond-haired actor, every American woman's ideal Englishman, was born Leslie Steiner to a Hungarian-Jewish father and Jewish mother.

"Churchill's the lone voice in the wilderness. A veritable Cassandra. Hitler's got everyone either mesmerized or terrified. Can't tell which. But it doesn't feel right being here with things the way they are. Know what I mean, Ozzie"?"

"Actually, not. When I disembarked at Pasadena eight years ago and felt the warm sunshine on my face, I said to myself: 'Osmond, this is paradise on earth. No more drafty dressing rooms. No more fog and damp. I shall lie in a hammock all year-round plucking oranges from the trees and live like Harun al-Rashid. I fought my war twenty years ago, Leslie, and my family suffered for it. If there is another, it will never come to America."

"Oh, Ozzie! You're so wrong. Hitler's a madman dedicated utterly to world domination. What are you up to Thursday evening?"

"Probably going to bed early with a volume of Trollope."

"There's a BIG dinner at the Ambassador. Hollywood Anti-Nazi League. Jurgen Schiller is going to speak. Know who he is?"

"'Know who he is'? That mad Austrian played Rupert of Hentzau to my Rassendyll on tour in *Prisoner of Zenda*. Haven't seen him in donkey's years."

"He gave up acting some time ago," said Howard. "Jurgen has dedicated his life to fighting fascism. Brilliant orator. Please, come with me, Ozzie. A show of solidarity from the creative community is so important."

"I might make an appearance if you put in a word with Selznick about our Flavia doing a screen test for that *Gone With The Wind* epic. I gather you're appearing in it."

"Is the poor girl mad?" Howard chuckled aloud. "They'll never cast an Englishwoman as Scarlett O'Hara. Not in a hundred years. The American public would never tolerate it. How is the lovely Hyacinth, by the way? Still traipsing up to Ojai in the thrall of her swami? Aren't you the least bit jealous of that chap?"

"They were children together in India," replied Radford. "And I would suggest, no saber rattling in front of my wife. She and Krishna are avowed pacifists."

"Unfortunately, Herr Hitler doesn't know the meaning of the word. Come along with me on Thursday, Ozzie, and you'll learn the true meaning of enlightenment."

FALLING IN LOVE AGAIN

The Packard scraped the running board as it screeched to a stop outside the entrance of the Trocadero, a popular, strictly black-tie nightclub on Sunset Boulevard.

"Hello, handsome." Flavia smiled at the car hop, tossing him her car key. "Good crowd tonight?"

"Packed to the rafters, Miss Radford."

Flavia had been club hopping for several hours. Her previous stop had been the Cafe Gala, a supper club frequented by homosexuals and lesbians, but also visited by heterosexuals fascinated by the lavender life.

Before leaving Best of Times for her night on the town, Flavia had asked their housekeeper if she might translate a few phrases for her into German.

"Willi darling, how would one say: 'Oh, baby, I'm so hot for you. I'm going to make you come all night.'"

The housekeeper's jaw dropped open at such a risqué declaration, but she felt obligated to write something for her employer's daughter. Armed with Willi's translation on a scrap of paper, Flavia grabbed a beaded bag and floated out the front door.

Entering the Cafe Gala on Horn Avenue just above the Strip, Flavia spotted Marlene Dietrich seated at a banquette with another woman.

"Am I late?" asked the chestnut-haired beauty, sliding enticingly into the booth opposite the beauteous Blue Angel and removing a Lucky Strike from her gold cigarette case.

"Did we have a previous assignation?" asked Dietrich, taking a long drag on her own cigarette, and gazing indifferently in Flavia's direction. A peculiar speech impediment caused the word to sound like 'pwevious'.

"Don't you remember me?" asked Flavia. "We met at Charlie Feldman's party. You said you'd like to see me again."

"I have a dreadful memory," said the Blue Angel. "But you have lovely eyes."

"My father is Sir Osmond Radford."

"And your mother is a radiant flower," replied Dietrich. "Wait! Wait! Hyacinth. Correct? The resemblance is striking. I adore your father. He's a Capricorn like me. We shared a dressing room at Paramount. By mistake. He graciously gave it up. Tell him that I'd love to do his radio show. You look remarkably like your mother. Are you still in school?"

Flavia blushed at the ridiculous question. Dietrich's eyes were boring into Flavia. The glamorous star's perfume was adding to the younger woman's arousal. The Blue Angel's theme song, Falling in Love Again, caromed off the walls of Flavia's brain. All she could think of was the sheer excitement of being in bed with the glamorous *Schauspieler*. Holding her, touching her, bringing her to climax with her mouth. "No. I'm an actress."

"Really?" Flavia's cigarette remained unlit. Dietrich took hold of the younger woman's hand, gracefully floating her own burning cigarette forward to ignite Flavia's Lucky Strike. "You abandoned your studies?" The Blue Angel's right leg was pressed against Flavia's. "Is there nothing more you can learn?"

Never wanted to. What am I to do? Can't help it.

"I've been practicing my German," said Flavia, trying hard not to faint. She clutched Dietrich's hand and returned her gaze. "Would you like to hear me say something?"

"Go ahead," said Dietrich. She withdrew her hand from Flavia's grasp and elevated it to touch the younger woman's cheek. "Don't be shy."

"I'm not."

"Well, then. *Was wollen Sie sagen, meine hübsche?*"

Flavia leaned forward and whispered the words Willi had scribbled on the scrap of paper into the movie star's ear. Dietrich exploded with laughter and placed her forehead on the table. Finally coming up for air, the Blue Angel looked pitifully at Flavia. "Poor darling! Why didn't you speak up sooner? There's nothing worse than a leaky carburetor. You must take your car to a mechanic immediately. And do give my regards to your parents."

Dietrich turned her attention back to her neglected date. Utterly humiliated, Flavia fled towards the exit.

* * *

No sooner had Flavia entered the Trocadero when she heard a familiar voice calling out in a thick Brooklyn accent: "Cigars, cigarettes, kewpie dolls! Cigars, cigarettes, kewpie dolls!"

Toby Winslow, a delicious little cigarette girl, was peddling her wares from a tray. Possessed of a perfect figure, the five-foot-nothing Toby wore a bow in her hair and the tiniest of skirts that showed off her incredible legs. She could easily have been the model for the kewpie dolls she sold.

"Hello, Toby!" Flavia absolutely adored the little bombshell from Flatbush. She had taken the 'dese-dem-and-dose' girl under her wing and made her her 'project'. "Finish the book yet?" Flavia was like an evangelist spreading the gospel of Margaret Mitchell to all who might listen.

"Not yet," replied Toby. "It's gotta lotta pages, y'know. But you are perfect to play Scarlett O'Hara."

"Tell David Selznick when he comes in." Flavia was searching the room for someone while she continued to speak. "And try not to say 'poifect'."

"My boyfriend don't mind," said Toby, who quickly corrected herself. "Doesn't mind. See? I can do it if I try hard."

"Still hot and heavy?"

"Torrid. Know what I mean? He's crazy about me. But his wife won't give him a divorce."

"Perhaps you should look elsewhere, Toby."

"Nah! I love him. Looking for your friends? They're in the powder room." Hugh Harcourt was dining at the other end of the restaurant with his wife Gwen, and another expatriate couple, the Pomfretts.

"Mosley's got the right idea," said Victor Pomfrett, a weasel-faced actor, who played weasel-faced villains in B-movies. "Mark my words. The British Union of Fascism is the wave of the future. Correction: the present. Look what Mussolini's done! Look at Hitler! Wait till the next election back home. The BUF will be swept into power and Oswald Mosley will be Prime Minister. Mark my words. I'll go one better: Charles Lindbergh will be the next President of the United States. Mark my words."

"Better not let Leslie Howard hear you," said Gwen Harcourt, a sharp-tongued, well-preserved redhead, who once had a successful stage career in England. "He'll have you charged with treason."

"Howard's a Jew," snarled Pomfrett, "even though he pretends otherwise. Just like his friend Korda. Just like all these Jews in Hollywood, who want to drag the world into another war. Mark my words."

"Careful, Vic," warned his wife Sybil, who had left home half-drunk and was now several sheets and a duvet to the wind, "You work for Jews."

"No need to remind me. Something wrong, Hugh?"

Harcourt had been watching Flavia's progress at the other end of the room. When she had disappeared into the powder room, he began tapping his chest repeatedly with the palms of his hands. Finally, he shrugged and said: "Thought I had another packet of ciggies. Need any, Vic? No? Back in a flash." Harcourt kissed his wife on the cheek and rose to his feet. "Try not to miss me, luv."

"It will be agony until you return, dearest."

Harcourt waded through the couples dancing on the tiny parquet floor until he came up behind Toby Winslow and said: "Might I have a packet of cigarettes, miss?"

Toby turned around and stared up at Hugh Harcourt's florid face. "Sure," she replied. "What brand?"

"What have you got?" Harcourt lowered his voice to a stage whisper and asked: "Could you hear my heart pounding from the other side of the room?"

"I thought it was the drummer."

"*'Nymph in thy orisons, be all my sins remembered'.*"

"I never know what yer talkin' about," whispered Toby, "but it always sounds so pretty. Are you hard?"

"Like fumed oak."

"Mmmm. I'm soakin' wet. Wanna come back to my place later?"

"Can't tonight, you delicious creature. Here with the wife and another couple."

"Yer a stinker. Y'know that?"

"Promise you'll spank me for being bad?"

"Natch."

Harcourt removed a folded five-dollar bill and slid the money gingerly into Toby's cleavage. He growled: "There's a little something extra for you." He took a packet of Pall Malls from her tray, readjusted his trousers, and returned to his wife.

* * *

Esther, the black attendant of the powder room, was shouting towards a cubicle as Flavia entered: "Y'all wanna act like that, go on down to Central Avenue."

"What is the cause of your consternation, Esther?" Flavia was always amused by the attendant's elevated state of dudgeon.

"Is that who I think it is?" Violet Purdy, a dyed blonde in her mid-twenties with a half-moon scar on her left cheek, stood up on a toilet seat. She peeped over the stall door and beamed at Flavia.

Esther shook an ebony forefinger at Violet and proclaimed: "Ain't no way for young white girls to behave!"

Violet stuck her tongue out at the attendant. It was mostly red but had a distinct coloration in the center of it.

An unseen voice inside the same stall called out: "Who you callin' a white girl?"

Esther stormed out of the powder room. A second later, the stall door opened. Violet emerged, followed by Consuela Gonzalez, a voluptuous twenty-year old from Guadalajara. Both wore the skimpiest of dresses held up by spaghetti straps.

Flavia's face lit up when she saw the two girls. "Hello, you bedizened cyprians."

"Heyyy!" echoed Consuela, taking mock offense. "I'm a convent girl. Don' talk to me like that, *puta*."

Flavia burst out laughing, embraced the two young women and kissed them full on the mouth. "Nothing like a leaky carburetor to get me going. What were you two novitiates up to in there?"

Violet produced a lit reefer from behind her back. "Want some loco weed, Limey? Consuela's cousin snuck it across the border."

"Is it strong?" asked Flavia.

"Holy mother of Jesus! I thought I was back in Milwaukee."

"Just what the doctor ordered."

Fifteen minutes later, a sky-high Flavia Radford sailed her Packard north towards Mulholland Drive while reciting aloud one of her favorite GWTW speeches: *'As God is my witness, they're not going to lick me. If I have to lie, steal, cheat, or kill, I'll never be hungry again.'* The incredibly potent marijuana had affected her sense of direction. Flavia cursed to herself upon realizing she was not taking her usual route home up Benedict Canyon but was actually two miles east on Laurel Canyon.

"Cockfosters!" She stuck her arm out to signal a left turn, then grabbed hold of the wheel and swung it hard.

At that exact moment, a man appeared out of nowhere in the headlights. Flavia slammed on the brakes. The man rolled up onto the hood and ended up plastered against the windscreen with a grotesque look on his face. Flavia jumped out of the car. The man rolled off the hood and tumbled to the ground.

SOME RATHER UNPLEASANT PEOPLE

Radford was tucked up in his bed reading *The Way We Live Now* when the telephone on the nightstand rang. It was almost midnight. The ringing would not disturb Hyacinth as she was on one of her frequent spiritual pilgrimages to Ojai. The actor-knight lifted the receiver and was greeted by a familiar voice, who offered neither an opening salutation nor an inquiry as to Radford's health: "Have you got two hundred dollars?" Swift and to the point, that was always Jasper Radford's *modus operandi.*

Jasper Radford was Osmond's older brother, a scoundrel and philanderer, who had arrived in Hollywood in 1935 following a well-publicized scandal in England. Shamelessly hitching on to his younger brother's coattails, the older Radford occasionally found work on screen playing butlers (usually with no lines). A dreadful actor when the camera was rolling, Jasper was an absolute delight off screen and a court jester at the weekly, high-stakes poker games attended by Selznick and his fellow moguls.

"In cash?" responded his younger brother.

"Of course," Jasper replied testily.

"What has occurred?"

"I left home without my purse," replied Jasper testily. "And some rather unpleasant people won't take a personal cheque."

Jasper proceeded to give his brother an address high in the hills to the east of the Cahuenga Pass. He expressly forbade Radford pulling up in his Rolls-Royce. In addition, he was to inquire as to the whereabouts of Dr. Livingstone. Charleston Brown, Radford's handsome, black chauffeur, heard the garage door open and insisted on driving his employer. The actor declined the offer, saying that he needed a solo excursion in his two-seater MG sports car to 'clear the cobwebs from his brain'. Half an hour later, Radford found himself ringing the doorbell of an antebellum mansion perched high above Grauman's Chinese Theatre. In keeping with the plantation style of architecture, the front door was opened by a vivacious colored maid, who curtsied as to the manner born.

"I've come to see Dr. Livingstone," said Radford.

"You must be Colonel Archibald!" said the maid, flashing the broadest of smiles. "Doctor's been expecting you. Do come in."

Radford stepped into the foyer just as a buxom, middle-aged blond descended the staircase. She comported herself exactly like Diamond Lil and addressed the Englishman in a voice more Mae West than Mae herself."

"Colonel Archibald!" she said "Your reputation has preceded you. Come into the parlor."

The overripe hostess undulated her way towards a set of pocket doors, parted them and gestured for the actor to precede her into the wood paneled parlor. Perched on a settee avidly reading that day's *Hollywood Reporter* were Ginger Rogers and Carole Lombard— most scantily clad, indeed and exhibiting more *poitrine* than their fans or even their husbands had ever seen in public. As Radford was well acquainted with both actresses, he thought it rather strange that neither one greeted him nor seemed to recognize him at all. Finally, he burst out laughing.

"Wanna share the joke?" asked the buxom hostess.

"My sentiments exactly," replied Radford. "I received a telephone call within the last hour asking me to come to Mae's."

"I'm Mae," said the hostess.

"Of course, you are, dear lady," replied Radford. "And doing a splendid job, if one may say so. Could we please end this charade and get down to the business at hand?"

The hostess placed a hand on her hip, turned her attention to the uncanny Rogers and Lombard lookalikes, and said: "Girls, haul freight. The Colonel and I need to talk."

The young women rose from the settee, approached Radford, and kissed him on both cheeks. The scent of their expensive perfume lingered long after they'd left the parlor.

"The resemblance is quite remarkable."

Mae ignored the Englishman's positive review and asked: "Didja bring the money?"

"What concern is that of yours?"" asked Radford.

"Dr. Livingstone's a naughty boy," she replied. "He took Merle upstairs a few hours ago and started battin' her around."

"Would that be Merle Oberon?"

"Around the house, she's simply known as Merle."

"Does Alex Korda know she's here?" asked Radford, referring to the English actress's Hungarian producer-lover.

"Let's talk turkey, Colonel. The Doc is no longer a welcome guest in my establishment. But he's run up quite a tab and he's not leavin' till he settles his account. Get my drift?"

"Crystal clear. Where is the good doctor now?"

"Where he can't cause any more trouble."

Mae led Radford to the far end of the parlor and pushed a panel which opened to her touch. The Englishman bent over to keep his head from hitting a beam. He followed her into semi-darkness and down a steep flight of rickety stairs.

"Will Boris Karloff be making an appearance next?" Radford asked with an amused smile.

"You got a good sense of humor, Colonel. Why don't you come see me some time?"

They had reached the bottom of the steps. Radford looked up from the cement floor that greeted him and gazed at row upon row of wine racks. The cellar was illuminated by a single, naked light bulb. Directly under the bulb, a plump, bald-pated, middle-aged man of medium height was flanked on either side by two Neanderthals in double breasted suits. Radford walked over to the man, who sat in a wooden chair sipping a glass of red wine and perspiring heavily. Without a scintilla of shame, the actor-knight uttered the immortal line: "Dr. Livingstone, I presume?"

"Took your bloody time getting here," growled Jasper Radford.

"If you'd rather I leave now...."

"No, no, no," said Jasper, holding his wine glass aloft. "Fancy a glass? It's a modest little plonk they're serving this evening. Chateau du San Pedro."

Radford removed an envelope from his inside jacket pocket and held it out to Jasper.

"Two hundred dollars. Per your request."

Mae stepped between the two brothers, took the envelope, and counted the money. The tally was correct.

"He's all yours, Colonel."

Jasper rose from the wooden chair and handed his wine glass to one of the Neanderthals. Tugging at the hem of his jacket, he remarked: "We must do this again at Whitsun."

All too aware that his older brother's false camaraderie was often a prelude to pugilistic exertions, Radford grabbed hold of Jasper's arm and steered him towards the exit. At the same moment, a nubile and fecund Merle Oberon look-alike raced down the stairs like one of the Furies. Her bare breasts were exposed under her silk wrapper. Her lip was swollen, and she had a black eye. The girl began hammering at Jasper's chest with her tiny fists.

"Son-of-a-bitch!" she shrieked.

Jasper grabbed hold of the girl's wrists to avert the blows. The larger of the two Neanderthals stepped in and pried Merle loose from the older Radford brother.

"Look what he done to me!" wailed Merle. "Look what the sick bastard done to me."

"Get him outta here, Colonel," said Mae.

Jasper trudged up the wooden stairs behind his younger brother, paused midway, turned back to the bristling madame, and, with all the solemnity of the Archbishop of Canterbury, said: "I shall report this regrettable lack of hospitality to *Les Freres Michelin.*"

UNWELCOME SOBRIETY

N o sooner had the man rolled off the Packard's hood, when Flavia began to consider her options. What would Scarlett O'Hara have done under the circumstances? *'I can't think about that right now. If I do, I'll go crazy. I'll think about that tomorrow.'* No, that plan of action wouldn't help one bit. Flavia had to get as far away from the body as possible.

She turned the key in the ignition. To her horror, the motor wouldn't start. Cockfosters! She'd have to walk. But where was one to go stranded in the middle of Laurel Canyon wearing evening dress and high heels?

Half an hour later, a weary and bedraggled Flavia arrived in the lobby of the Chateau Marmont on Sunset Boulevard. "Might I use your telephone?" She had caught the attention of the drowsy night clerk, who stared up at the beautiful, barefoot actress.

Twenty minutes later, Charleston Brown beeped the horn in front of the Marmont. Flavia climbed into the front seat of the Rolls-Royce next to the black chauffeur and they made their way back up Laurel Canyon where they caught sight of the abandoned Packard— but no body.

"What's goin' on, Miss Flavia?"

"It was here an hour ago. I promise you, Charleston. Lying in the road. Big as life. Or death."

"How much reefer did you smoke tonight?"

"I beg your pardon?"

"Was there really a body or did you just dream it up?"

"I promise you there was a man and— God forgive me— I hit him. Oh, no!" Flavia gripped Charleston's arm in terror. "What if the police have already been here? What if they've taken the body to the morgue?"

"Cops haven't been here," said Charleston. "Otherwise, they'd have taken the Packard. You okay to drive?"

"The events of the evening have reduced me to an unwelcome sobriety."

"Good. Just in case, you follow me back to Best of Times. Okay?"

They were about to get into their respective vehicles when a mounted policeman screeched his motorcycle to a halt in front of them. The cop warily eyed Charleston, who was not dressed in his usual chauffeur's livery, but was wearing a stylish sports jacket and spectator shoes.

"Aren't you outta your neighborhood, boy?" asked the cop.

"Mr. Brown is in my employ," said Flavia.

"And who the hell are you?" asked the cop, staring at the barefoot English actress.

"She was havin' trouble wit' her engine, boss." Charleston was staring at the ground and shuffling his feet like a blackface actor in a stock company production of *Uncle Tom's Cabin*. "She done sent for me to fix it. Sho nuff."

The cop stared at them both suspiciously, then said: "Well, make it snappy, Snowflake, and get on your way. Both of ya."

"Yassuh, boss."

The cop got back on his motorcycle, revved it up and drove off.

Flavia stared incredulously at Charleston. "Why did you behave in that outrageous manner?"

"Cuz I'm not white," replied the chauffeur, enumerating his responses on his long, thin fingers. "I don't want to be mounted over his fireplace. And your Daddy don't need that kind of publicity."

"But it's not fair! Having to behave like Stepin Fetchit to assuage that vulgar policeman."

"Welcome to America."

Charleston drove the Rolls perilously close to the speed limit on his way west on Sunset. Flavia had difficulty keeping up with him. By the time the Packard reached Benedict Canyon, the chauffeur was nowhere in sight. The actress had the pedal to the floor as she turned sharply onto Tower Road. In her haste, she almost ran over a man in bathrobe and pajamas walking his pet Dachshund.

FOUR ABSOLUTES

45

The Radford brothers drove in silence through Hollywood for several minutes after departing the hillside brothel. Sir Osmond finally spoke: "You might thank me for what I did."

Jasper stared up at the night sky for a length of time, then murmured a perfunctory: "Thank you."

"What the devil was all that?" asked Radford.

"Oh, please, Ozzie. I know you and Hyacinth are a proper Darby and Joan, but there was a time when you weren't married. It's a bordello."

"I realized that. But those girls! They looked exactly—"

"The wonders of modern surgery," said Jasper. "The ultimate fantasy. Being able to shag one's favorite film star. With Mae West reigning as the madame supreme. God bless America, what? The Prince of Wales visited Mae's."

"He didn't!"

"I promise you. Mrs. Simpson sent him. Post-graduate work."

"But why all the aliases? Dr. Livingstone and Colonel Whosit."

"To protect the clients. The girls may well resemble Claudette Colbert and Joan Crawford, but they aren't really. Similarly, a chap, who looks remarkably like Sir Osmond Radford turns out to be someone called Colonel Archibald."

"For the police blotter?"

"Fear not. The Chief of Police is one of Mae's regulars. Perversely, I am often mistaken for one of the staff and asked by some yahoo to fetch him a drink. 'Fetch it yourself, you insignificant mollusk. I am not the butler. I merely play one on screen.'"

Jasper Radford was the epitome of the hapless middle child. His older brother Priam was the heir to the family estate in Kent and made a good living from it. His little brother Osmond shocked the family by running off to London and becoming an actor. The scandal of the county. Until he married Hyacinth Talbot.

It was as if he'd married into the Royal Family. When Osmond became a West End star, Jasper turned up in London on his coattails. He still possessed a thick head of hair in those days, and the most devilish mustache. Jasper was a compulsive gambler. His addiction drove his poor wife Pamela, a lovely woman from a wealthy family to distraction. Her parents had begged her not to marry Jasper. But she did and had two children with him. Jasper embezzled a fortune from a business venture, and it was later discovered he'd been having an affair with his partner's wife. Pamela subsequently sued him for divorce. Every door that had previously welcomed Jasper turned him away. He was branded a bounder, a cad, and a pariah. No decent woman would be seen in his company. Except for Eunice.

"Are you working these days?" asked Radford.

"Last week at RKO," replied Jasper. "Musical with Fred and Ginger. He's quite a nice chap. Invited me out to the track."

"I haven't worked in six months."

"Weren't you on the wireless last Saturday?"

"That's not work, Jas. It's reading. I need something to sink my teeth into. A proper acting role." Radford debated whether to tell his older brother about the pending Sherlock Holmes screen test but decided against it. Jasper delighted in sticking the needle into his younger brother's rib cage any chance he had.

"Pity about *Dombey and Son*."

"Sank like a stone," said Radford. "Freddy Bartholomew was far too old."

"He wasn't the old one. "Radford stared questioningly at his older brother. "Well, you *are* getting on, old boy."

"What's really the problem?" asked Radford, turning the MG north on Doheny Drive.

"When you were cast in *Dombey and Son*, I begged you to get me a part. A humble day's work would have sufficed. What did you say in response? 'Sorry, Jas. They don't need any butlers.' Your words were like an ice pick bludgeoning my heart! There's so much more to me than being a butler. All my years in the City. I was in great demand as an after-dinner speaker. But have you once asked me to appear on your radio show? No!"

"Be realistic, Jasper. You're not an actor. You make faces and people laugh at you. But you can't handle a speech of any consequence. You turned up here after the scandal in England thinking you could 'make a fast buck' in the movies. Your very words. Remember? Have you managed to save one penny? No! You gamble it away and spend what's left on whores." Radford pulled the car over to the curb and turned to his brother: "Sorry, Jas. I didn't mean what I said."

"How easy it is for you," replied Jasper. "Blessed with the gifts of great height, a handsome head of hair and those ridiculous eyebrows. I can assure you if I'd kept my curly locks and worn lifts in my shoes, I'd have given you a run for your money. The truth be known, Ozzie, all you really do is ape our late lamented father. Those stern looks and pensive pauses that made the matinee ladies swoon. The clenched fist raised so dramatically to the brow. It's just dear old Papa, isn't it? But no one knows that except me. Good night, little brother." Jasper grabbed hold of the handle and got out of the car.

Radford called after him: "Come back, Jasper! Please! Let me drive you home!"

His older brother turned around and pointed to the tiny bungalow at the end of the walkway. "I *am* home. Sorry you don't recognize my humble abode."

Jasper had no sooner placed his key in the lock and stepped across the threshold when he heard his wife's voice: "Where have you been? Two o'clock in the morning. I've been worried half to death."

"I've been out with my brother. The Masquer's Club."

"Ohhh! Lady Muck let him off the chain, did she?"

Eunice Radford usually sounded remarkably like the dowager Queen Mary, except when she was emotionally rattled and her voice moved hundreds of miles north of Westminster.

When London society had turned on Jasper Radford, only his solicitor's secretary stood by him. Originally from Manchester, Eunice Wrench possessed a Northern accent one could slice with a scimitar. Her first bit of employment in London was at a factory in the East End, but she was laid off with two dozen other workers after a few weeks. Walking along Waterloo Bridge one fogbound evening in a state of despair and down to her last farthing, the buxom Mancunian redhead was mistaken for a lady of the night. "What price pleasure, m'dear?" asked the toff. Does he take me for a tart? thought Eunice. Well, why not? Money for old rope.

Three months later, she had saved enough money for a room in Shepherd's Market and a new wardrobe. She remained on the game in Mayfair for the next year. Being by nature an extremely ambitious creature, Miss Wrench realized that ultimately there was no long-term future in prostitution, despite the money she was raking in on her back. She enrolled in a secretarial school by day and took elocution lessons by night. Upon graduation Miss Wrench found employment at the Inns of Court as a general secretary to a prestigious firm of solicitors.

It was there that Eunice met the outrageous, but ever-so-nice Jasper Radford, who was going through a painful divorce and looking for a sympathetic shoulder and ample bosom to cry on. Eunice, who always fancied bald men, found Jasper to be a fervent lover, although his sexual predilections tended to run towards the hunt more than the bedroom. She made it clear that the use of riding crops and such paraphernalia could only occur on very special occasions, such as birthdays and coronations.

Within a year, she had become Eunice Radford. Not even Jasper knew of her earlier life in the *demimonde*. Moving to America made the likelihood of the former Miss Wrench running into anyone from her salad days on the game extremely remote. Her posh accent brought her prompt service in Los Angeles department stores and exceptional seating in restaurants. But she was kept at a frosty arms' length by the memsahibs of the Hollywood Raj. Eunice thought this was due to a slight but uncanny resemblance to Gwendolyn Harcourt, who refused to be in the same room with her.

Being Mrs. Jasper Radford had not turned out to be the nirvana Eunice had hoped for. She grew more and more depressed with her situation until the afternoon a complete stranger found her weeping in the third-floor ladies room of Bullock's Wilshire Department store. Her name was Bijou Destino and she took Eunice to her first Oxford Group meeting.

"Have you had a coffee enema again?" asked Jasper. "They always make you so jumpy."

"I went to a meeting tonight," Eunice said fervently. "With Bijou. She drove."

"What sort of meeting?"

"The Oxford Group. Oh, I do wish you'd go with me, Jas. It would change your life."

"Can you imagine me a Buchmanite? Really, old girl." Jasper disdained the Christian organization of which Eunice was so enthralled. Founded by an American Lutheran minister named Frank Buchman, his followers were taught that the root of all problems was derived from fear and selfishness. Buchmanites strove to attain the unattainable Four Absolutes: honesty, purity, unselfishness and love. Jasper thought it was a cult.

"Dr. Buchman is going to meet Hitler." Eunice could barely control her excitement at the prospect of these two powerful forces colliding head on.

"I've got a blinding headache, Eunice. Do you mind awfully if I retire for the—?"

Eunice grabbed hold of a yellow legal pad and barred her husband's path to the bedroom. "Look what I wrote during my Quiet Time."

"Quiet time?"

"Oh, Jas! You never listen to me. We always have Quiet Time at the meetings where we commune with the Divine and write down any inspirational thoughts that come to us."

Eunice thrust the yellow legal pad in Jasper's face. He stared without a whit of comprehension at the name his wife had printed in large block letters.

"Who the devil is Gerald O'Hara?"

"The father in *Gone With The Wind*. The book your beloved niece is so obsessed with. David O. Selznick is making a movie of it. Even I know that. Everyone in Hollywood knows that."

"But what does this have to do with—?"

"YOU … are going to play Gerald O'Hara. You, Jasper Radford, are finally going to be a film star. You will probably win an Academy Award."

"Have you been drinking?"

Eunice grabbed hold of her husband's hands and squeezed them until he winced. "It came to me tonight, Jasper. God wants you to play this role."

"I think not."

"You're so much more than a butler." Eunice all but spat out the last word.

"That's not what my little brother thinks."

"Jealousy— plain and simple. You have the makings of a great actor, Jasper. This is your chance, lad. Seize it!"

It wasn't exactly the St. Crispin's Day speech, but Jasper was quite aroused by it. Seizing hold of his wife, he crushed her into him. Eunice was trembling as she stared down at her husband's bulging crotch.

"Oh, Jasper!"

"Let's go to bed," he growled.

"Yes, yes, yes." Then she caught herself. "No whips.

BLATANT DISREGARD FOR HUMANITY

Over one hundred pro-Nazi picketers marched in front of the Ambassador Hotel on Wilshire Boulevard that evening. Some carried placards that read: "America First Forever" and "Hitler is Right!" The various film stars, who emerged from their cars to attend the Hollywood Anti-Nazi League event inside, were pelted by the picketers with eggs and rotten tomatoes. One even tossed a damp paper bag filled with feces.

"Didja get a picture of that?" growled veteran FBI Special Agent Floyd Hightower from the safety of his Ford parked across the way from the hotel's main entrance. The G-Man was in his mid-40s, well over six feet tall with a hawk nose and a pock marked face stretched across high cheekbones (a legacy passed down from his Cherokee grandmother). His boss, Dixon Kirby, once described Hightower's deep Oklahoma growl as 'forty miles of bad road.' "Mink and shit. See what a dry cleaner can do with that. Even in Beverly Hills. Who we got so far?"

"Still no trace of Hesselberg. Or Bickel, Goldenberg, Rothschild and the other ones." Hightower's partner, Matt Corcoran, peered through his camera's telephoto lens.

"How many times I gotta tell you, Matt? They're using aliases. Those sheenies are trying to pass for God-fearing Christians. Calling themselves Melvyn Douglas, Fredric March, Edward G. Robinson, and Dorothy Parker."

"My wife is crazy about Fredric March. Are you sure he's a Jew?"

"Might as well be. He's leans so far left, he couldn't stand up straight if his life depended on it."

"Aren't all Commies Jews?"

"Not necessarily," replied Hightower. "But they sure as hell aren't Americans. They don't pledge allegiance to Uncle Sam. Just to Uncle Izzy and all the other Hebes, who own the banks. Ever notice how no Jews went broke after the stock market crashed? That's cause they manipulated the whole thing. Hitler's got the right idea. Round 'em all up and put 'em in camps."

"Hey! Isn't that Leslie Howard?" asked Corcoran.

"Another Hebe," said Hightower scornfully.

"Jesus, Floyd! You're gonna break my wife's heart. She saw *The Scarlet Pimpernel* five times."

"That's how they do it. See? The kikes that run the studios make our women fall in love with these impersonators. They manipulate their emotions. World domination. That's what the Jews and the Commies are after. I tell Ethel this all the time."

"How is Ethel?"

"The same," growled Hightower.

"Who's the tall guy with Leslie Howard?"

"Sir Osmond Radford."

"Jew?"

"Nah. Some old English actor. Does a weekly radio show on CBS. We got nothing on him."

"What about this guy?" Corcoran passed his partner the telephoto lens. "Look familiar?"

"Lemme see," replied Hightower, flipping rapidly through the thick file of surveillance photos in his lap. "Got him in here someplace. Yup. Beverly Hills lawyer. He's definitely a person of interest. Name's Chester Lowenthal. Another Hebe. From San Francisco."

"They got Jews in San Francisco?"

"They got 'em everywhere."

* * *

Chester Lowenthal had met Paul Merlin his first day at Stanford Law School in 1930. Merlin, a blond, towering Adonis, had come west from Rochester, New York, with a tennis racquet in one hand and his cock in the other. Lowenthal marveled at Merlin's ability to absorb the finer points of jurisprudence while effortlessly hopping from bed to bed with some of the wealthiest girls in in the Bay area. Smart and extremely good-looking, Chet Lowenthal's non-observant Jewish family had lived in Northern California for three generations. After graduation, Merlin headed south to article with a Los

Angeles law firm while the naturally conservative Lowenthal remained in San Francisco clerking for a firm of stodgy maritime attorneys. After two years of radio silence, Lowenthal received a telegram from Merlin:

PACK YOUR BAGS STOP FORTUNE TO BE MADE IN DIVORCE STOP WOMEN ARE SO GRATEFUL DON'T STOP PAUL

* * *

Lowenthal wasn't sure what the telegram meant. Was it a gag? Always something of a joker, Merlin had listed 'DRINKING' just below 'TENNIS' as a special skill on his résumé. When Lowenthal didn't reply to his wire, Merlin telephoned him long distance two days later and expressed deep concern. Had Lowenthal been run over by a trolley car and killed? What other reason could he have for not responding? Merlin rhapsodized about Beverly Hills, its glorious weather, its palm trees and the remarkable beauty of its women, whom he claimed he'd been stacking up like cordwood next to his fireplace in anticipation of Lowenthal's arrival.

The law office was situated above a clothing store on Rodeo Drive. It wasn't at all what Lowenthal had expected— particularly after two years in a conservative corporate environment. How many lawyers were employed in the firm? The question was answered when Merlin steered his old college buddy towards a door halfway down the hall and pointed out a sign which read "Blaine, Merlin & Lowenthal, Attorneys at Law."

"Who's Blaine?" asked Lowenthal, not fully registering he'd gone with a single train ride from low man on the totem pole in San Francisco to full partner in a Beverly Hills law firm.

"F. Sedgwick Blaine. The old lush fronting for us," smiled Merlin, opening the door, and gesturing for Lowenthal to walk in ahead of him. "Spends most of the week in Montecito with his Bolivian mistress. Actually, Juanita is his housekeeper. But Mrs. Blaine has no idea her husband's been doing the nasty with her— that is when he's sober enough to maintain an erection. Hello, Gladdie."

Gladdie was Gladys McNutt, a big-as-a-minute, freckle-faced redhead, who sat perched behind her Underwood all day typing letters and answering the phone. "Kay Francis called," said Gladys, not looking up from her typing.

"Is she getting a divorce?" asked Merlin.

"No. But she heard Joan Blondell is and she's 'vewy, vewy intewested'."

"Please, Gladys, let's not give my new partner the wrong impression."

"Are you Mr. Lowenthal?" asked Gladys, who rose to her full height of five feet and shook his hand with a remarkably strong grip. "I thought he made you up as a tax deduction."

"You'll get used to Gladys," said Merlin, shepherding Lowenthal into his private office. "I inherited her from old man Blaine. Want to see your office?"

"Paul, you've bamboozled me."

"What are you talking about, buddy? Didn't I bring you all the way down here? First class."

"To do what?"

"Divorces! Didn't you read my telegram? It's the wave of the future out here, buddy. These people live in a dream world. They make five pictures a year. Five different identities. Pretend husbands. Pretend wives. Kissing each other passionately all day long. Gets confusing. What's the movie and what's real? They don't know but— bottom line— they're not happy. They try a new partner to see if the grass is more verdant on the other side of Mulholland Drive. Divorce is in the air, buddy, and I'm flying high. Building quite the reputation for myself. When women want to untie the knot, they think of Merlin the Divorce Magician."

"Did you dream up that moniker yourself?"

"No, no. That's vintage Russell Birdwell. David Selznick's publicist. Man's a genius. I pay him on the QT and he keeps my name in all the gossip columns. Took me a while to figure out the secret to my success: represent the women. Judges are always sympathetic to them, and they are so fucking grateful to the man, who got them their freedom and a big fat settlement. Plus, they like the way I hold their hands in court. I'm sensitive, see. And, brother, do I get laid! So? What do you think, buddy?"

Lowenthal seriously considered taking the next train back to San Francisco, but Merlin never took no for an answer. Those two little letters were anathema to him. So Lowenthal joined him in the divorce business and the two performed very well. Both legally and in bed. Merlin was nothing short of a wizard with women. Gazing tenderly at them, the pride of Rochester would pat their hands and rub their spines gently all through the court room proceedings. They, in turn, did not forget his kindness. Particularly when they found themselves alone abruptly after years of unhappy marriages.

The two attorneys were hugely successful. So much so that Sedgwick Blaine sobered up long enough to read his contract and discovered that his junior partners were in arrears for thirty per cent of the company's income that they were obliged to pay him.

"How could you have done that?" Lowenthal asked Merlin, after reading the latest demand from their senior partner. "How could you sign a contract like that?"

"I never dreamt you'd be this good," said an embarrassed Merlin. "You get settlements for these women I never dreamt of. How do you do it, Chet? What an amazing negotiator! I always take the first offer."

"Not anymore. You've got to bring in more money, Paul. If we're going to keep paying Blaine his pound of flesh."

The senior partner's appetite grew more avaricious. With their backs up against the wall threatening to break through into the next room, Lowenthal masterminded a solution to the Sedgwick Blaine dilemma. He assigned Francis X. Doherty, a retired LAPD detective and the firm's in-house private investigator, to get the dirt on their adulterous senior partner. Armed with explicit photographs of her darling husband in compromising positions with the ungrateful Bolivian strumpet, the boys persuaded the plump, hitherto unsuspecting Mrs. Blaine to file suit for divorce.

Sedgwick was so apoplectic when served by his traitorous junior partners that he succumbed to a fatal coronary. Mrs. Blaine inherited the entire estate and promptly took an around the world cruise. Out of gratitude, she released Merlin and Lowenthal from any future fiduciary responsibilities.

They moved out of their Charleville apartment and leased a beautiful Spanish villa on Tower Road across the street from Best of Times.

As a housewarming present, Gladys bought her employers a female Dachshund, whom she'd named Marlene. The attorneys had been living on Tower Road for almost a month without ever meeting their titled neighbors across the street. Lowenthal had established a nodding acquaintanceship with the Radfords' housekeeper, whom the lawyer would occasionally encounter while picking up the morning newspapers.

Of course, there had been the rather dramatic incident in the wee hours of that morning when a Packard had almost run Lowenthal down while he was taking Marlene for a walk. The beautiful, chestnut-haired woman behind the wheel of the Packard disappeared inside the garage of Best of Times and hadn't the decency to make inquiries as to her neighbor's well-being.

Lowenthal found himself seated one table over from Best of Times's owner in the ballroom of the Ambassador Hotel where both men were attending the Hollywood Anti-Nazi League fundraiser. Radford was gazing indifferently into space. Leslie Howard was engaged in conversation with Martin Kohlinger, a powerful man in his mid-40s with short-cropped hair and a walrus mustache, who looked more like a wrestler than a movie director.

Despite his formidable physique, Kohlinger seemed weighed down by a great sadness. Lowenthal rose from his chair and walked over to the next table.

"Sir Osmond?"

Radford looked up at the young lawyer: "You have the advantage of me, sir."

"Chester Lowenthal. I'm your neighbor. Across the street."

Radford stared blankly at the young lawyer. Finally, he said: "The little Dachshund."

"Yes. Marlene."

"Is she perpetually on heat?"

"Sir?"

"Your little bitch is forever trotting around our front lawn. Driving my Great Danes to distraction. I daren't let them out when she's abroad."

"I can assure you, she's not that kind of broad."

The two neighbors stared at each other failing to comprehend what the other one meant.

"Have you completed your construction?" asked Radford. "The one you pursue on Sundays."

"The gazebo? So sorry. Yes, it's finished. Sunday was the only time those guys were available. If they've disturbed-"

"Not at all, my dear chap. I'm indebted to you. Might have been late for cricket the other day. Don't suppose you play?"

"Golf."

"What's your handicap?"

"None."

"Indeed? You should meet my eldest daughter. Quite the golfer. Hmm. Perhaps not."

The myopic Howard turned around at that moment to see who the actor-knight was chatting up so amiably.

"Hello," said the former Leslie Steiner, smiling and squinting at the same time.

"Hi."

This American voice was one Howard couldn't identify. Reaching into his breast pocket for his spectacles, he placed them his on his nose. The face came into focus but meant nothing to the actor.

"Leslie Howard." He held out his hand to the younger man. "Chester Lowenthal. Call me Chet."

"Lowenthal," repeated Howard. "Lowenthal. Don't you do legal work for us at the Anti-Nazi League?"

"*Pro bono*. Makes up for all the divorces."

"Lowenthal?" Kohlinger stared curiously at the young divorce lawyer. "German?"

"My great-grandfather Rudolf came over from Hamburg in 1848. He was a junior clerk at a bank, and they sent him all the way around the world to collect a debt. Never went back."

"Did he collect the debt?"

"That is an amazing part of family lore, Mr. Kohlinger. It would make a great movie."

"Really?" Kohlinger's face lit up. "Perhaps, we could talk about it some time. Sounds much better than the B-nonsense I have been churning out lately for the Brothers Warner. And, please, call me Marty. We shall be great friends. One cannot have enough friends."

The director's eyes began to tear up. Howard squeezed Kohlinger's arm and whispered to Lowenthal: "The Nazis killed his entire family."

The microphone at the dais made a high-pitched electronic squeal. The urbane Melvyn Douglas, who was standing behind it, apologized to the well-heeled crowd gathered in the ballroom: "Standing here this evening, looking out at so many familiar faces, I am honored to introduce a true hero. We in Hollywood pretend to be Lochinvars up there on the big screen, but our speaker is the real McCoy. A man, who fearlessly spoke up against tyranny and oppression when no one else dared voice their true opinions. It's rumored that Hitler has put a bounty on his head. That's how afraid the *Führer* is of this man. As well he should be. Without further ado, I give you Jurgen Schiller."

Radford sat up in his chair and watched as his old dueling partner strode from the wings onto the dais. Schiller was of medium height, possessed a good head of hair, still dark like his thick eyebrows, and rakish mustache. When he spoke— in perfect English— it was clear that the Austrian had lost none of his ability to hold an audience's attention.

"I came to Hollywood as an actor ten years ago," said Schiller, with an engaging twinkle in his eyes. "A not very young *Schauspieler* determined to conquer the world. This did not happen. It is not one's destiny to conquer the world. History has proved it to us countless times. But always there is a twisted mind that believes that they are the one that will break the mold. It is they, who will bring the planet to its knees. Such a man sits in Berlin today. Determined to rule the globe.

"He is dedicated to exterminating the Jews, the gypsies, the homosexuals. No one dares defy him. Even here in Los Angeles— thousands of miles away from Germany— this monster attempts to rule. And your employers bow to his will, aided and abetted by the Motion Picture Production Code. How can this be you ask? I will tell you.

"Georg Gyssling is the German Consul here in your city. A man who takes his orders directly from the High Command in Berlin. There are some who don't take him seriously. They dismiss him as a buffoon, who took too many spills on his bobsled. Oh, you didn't know. Herr Gyssling finished last in the 1932 Winter Olympics in Lake Placid. When he weighed a hundred pounds less. No. Despite his excess weight, Gyssling has great power and influence in the motion picture industry. More than you can imagine. For the past seven years, he has been regularly invited to view screenings of studio motion pictures and allowed to censor these films. More than Joseph Breen at the MPPC. Don't you find it most peculiar that Warner Brothers made a movie, *The Life of Emile Zola*, that did not once contain the word 'Jew'? What was Alfred Dreyfus? A Seventh Day Adventist? This systematic elimination of the Jews from American consciousness was not Gyssling's private and personal animosity rising to the surface. No! Georg Gyssling is a puppet, whose strings are pulled by the monster puppeteer in Berlin. Don't think this is peculiar to the Warner Brothers. Oh, no! All the other studios are predominantly run by Jews. They, too, have acquiesced to the Nazis' demands because they fear the loss of the lucrative German market. German Paramount and German Fox newsreels are little more than propaganda organs for the Third Reich. MGM— which has no newsreels— has reinvested its blocked earnings into German armaments. Only the other week, Mr. Louis B. Mayer, a man who serves his beloved mother's chicken soup in the studio commissary, hosted a luncheon for the editors of ten German newspapers. Afterwards, he personally led them on a guided tour of the studio. Shame on you, Mr. Mayer! Shame on Hollywood!

"What are we to do? What are the outraged citizens of the diminishing free world to do to combat this blatant disregard for humanity? How can we fight back when your great heroes like Charles Lindbergh embrace the philosophy of America First? The same Lucky Lindy, who is wined and dined by Adolf Hitler and gives interviews saying what 'a great guy' the Fuhrer is. What hope is there? What defense? Propaganda, my friends, is the new weapon of war. And, potentially, its most affective. Herr Hitler has managed to lead the cowed German people into mass madness by creating a culture of round the clock lies. Books, newspapers, billboards and— most importantly— motion pictures. Under the direction of his personal Circe, Leni Riefenstahl, who brought the masses to their feet with her film, *Triumph of the Will*. A brilliant advertisement for the Third Reich. You, the artists of America, must fight back. Sneak anti-Nazi messages into your creations. Fool Herr Gyssling, Herr Goebbels, and even Mr. Joseph Breen, the Hollywood censor. Use your God-given talents to defeat these little men, who arrogantly think they are gods."

The audience went wild, cheering, whistling, and pounding the tables. What they would do the next day was open to conjecture. But, at that moment, they were ready to stand up to the beast in Berlin.

Everyone in the Ambassador ballroom wanted to shake Jurgen Schiller's hand and praise his brave eloquence. Leslie Howard managed somehow to steer the charismatic Austrian over to his table where he reunited Schiller with Radford.

"Ozzie!" Schiller embraced the actor-knight and kissed him on both cheeks. "*Etschuldigen Sie mich*, Sir Osmond. Look at you, *mein Freund*! Handsome, as ever. Haven't gained a pound. How long has it been? Don't tell me. Look! I still have the scar where the tip of your foil came off on stage." The Austrian turned to the others at the table and explained: "Eight times a week, we fought to the death. Only make believe. But now, I fight for real. Have you been back to England recently?"

"Not for years," replied Radford.

"You wouldn't recognize it. Mosley's black shirts march on the streets. It is disgusting. That poor, uninformed Chamberlain treats Hitler as he would a gentleman. This is not the case. He is no gentleman. *Ach*, but I gave my speech already this evening. How is Hyacinth? The fairest maiden in all of England. I would love to see her again."

"She's away for a few days. How long are you here, Jurgen?"

"I take the train to San Francisco in the morning then on to Seattle. The next day I fly to Milwaukee, Minneapolis, and Chicago. After that I don't know. But I'll be back. Think of me as a Viennese Paul Revere. 'The Nazis are coming! The Nazis are coming!' People must listen, Ozzie. They must."

* * *

It was almost midnight by the time Martin Kohlinger returned to his bungalow on the Los Angeles-Beverly Hills border. A cat was crying as the director parked his La Salle in the detached garage at the rear of the driveway. "*Ja, ja, ja!*" Kohlinger called out from the garage. "*Ich komme! Ich komme!*" The expatriate director wondered if the marmalade stray understood a word of German. But hunger was the same word in English or German. The cat, whom he had dubbed Felix, was a living creature with whom he could still speak his native tongue.

Kohlinger walked into the kitchen, opened the icebox, and poured out a saucer full of milk. It smelled sour but Felix wouldn't mind.

"Es ist gut, Felix? Ich muss arbeiten."

Kohlinger walked into his wood paneled study, turned on the light over his desk and began typing. Who were all those people gathered there tonight? He must remember all the names. Very important. He must also regurgitate every word Jurgen Schiller had spoken.

It was half past one in the morning when Kohlinger finally finished compiling his list. He would reward his labors with a drink. It was important to have remained sober at the dinner. It was far too easy to fall into an alcoholic stupor. Opening the bottom drawer, the director withdrew a bottle of Irish whisky and a shot glass. A framed faded photograph of his late wife and two children stared down at him from the wall. He raised his glass and toasted them. Felix leapt up into his lap and began purring. Kohlinger stroked the cat three times and lifted him off his knees with his powerful hands. *"Später, Felix. Später. Ich habe Sie gern, aber…"*

Did he dare have another whisky before making the dreaded phone call? No! Martin Kohlinger lifted the receiver and dialed the number.

The voice at the other end of the phone was not pleased to be wakened at that late hour.

"You told me to phone right after the dinner," said Kohlinger, who feared the wrath of the man at the other end of the line. "It went late. Schiller is very popular."

"Who was there?" asked the voice at the other end. Kohlinger read the list of almost three hundred names. "Type them up for me and leave them at the usual drop."

"It is already done, Herr Gyssling."

"Do not use my name on the telephone. Ever!"

Martin Kohlinger despised the German Consul and resented having to report to him. He was tempted to report how Schiller had referred to Gyssling as a buffoon. But that might result in possible consequences the director chose not to contemplate. Replacing the receiver on its cradle, Kohlinger poured himself a second drink and stared once more at the faded framed picture of his family on the wall. He wondered who the women and children really were. Where had Georg Gyssling found that perfect bit of set dressing?

BLINDED BY THE SUN

Lady Radford could scarcely believe she'd been away from Best of Times for over a week. Her sleep at Arya Vihara was always deep and uninterrupted. The air in the hills high above Ojai was pure and the proximity to Krishna always brought a great serenity to her.

That night was decidedly different. Dreams had been a constant danger for Hyacinth ever since childhood. She would see things that often came true. Never daring to tell anyone about her visions, she feared the consequences of this strange, unwanted gift.

In her dream, a younger version of herself was back in India riding a gaudily decorated elephant. The proud pachyderm delivered her up a long driveway to a magnificent palace, where turbaned servants stood on the grounds awaiting her arrival. Fussing over her and sweeping her pathway with brooms made from the branches of pomegranate trees, the little English girl was escorted into a garden filled with exotic flowers and climbing vines, the likes of which she had never seen before.

A drum heralded the entrance of a younger version of Krishna. Not the way he had looked all those years before in Madras, frail and lice ridden. This Krishna was cleaner and healthier.

"I have friends for you to meet," Krishna said, beaming at her with delight. "We can all play together."

The future World Teacher introduced Hyacinth to younger versions of Alec and Ito. Alec took her to one side and tried to kiss her. She pushed him away.

"What are you doing?" said the little English girl, outraged by the boy's behavior. "That's no way to treat your mother."

"Don't like this game," said Alec. "Don't know how to play it." The boy stormed off, climbing up the twisted roots of a banyan tree.

Ito knelt on the ground, planting row upon row of seeds in the rich soil. Miraculously, flowers began to grow and bloom within seconds.

"How on earth did you do that?" asked Hyacinth.

Alec reappeared at that moment. With great ferocity, he ripped the trowel loose from Ito's hand. Then he shoved the Japanese boy down on the ground, crushing the flowers that had just sprung up from the ground.

"Bad boy!" shouted Hyacinth, immediately regretting her harsh words.

"Mummy! Mummy!"

Hyacinth looked around to see Ito, holding his arms out to her.

"Come see what I have done, Mummy."

"Here I am, darling. What did you want me to see?"

The Japanese boy removed his spectacles and handed them to her. He seemed older, as well. "Put them on and look into the sun."

"No. It could cause blindness."

"Do as I say!" Ito's voice possessed a harshness Hyacinth had never heard before. "Quickly! Before it goes away."

Hyacinth put on Ito's spectacles and raised her vision skyward. The bright yellow sun was a mere backdrop to the awesome vision she beheld. Hundreds of airplanes were coming out of the overpowering sun dropping bombs. Ripping the spectacles from her face, she threw them to the ground.

"Something wrong, darling?"

A terrified Hyacinth rushed into her husband's arms. But the man she clung to fiercely wasn't Osmond. He was several inches shorter, but devilishly attractive all the same. It was difficult to make out his face because the clinging vines were aggressively on the move obscuring most of the garden's other visitors from sight.

"What is it, old girl? Have you seen a ghost?"

"Dickie?"

"Sir Richard. And you are Lady Ives-Curtis. Whenever we are in public. Please, try and remember that."

"But where is Ozzie?" None of this made any sense to Hyacinth. She had always adored Dickie. But not in that way. "What has happened to Osmond?"

"I'm frightfully sorry," said Dickie, bowing his head, the image of contrition, "But I had to take him away."

"No, no, no!" she howled.

There was a gentle knocking at the door.

"Hyacinth? Is everything alright? I heard you cry out."

"Krishna? Come in, please."

The door swung open. A handsome Indian man in his early 40s entered the room. His eyes were large and dark, his nose long and precipitous. At the ripe age of ten, Jiddu Krishnamurti had been plucked from obscurity and groomed to be the World Teacher of the Theosophical Society. He took his responsibilities seriously but never lost the sense of playfulness, which he and Hyacinth had shared so many years before. Pulling up a wooden chair, he sat at the end of the bed and trained his dark, soulful eyes on her.

"Was it a bad dream?" asked Krishna. "Tell it to me. Perhaps, you will feel better."

Hyacinth recounted the events as best she could (omitting the detail of the airplanes coming out of the sun). As a child, she dreamt that Krishna's mother had died. She never shared the dream with her playmate. Two weeks later, Krishna's mother fell ill and passed away. Hyacinth reluctantly attended the funeral— convinced that her dream had caused the woman's death. She was relieved when her parents took her home to England a month later.

"Are you familiar with Shinto?" asked Hyacinth.

"It is the indigenous faith of the Japanese people," replied Krishna. "As old as the country itself. More a way of life than a religion. One can adhere to a belief in Shinto and also be a Buddhist. It is said that Shinto helps one to live. Buddhism helps one to die."

"How do you know all this?" Hyacinth shook her head, amazed as always by her friend's vast storehouse of knowledge.

"I read books," shrugged the World Teacher.

"Earlier this year, I was asked to give a lecture on interior design at USC. Ito Hashimuro was in the audience. He hung on my every word with a rapt attention that I frankly found embarrassing."

Krishna folded his legs underneath his torso like a little boy waiting for a bedtime story.

"Ito adored his mother and her stories. His father was a commander in the Royal Japanese Navy and had no time for the boy. Ito said that when his mother spoke her voice sounded like tiny crystals in the breeze. He told her she was the goddess *Izanami* and he was her consort *Izanagi*. She hugged her son and said: 'Tell no one. It is our secret.'

"When Ito was ten, his mother became very ill. He would sit at her bedside for hours holding her hand. Mrs. Hashimuro tried to comfort her beloved child. 'I won't leave you alone. I promise.' The boy was desolate when she died. He had lost his *Izanami*.

"Commander Hashimuro could not or would not console him. He was too busy building a great navy. Ito was raised by his older sisters, who taught him to paint and love flowers. The boy had no interest in becoming a sailor like his father or inflicting harm on others. He is a pacifist like us, Krishna.

"When I had finished my lecture, Ito presented himself to me, bowed deeply and told me the story I have just related to you. He said that when I spoke the long-forgotten sound of tiny crystals in the breeze resonated in his brain. He remembered the promise his mother had made to him on her death bed. *I won't leave you alone.* He believed that the *kami*— the spirit— of his mother had migrated inside of me. I was his new *Izanami*. He looked at me with such love, Krishna, that my heart melted. I felt as one with him as I do with you. How could I explain this feeling to Osmond? He's a good man and I love him, but he's bound to the earth. So I engaged Ito as our gardener. He has transformed Best of Times into a paradise. I tutor him in Theosophy; he teaches me about Shinto. We practice yoga; take walks by the ocean; climb up into the mountains; seek the Great Peace."

"How wonderful for you," said Krishna. "But not for Alec. He is jealous of Ito."

"Did I tell you that?"

"Your dream did. Knocking Ito to the ground. Crushing his flowers. Wanting you for himself. The kisses he can't have. A father who's not there. Tell me more about Ito."

"He's an absolute delight. The world takes on a different complexion through his eyes. He bought a model T-Ford. It's always breaking down, which doesn't seem to bother him. The fast-talking car salesman swore up and down that it had once belonged to Henry Ford. Ito feels it is sacred."

Krishna giggled, then asked: "Have you seen him recently?"

"He came round to the house Sunday before last in a state of distress. Tears streaming down his face. He had received a letter from Japan. We were in the midst of a photo shoot. Publicity for Osmond's radio show. I had asked Ito to wait inside the house until we were done. But, when I finally entered the library, he wasn't there. Haven't heard a word from him since. I'm concerned."

HOLLYWOODUS IN LATRINA

Radford was taken aback when his agent informed him the Sherlock Holmes screen test would not be shot on Twentieth Century Fox's sprawling Pico Boulevard lot. Instead, the actor-knight was to report to hair and makeup at the original William Fox studio on Western Avenue near Sunset. This was where B-movies like Peter Lorre's *Mr. Moto* series were cranked out in record time.

Having made himself up for years in the theatre, Radford always felt decidedly odd having another man apply pancake to his face. But it did feel good to be back in a makeup chair again even though Buck, the makeup man, had never heard of the actor-knight.

"You from back east?" asked Buck, a walking cadaver with nicotine-stained fingers, and a voice that belied a lifetime of smoking. He was also that rarest of species: a native Angeleno.

"England, actually."

"Well, that's east, ain't it?" asked Buck. "Unless you wanna go the long way round. Theatre guy?"

"Yes."

"Thought so. Your voice. Ever do silents?"

"No."

"Those were the days," said Buck, slapping some powder on Radford's forehead. "Lemme tell ya. I was a kid actor in a couple of 'em. Back in the teens. My mom ran a boardin' house on El Centro. Them actors! They'd be up all night drinkin' and whorin'. Didn't matter. Didn't have no lines to learn. And if they looked like shit the next morning, I'd fix 'em up. Some of 'em had screechy voices like chalk on a blackboard. Didn't matter. No lines to memorize. Just had to look good. Anyone could act in movies. Jolson fucked it up. Lemme tell ya. Good news for you theatre guys. Been here long?"

"Eight years."

"Want me to fix them eyebrows? They can't figure out which way to grow."

Radford was about to inform Buck that his upside down parentheses had been his trademark for years when an assistant director stuck his head in the dressing room. "We're ready for you, Sir Osmond."

The actor-knight rose from the makeup chair, grabbed his Inverness cape and started out of the room.

Buck bade him a farewell: "Just keep sluggin', limey. You'll make it yet." Radford nodded gratefully and followed the assistant director down the corridor and onto the small soundstage. The actor-knight stepped gingerly over coiled cables and tried to avoid tripping on the apple boxes dotted about. A special effects man holding a thick hose was pumping something that was supposed to be fog onto the bare stage. The desired affect was something vaguely akin to the English moors. The effect on Radford was something he hadn't experienced since the Great War.

"Hell's bells! What is that noxious nebula?" Radford asked a grip walking past him.

"Ask props."

Gil Hutchins, a long-time dialog director on the Pico lot, had been given the opportunity to direct the test. Hutchins walked over to Radford, shook his hand, and gave the actor-knight's costume the once over. "Looks great, Sir Osmond. Meerschaum pipe's a nice touch."

"Brought it from home. Good thing. The wardrobe lady gave me one wasn't at all right."

"Do you know the lines?" Hutchins asked abruptly.

"Of course." Flavia had spent the previous evening going through the sides repeatedly with her extremely nervous father.

"Then let's put one in the can." Hutchins clapped his hands together resolutely. "How we doing with the fog, Gus? Seems to be losing its oomph. Wanna freshen it up a little bit? If you'd just step onto the set, Sir Osmond."

"Could we possibly do without the fog?" asked Radford, who felt his own oomph slipping away. "Reminds one of mustard gas."

"Mustard gas?"

"From the war."

"This isn't mustard gas," said Hutchins.

"Of course not. We'd all be dead. But it's positively toxic."

Hutchins took the actor-knight to one side, and spoke in hushed tones:

"Look, Sir Osmond, this is just a test. Mr. Zanuck tossed me a bone letting me direct it. I'm 35-years-old. Been waiting a long time. Know what I mean? Don't make me look bad in the production report."

"So, we're both auditioning?" asked a sympathetic Radford.

"One way of looking at it." Hutchins had a desperate expression on his face. The actor-knight nodded in complete sympathy with the man's situation.

"Ready when you are," said Radford, finding his mark on the soundstage.

A bell rang signifying the set was locked. The man with the clapper board shouted: "Baskervilles Test. Take One." Hutchins called 'Ready', then nodded to Radford and said: "Action!"

"Remember that missing boot, Watson?" asked Radford in his best Holmesian tone. "Why do you suppose the brown one was so mysteriously replaced and the black one taken? Because the brown one would never have had the scent of the owner— and the black one had!"

"Cut!"

The bell sounded abruptly, and the fog evaporated, as if by magic. Hutchins ran over to a bewildered Radford and began pumping the actor-knight's hand.

"That was great, Sir Osmond! Just great. Exactly what Mr. Zanuck wanted."

"But there was much more to the speech," protested Radford. "It went on for another half page." The wardrobe lady was struggling to remove the Inverness cape from the actor-knight's shoulders. "Madame, I-I-I must ask you to desist."

"Stop squirming, willya!" said the wardrobe lady, a lit cigarette dangling from her mouth. "Gotta get this over to Pico. They need it for C. Aubrey Smith."

Ignoring the woman's obsessive exertions, Radford asked Hutchins: "Are you positive you wouldn't like another take? You have as much riding on this as I do. Just a moment. That's *my* pipe! I-I-I brought it from home." The last remark was addressed to an overzealous prop man, attempting to wrest the Meerschaum away from the actor-knight.

"Do you feel you could do it better?" asked a now uncertain Hutchins. "I thought it was perfect."

Before Radford could respond, a disheveled man in a top hat, cutaway coat and striped trousers meandered onto the set. Had it been ten years earlier, the man would have been surrounded by an entourage fending off a swarm of photographers and swooning fans. Known as 'The Great Profile', John

Barrymore had been the highest paid actor in movies. He was now a bloated alcoholic performing a tragic parody of himself on the radio. When he did find employment in the movies, the foremost actor of his generation was pathologically unable to remember his lines. This explained the small chalkboard he clutched like a sacred totem to his chest.

Radford was stunned by the sight of the man, whom he had idolized and played opposite in *Hamlet* so many years before in London. Only six years Radford's senior, the Great Profile now looked two decades older. The two were neighbors on Tower Road, albeit several blocks apart. Barrymore lived the life of a recluse and the actor-knight had not wanted to presume on their past friendship or run the risk of not being remembered.

"Forgive my tardiness," said Barrymore, in unmistakable and inimitable tones, "but my chauffeur has eloped with the four-square Amy Semple McPherson and I was forced to take a Yellow Cab. This is *Hold That Co-Ed*, is it not? Where are all the freshmen and their concubines?"

"Sorry, Mr. Barrymore," said Hutchins. "*Co-Ed* is shooting on the Pico lot."

"'The Pico lot'? Where the hell is that? I fear that I am hopelessly lost." Barrymore held out his chalkboard with childlike helplessness and pointed to his scribbling. "I specifically instructed the albino cab man to drive me to Fox and this is where he brought me. See the address. I copied it from the telephone directory."

"Must have been an old phone book," snorted the prop man.

"Dost mock me, varlet?" asked Barrymore. "I came ready to work. Am I responsible for the change of venue?"

"It's alright, Jack." Radford finally broke his silence. "I'll drive you to Pico."

"The Good Samaritan. What is your name, kind sir? It shall be written in the Book of Deeds."

"Osmond Radford. I was your Laertes in London."

Barrymore walked over to the actor-knight until they were toe to toe. Withdrawing a pair of spectacles from his inside pocket, the Great Profile examined Radford's face. His eyes lit up as he recited:

I'll be your foil, Laertes: in mine ignorance

Your skill shall, like a star i' the darkest night,

Stick fiery off indeed.

Radford smiled and picked up the cue: "You mock me, sir."

Barrymore cackled with delight, and heartily embraced the actor-knight. "Dear Ozzie! Most worthy of opponents. Do you know I still have marks on my throat from your throttling me atop Ophelia's grave?"

"Purely self-defense. You scared the hell out of me every night, Jack."

"What brings you to this dermoid cyst? *Hollywoodus in latrina.*"

"I live here. In fact, we're neighbors on Tower Road."

"Are we, indeed? Did I know that? *Yea, from the table of my memory, I'll wipe away…* all memory." Barrymore held up the chalkboard. "Lost without this bit of slate." He folded his arms across his chest and took Radford's measure. "Tell me, Ozzie. Have they eased you onto a gentler horse yet?"

"Don't quite follow, Jack."

"Neither one of us is in the running for Prince Charming anymore…. Neighbors, are we? You must pay me a visit. I'm sure there's still a cask of amontillado we can imbibe together. Why don't we have lunch today? Fuck this acting shit!"

"I'm afraid Sir Osmond is having lunch with me," said an unseen voice from the shadows.

Radford knew that voice as surely as he knew his own. Its owner stepped out of the darkness and walked towards the actor-knight clutching a briefcase. His hair had been dark when they'd first known each other. When he emerged from the hole after a month in solitary, it had turned grey. But Richard Ives-Curtis's chiseled features and piercing blue eyes were unmistakable.

"Dickie! Is it really you?"

ALL A SMOKE SCREEN

John Barrymore and the Inverness cape were both bundled into a studio vehicle and dispatched posthaste to the main Fox lot on Pico. Radford escorted Ives-Curtis out to the parking lot where Charleston Brown sat behind the wheel of the Rolls reading a racing form. Tossing the paper to one side, the faithful chauffeur zipped out of the car and opened the back door for his employer and his guest.

"What good fortune the Ambassador Hotel should be at Wilshire and Western and you working at Western and Sunset." Ives-Curtis stared with unabashed affection at his former comrade-in-arms. "I simply walked north. Hotel staff were appalled. Apparently, it's the height of *mauvais temps* to ever use one's feet in Hollywood. Except to test the temperature of a swimming pool."

"How ever did you find me, Dickie? How did you get on the lot? It's guarded like the Tower of London." The actor-knight was still in a profound state of shock at the presence of the enigmatic Richard Ives-Curtis, whom he had not set eyes on for ten years.

"I'm not entirely without resources, Ozzie. Surely, you of all people haven't forgotten." Richard Ives-Curtis had attempted no less than four escapes from the German prisoner-of-war camp where they had both been incarcerated twenty years earlier. "Can't keep me in; can't keep me out. Hope you're hungry, old boy. I'm positively ravenous."

"What about Musso and Frank's? On Hollywood Boulevard. It's not far from here and they do quite a good fish."

"No, no. When I arrived at the hotel yesterday, I beheld a gigantic bowler hat across the street. To my utter amazement, the concierge informed me that it was a restaurant. The Brown Derby. We must eat there. Edwina will never believe I ate a meal inside a hat."

"How is Edwina?"

"Radiant. She presented me with a son last week. His name is Anthony. Rather hoping you'd be his godfather."

"After all these years?"

"We share a history, Ozzie. All the more reason."

* * *

After several martinis, the two old friends sang the unofficial Flying Corps anthem.

Stand, stand to your glasses steady,

And drink to your comrades' eyes,

Here's a cup for the dead already,

And hurrah for the next man that dies.

They burst into laughter at the end of the chorus, oblivious to the curious looks of their fellow diners inside "The Hat", as Ives-Curtis steadfastly insisted on referring to the popular entertainment industry restaurant.

"Are you still with the trade legation?" asked Radford.

"Not for donkey's years. I write now. Travel books. Ever heard of Rupert Templeton?"

"Is that you? We have a few of your books tucked away at home. They'll be on prominent display now. Paid to travel. How remarkable, Dickie! Get to use some of your languages, as well?"

"Comes in handy occasionally. But tell me about the Holmes film. Wondered when you'd finally get around to filming it."

Radford recounted the indignities he had suffered during his screen test that morning. Ives-Curtis's laughter grew louder with every twist and turn in the tale.

"Glad you find it amusing, Ives-Curtis. It was one of the most humiliating experiences of my career." The actor-knight signaled the waiter to bring him another martini.

"Perhaps it's time you took up a new career, Ozzie. Writing on the wall and all that tosh."

"I'm 50-years-old, Dickie. Acting has been my entire life."

"Except for those four years serving King and country," said Ives-Curtis pointedly.

"Three years of which were spent in a bloody prison camp."

The waiter brought the martini. Radford belted it down in one go.

"Steady on, old boy," warned Ives-Curtis. "Haven't had our pudding yet."

A dowdy, middle-aged woman walked over to their table giggling with delight. Radford leapt to his feet.

"Oh, you British!" said the dowdy woman in a mid-West accent. She playfully pushed Radford back onto the banquette. "Always so proper. I was watching you across the room, Osmond. Thought I knew every actor in town, but this handsome gentleman is a complete mystery to me.

"Lolly, this is one my oldest friends. We served in the Royal Flying Corps together. Sir Richard Ives-Curtis."

"Sir Osmond and Sir Richard," said the dowdy woman, pointing to them like a set of collectibles in a shop on Brighton Way. "Mother told me there'd be knights like these. Hmm. That's a good one, Lolly. Write it down. And you're not an actor, Richard? So attractive."

"No," replied Ives-Curtis. "I write travel books."

"The screen's loss." The dowdy woman leaned over, touched Radford's cheek fondly and whispered: "The grapevine says your Sherlock Holmes test was outstanding. Better than Rathbone's."

"Basil tested?"

"You didn't hear it from me. Bye-bye, Richard."

"Who was that extraordinary creature?" asked Ives-Curtis, lighting up a cigarette after the dowdy woman had returned to her seat on the other side of the restaurant. "Bit of a gorgon, what?"

"Her name is Louella Parsons," replied Radford, "She's a stindicated-syndicated-gossip columnist. With another harpy named Hedda Hopper, they run a proper reign of terror throughout the town. She's also incontinent. Pees on everyone's sofa. Hyacinth won't have her in the house. The woman possesses a vast network of spies that makes the British Trade Legation look pale by comparison."

"What the deuce are you talking about, Ozzie? Perhaps, you've had more than your ration of martinis."

"Do you think me a complete fool?" asked Radford. "Travel writer. Trade Legation. All a smoke screen, isn't it, old son? You're in the Secret Service. I've suspected it for years. All those postcards from exotic locales. Always followed by a civil war or some nasty chap meeting an even nastier end."

"What a marvelous imagination you have, Osmond. But I suppose an actor must have one to go along with his makeup box. You were very good in *The Scarlet Pimpernel*, by the way. Loved your disguises."

"I was bloody brilliant as Pershy Blakeney!" Radford was quite crocked by this time. "Shidney Carton, as well. Sidney, dammit! But did they cast me in the movie versions? Nooo! Youth must be served! Leslie Howard and Ronnie Colman were their choices. Hell's bells! They're only four years my junior. But now I-I-I finally have a chance for immortality. Sherlock Holmes is the role of a lifetime. I'm bound and determined to mimortalize—immortalize it, dammit— on the silver screen."

"Best of British luck, old boy."

"Luck be damned. It's kismet. Part belongs to me, Dickie. Conan Doyle said it to my face. 'Best Sherlock ever!' Could one ever ask for a better endorsement? Hyacinth is up in Ojai praying for me. Wonderful woman! Blessed to have her by my side. Oh, dear! Need to spend a penny, as the ladies say. Be right back, Dickie. And don't think of picking up the cheque. No, no. This lunch was brought to you by Kellogg's Corn Flakes."

The actor-knight was listing leeward like a bosun's mate in a force ten gale. Steady as she goes. Once round the Horn, then smooth sailing past the *maitre d's* podium and straight on to the gents. Why was the room continuing to spin? Hard to starboard! What was happening? Why was everything going out of focus?

Radford collided with a waiter and crumbled to the floor, carrying two blue plate specials with him. The normally jaded patrons of The Brown Derby gasped as one in shock. Bolting to his feet a second later, Ives-Curtis raced towards his old comrade-at-arms. Ever on the lookout for a scoop, Louella Parsons removed a Mark Cross pen and notebook from her Vuitton handbag and began scribbling.

IMMINENT DANGER

I t was almost eight the next morning when Hyacinth dashed inside the house. Willi was dusting various *objets* in the hallway as Lady Radford dropped her valise and asked the housekeeper: "Where is Sir Osmond? Is he alright?"

"In the bedroom," replied Willi, surprised and a trifle alarmed by Lady Radford's dramatic entrance.

Taking the stairs two at a time, Hyacinth burst into the master suite where she found her husband sitting up in their four-poster bed talking agitatedly on the telephone.

"Don't be an ass, Hughie. I-I-I'm fine. Would I be talking to you otherwise? … Of course not. I'm doing my broadcast tomorrow evening and— Ah! Here's Hy. We'll speak anon." Radford replaced the receiver and stared quizzically at his wife. "Home so soon?"

"I came as soon as I heard." Hyacinth hared over to the bed, touched her husband's forehead, and embraced him fervently.

"Heard what? Bloody telephone's been ringing off the hook all morning with inquiries as to my health. Do I-I-I look unwell?"

"Not really."

"Are you disappointed that I'm not? How did you get down here, by the way?"

"Krishna drove me. When he saw how upset I was—"

"But why were you upset?"

"Gwen rang Aya Vihara at dawn. Fortunately, everyone was awake for Sadhana. She called about the blind item in Louella Parsons' column."

"Hell's bells! I'd forgotten the dreaded Lolly was there. What did that gorgon write? My death knell?"

"She didn't mention you by name. 'What titled British thespian passed out inside what famous restaurant at lunch yesterday?' Our Gwen's always been a clever boots. Reckoned it was either you or Cedric. What did happen, Ozzie?"

"The room began to spin and down I went like the proverbial ton of bricks. Promise you won't laugh," said Radford, "but I-I-I think I was drugged."

"Who on earth would do that?"

"No idea. Always thought of myself a beloved figure."

"*My* beloved figure." Hyacinth lay down on the bed and wrapped her arms around her husband. "Did you go to the hospital?"

"Nooo. Charleston and Dickie brought me home."

"Dickie?" A cold chill ran down Hyacinth's spine. "Dickie!"

"Richard Ives-Curtis."

"Yes, darling. I know who Dickie is. Where did he come from?"

"Down the chimney like Father Christmas. I'd just finished my screen test when he materialized out of nowhere and took me to lunch." Hyacinth rose abruptly from the bed and walked over to the bay window. "What's wrong, darling?"

"Dickie was in my dream two nights ago. Very disturbing."

"Why were you dreaming about Dickie?"

"Oh, don't be an ass, Osmond. Where is he now?"

"Actually, I'm right here," said Ives-Curtis, standing impishly in the doorway. "Hello, Hyacinth. Beautiful, as ever! 'Age cannot wither' and all that Shakespeare falderal."

"It is customary, Richard, to inform old friends in advance when one is going to pay a surprise visit."

"Then it wouldn't be a surprise. Sorry, Nanny. Going to spank my bottom? Shan't do it again." Ives-Curtis entered the bedroom and embraced Hyacinth.

"Hadn't really planned on being here at all. I was making a connection to Mexico City and thought to myself: 'How can one stop in Los Angeles and not see the Radfords?'"

"Mexico City? What on earth—?"

"Travel books, old girl. My new dodge." Ives-Curtis released her from his embrace and walked over to the bed. "Looking much better today, Ozzie. Green is not a good color for you. Pallor wise. What a lovely home you have, Hy. And how your children have grown!"

"When did you see the children?" asked Radford.

"Middle of the night. Your Mr. Brown and I had put you to bed some hours earlier. Dead to the world, you were. I fell asleep in that chair watching over you like the good shepherd. Then I woke up rather keen to go to the loo. Didn't want to turn a light on. I stumbled down the passageway looking for the w.c. when I was seized from behind in a vice-like grip. An imperious voice demanded to know who the hell I was and what I was doing here. My powerful assailant identified himself as Alec Radford. "Impossible," said I. 'Alec Radford's a little boy'. This grown-up Alec didn't remember me at all. No idea who I was. Then the front door opened downstairs, and an exquisite vision tiptoed up to the second floor fresh from an evening's revelry. It was my goddaughter. Mercifully, Flavia not only remembered her Uncle Dickie, but offered me a bed to sleep in. Not to fear. It was her baby sister's. Where is Julia, by the way?"

"We don't know," said Hyacinth.

"In New York," replied Radford brusquely.

"Not a peep from her since her play closed in Boston."

"She's fine," said Radford. "Or we would have heard."

"Have you had any breakfast, Dickie?" asked Hyacinth, not wishing to pursue the matter of their errant daughter any further.

"No. Thought I'd get something back at the hotel."

"Nonsense. You'll stay for breakfast. Entertain our guest, Ozzie, while I have Willi whip up something special in the kitchen."

Lady Radford took her leave of the two old comrades-in-arms and went downstairs. Ives-Curtis grinned as he sat on the edge of the bed.

"Didn't want to say anything in front of Hy but you did scare the hell out of me yesterday. What's wrong, Ozzie? One could plant apple seeds in the furrows of your brow."

Radford stared in silence at his old friend. Finally, he asked: "Why are you here, Dickie? And spare me the fantasy about Mexico City."

"Care to see my airplane ticket?"

"What I would like is the truth, Richard."

"Hmmm. You've guessed a bit of it already. My globe hopping isn't all meant for the printed page."

"Then you *are* with the Secret Service?"

Ives-Curtis did not answer Radford's question. Instead, he posed one of his own: "Ever think about the war?"

"Not much. Ancient history."

"Afraid there's going to be another one, old boy. Matter of weeks. Months. Most definitely within a year."

"What about the Munich Accord?"

"'Peace for our time'? Poor old Neville. It's going to be a truly global conflict, Ozzie. Not just Europe."

"You sound like Leslie Howard."

"God bless him. And Jurgen Schiller. They don't wear rose-colored glasses. We are in imminent danger."

"Is nothing to be done?"

"Certainly," replied Ives-Curtis. "We can all learn to speak German. *So schnell wie möglich.* For a vegetarian, Herr Hitler has demonstrated a most carnivorous appetite for devouring entire countries. England is next on the menu. I'm part of a shadow government waiting in the wings for Churchill to become the new Prime Minister."

"Should you be telling me this?"

Ives-Curtis looked about the room and asked wryly: "We are alone, aren't we?" He pulled his briefcase up from the floor, withdrew a document and fountain pen from inside and offered them to Radford: "Sign this."

"What is it?"

"Official Secrets Act. I want you to work for me." Ives-Curtis hastily corrected himself. "For England."

Radford stared at the document. "You bastard! *You* drugged my drink. It was all a macabre scheme of yours to have me join the Secret Service."

"Brilliant! You figured it out with that insightful, deductive mind of yours. Bravo, Ozzie! Always knew you were the right man for the job. Sorry it had to be done this way but there was no other option."

"Get out, Dickie! Leave my house at once. Do you realize what you've done? To my reputation? An actor in ill-health is virtually unemployable in this town. He can't be insured by any movie studio."

"Quit deluding yourself, Osmond. You don't have a movie career."

"I am going to play Sherlock Holmes. It's the part of a lifetime."

"Twentieth Century Fox will announce today that Basil Rathbone will be playing Holmes. Let go of it, Ozzie. *I* am offering you the true role of a lifetime."

"Get out!"

Ives-Curtis pointed to the government document lying atop the bed. "Think about it."

* * *

Hyacinth knew something was wrong when Ives-Curtis changed his mind about breakfast. She refused to let him phone for a cab and insisted that Charleston drive him back to the Ambassador.

"When do you leave for Mexico?"

"Tomorrow."

"Perhaps when you return, we could host a dinner party for you. So many members of the colony would love to meet you. Do you know Aubrey Smith?"

"He and my father were at Charterhouse. On the cricket team together."

"Indeed! Then we must plan a dinner. Do give my love to Edwina. And congratulations on the baby. I'll be sending a gift."

Alec awoke in his room with what he decided was a brilliant notion. He'd been giving the old man a bit of a rough time, and this might be the way to pave a new inroad to furthering his career. Clad in his pajamas, he entered the master suite without knocking. With characteristic lack of intuition, Alec was oblivious to his father's foul mood.

"I say," said the younger Radford, propelling himself into the room under the full sail of his enthusiasm. "I have the most ripping idea."

The actor-knight had just hung up on Charles Feldman, his agent, who confirmed that Fox was not going to cast him as Sherlock Holmes. "They went another way," said Feldman, either ignorant of or not wishing to mention that Basil Rathbone was about to reinvent himself in the public's perception.

"Father?" Alec decided that the more respectful term of paternity was appropriate to the moment.

"What is it?"

"Know those Mowgli stories of Kipling's?"

"Mowgli?"

"The boy who was raised by wolves. Why don't I read one of them on your radio program? We could read them together. Father and son. You could be Baloo the bear. Or Shere Khan the tiger. Or both. What do you think?"

"Unfortunately, Alec, I don't cast the show. Merely a mill hand, as it were. And— quite bluntly— you're not a star. We have guests like Clark Gable and Bette Davis. Big stars."

"Flavia's been on the show."

"She did do that film with David Manners— "

"At Monogram. Which barely counts. I'm opening next month in *The Dawn Patrol* with Errol-bloody-Flynn. Doesn't that mean anything to you? Oh, why do I bother?" With that hysterical outburst, Alec fled the bedroom.

Radford heaved a sigh of despair, curled up in the bed and sank into a deep, dreamless sleep. He was awakened sometime later by his wife gently touching his shoulder.

"Osmond? Wake up, darling. Dickie's come back and he's brought someone special to see you."

Not quite awake, Radford misheard what Hyacinth had said to him and grumbled: "I have no need of a specialist. There's nothing wrong with me, as he well knows."

The disgraced former comrade-at-arms glided into the room, placed his hands on Hyacinth's shoulders and whispered: "Best let me handle this alone." His wife nodded and departed the bedroom.

"What is it now, Rupert?" The name was meant as a dig at Dickie's pseudonym. "Or would you prefer some other secret identity?"

"*Mea culpa,*" said Dickie, thumping his heart with his fist. "One realizes how shocking and frightening yesterday's incident inside The Hat must have been for you. Especially when one has always prided oneself on a healthy regimen. To have seemingly lost control in public must have been utterly humiliating. But necessary to the job that lies ahead."

"How did you persuade Lolly to be your collaborator?"

"Contrary to what you may believe, the presence of the Parsons woman was not orchestrated. Fate was on our side, Ozzie. Kismet! Her veiled reportage only aided the libretto. It was for the Greater Good."

"I don't want to go back to England."

"And why should you?" asked Ives-Curtis. "The work I have in mind for you is right here in Hollywood."

"But my career—"

"Will continue. In fact, it's vital. You will still host your radio show on Saturday evenings. But no more testing for films. You need your days freed up for other activities."

"What sort of activities? You're more cryptic than ever." Raucous laughter could be heard from the sitting room.

"What's going on down there?" asked Radford. "Is it a bank holiday?"

"Never mind that," said Ives-Curtis. "We need to clear the air. You are a born actor, Osmond. No question about that. I want you to resurrect *The Scarlet Pimpernel*. Not on stage. In the real world. Create another persona for yourself. Dithering, harmless, ineffectual, with a rumored heart condition. All the while, you shall be my eyes and ears in the film colony. A great many European émigrés have flooded into Hollywood. Mostly fleeing Hitler and Mussolini's repressive regimes. But many of those refugees are secret fascist sympathizers. Bunds, inspired by the Third Reich, are dotted from coast to coast. Holding secret and not-so-secret meetings. Pelley's Silver Shirts walk the streets of Los Angeles wearing swastika arm bands. They must not be allowed to proliferate,"

"Can't Washington do something about it?" Radford asked innocently.

"Steady on, old boy. This *is* a democracy." Ives-Curtis shook his head in despair. "The U.S. Congress has convinced itself that this will be strictly a European conflict. Exactly what the bloody fools thought last time. War is inevitable— despite the efforts of Chamberlain, Kennedy, Lindbergh and their ilk to appease Hitler. Trust me, Ozzie. I need you. More importantly, England needs you. Just as it needs Alec."

"Alec? My son? Silly ass thinks Hitler walks on water."

"I know how the boy irks you. The days when a well-bred young Englishman could be defined as good at a hunt ball and invaluable in a shipwreck are sadly over. This coming war will be the making of Alec. Remember how impossible we were during our salad days in the Flying Corps? Almost court-martialed for our outlandish pranks. Quaffing down magnums of the Widow while foolishly thinking we'd live forever. We grew up quickly after flying those first few missions. Rest assured; the next go round will do the same for young Alec."

The laughter from the sitting room grew louder. "Would you please tell me the source of all that mirth?"

"Please," said Ives-Curtis, ignoring Radford yet again. "Apply some balm to your bruised ego. Rathbone will be fine as Sherlock. He *is* younger than you, old boy. Hard as it is to swallow. What did your chum Jack Barrymore say about 'being eased onto a gentler horse'? Your new steed may seem gentler, Ozzie, but he's far more powerful."

There was a knock at the bedroom door. A slight man in his late 30s, with sandy hair, pug nose and a boyish demeanor, stuck his head in the door. With a pronounced Cockney accent, he asked: "Is the deed done, guv?"

"Boggs!" Sir Osmond's face lit up with delight. "What on earth— Dickie! Have I gone mad?"

"Quite the welcome 'ome the ladies give me downstairs," said Len Boggs, Radford's former dresser. "If I'd known they'd be this 'appy to see me, I'd 'ave turned up a lot sooner."

"Where have you been, Boggs? The letters I wrote you were all returned 'Address Unknown'."

A sheepish look came over Boggs's face and he turned to Ives-Curtis for assistance.

"Boggs has been a guest of His Majesty's Prison System for the past few years. Wormwood Scrubs."

"Victim of circumstances, guv. Fortunately, Sir Richard 'ere came to my rescue and brought me on board."

"On board?" asked Radford.

"Boggs has already signed the OSA," said Ives-Curtis. "In light of your rumored health problems— which no one believes for a moment— it might be best if you took on a valet cum personal assistant. You and Boggs always had a special rapport in the camp. And he was invaluable as your dresser in the West End."

"Hell's bells! Have you no shame, Dickie?"

"Please, guv!" pleaded Boggs. "Do what 'e says. Otherwise, it's back to the Scrubs for me."

The actor-knight's eyes darted back and forth between the spymaster and his former dresser. "Does Hyacinth know about this?

Ives-Curtis shook his head. "It's our little secret. No one else can ever know."

The actor-knight heaved a sigh and asked: "Where did I put that bloody document?"

HALLOWE'EN PRANK

The siren's wailing finally stopped as the ambulance pulled up in front of the CBS flag ship on Madison Avenue. John Houseman raced outside from the lobby, clutching a script in his hand and opened the back door of the ambulance. A tall, young man with a grinning baby face emerged intact waving a large Havana cigar like a baton.

"They'll arrest you for this one day," said the Rumanian-born Houseman in his hothouse British accent. "It's a serious offense to fraudulently travel in an ambulance."

"Always doom and gloom, Jack," countered the 23-year-old Orson Welles, patting his producing partner on the shoulder. Without breaking stride, the Boy Wonder entered the building. "Can you think of a faster way to get around the city? Traffic here is worse than Hong Kong. How much have we got in petty cash? Can you pay the driver? He's a sweet guy and his wife's expecting their ninth child. Maybe it's the tenth. How're the rewrites going?"

"How's *Danton's Death*?" countered Houseman, referring to their latest Mercury Theatre stage production, which was set to open in less than a week.

"Brilliant, if I say so myself. Which I just did." The Boy Wonder stood before a bank of elevators staring at the radio script his partner had handed him.

"What are all these red lines, Jack?" Welles rumbled in his best bass-baritone. "St. Patrick's Cathedral? Princeton University? Biltmore Hotel?"

"Notes from the network, Orson. They want all the names changed to fictional ones."

"Whyyy?" whined Welles, inadvertently raising his voice several octaves. "It kills all the fun. This is a Hallowe'en prank, Jack. We want the audience to momentarily suspend disbelief and think Martians have really invaded America. Like King Kong on the Empire State Building. All smoke and mirrors."

"They're afraid people might take it seriously, Orson."

"Oh, for Chrissake, Jack! We tell them right off the top it's an adaptation. Nobody listens to our fucking show. It's positively anti-American to like literature, let alone listen to it. No, Jack! The Great Unwashed are tuned in to Edgar Bergen and Charlie McCarthy sticking it to W.C. Fields. That's the problem with our show. We don't have a dummy. They're all ensconced upstairs in the executive boardroom." Welles exhaled the sigh of the ages and lit his cigar.

"What I don't do for my fucking art! Could someone please phone Sardi's and have them send over three porterhouse steaks and a pailful of oysters? I'm feeling peckish, Jack. Are we still doing the adaptation of *Rebecca* next month? There's a little English girl I met. Perfect to play the second Mrs. DeWinter."

"Don't you ever get tired of being Peck's Bad Boy?" asked Houseman.

"It's nothing like that! She's a West End actress. Her show just closed out-of-town. What the hell's her name? Father was a big star back in England. Judy Radford. No! Not Judy… Julia. We should try and find her, Jack. She's quite special. Possessed of that infuriatingly British prim exterior which belies the sex-crazed Delilah desperate to escape from within."

"Orson, how much have you had to drink today?"

"Fuck off, Houseman! You pretentious bean counter! I'm going to work."

Welles look at the script and intoned: "'We know now that in the early years of the twentieth century this world was being watched closely by intelligences greater than man's.' Yeah, Charlie McCarthy's. Come on over, Adolf! No one here's going to stop you."

* * *

Unaware of Orson Welles's interest in her, a desperate and forlorn Julia Radford, wandered about the east side of Manhattan pondering a torturous decision. She wore a long black cloak and hood, which made her resemble *The Scarlet Letter*'s Hester Prynne. Several hours had passed since she'd arrived from Boston and checked her suitcase in a locker at Penn Station. Because the next day was Hallowe'en, no one took notice of the actress's melodramatic attire. She removed an envelope from inside her purse for the hundredth time and withdrew a folded, hand-written letter. It was from

Lansing Wallace, the man to whom she had surrendered her virginity a month earlier. The same man, who had promised to make her his wife. The blackguard, who had driven her to the brink of suicide.

Dear Julia:

This is probably the hardest letter I ever had to write anyone. You're going to think I'm the world's biggest heel, but I owe you the truth. I didn't go back to Michigan. My mother died two years ago. I just couldn't bring myself to tell you the truth.

These weeks working with you on The Conflicted Heart was one of the truly extraordinary experiences of my career. You're a great kid, Julia. And a great lover. Besides being beautiful and talented, you are the greatest lay I've ever had. Even now, sitting here and writing about it, I feel myself aroused. There were nights on stage when I had trouble remembering my lines because I just wanted to grab you and bang your brains out. Which is completely separate from your talent as an actress. You have a great future ahead of you, kid.

But there's no place for me in that future. There can't be. I haven't been completely honest with you, Julia. Not just the lie about my mother. I'm married. And I have two children.

What we shared was real magic, Your Ladyship. All part of the special world of the theatre which we inhabit. But there was no reality beyond the run of the play. So long as we were on stage at the Colonial and all those glorious nights we shared afterwards, we had a bond that belonged only to us.

But I'm home with my family now. Back in the real world of mowing the lawn, fixing the drip in the kitchen sink, putting iodine on my little boy's knees when he scrapes them. And trying to get another show. That's my real life, Julia.

I will always remember and cherish the magic we shared. But we can never and must never see each other again. Please, don't try to contact me.

Our show was aptly named The Conflicted Heart. But, like the play, we folded in Boston.

Best of luck in the future!

Wally

Julia had decided that if she couldn't have Wallace Lansing (his real name), no one else would either. She would travel to the dreary little town in New Jersey where he lived and murder the mendacious swine. In full view of his wife and children. Hang the consequences! No jury would ever convict her once they'd heard her pathetic tale. She would shoot the bastard point blank. But with what weapon? Julia had spent an entire afternoon combing through a Boston pawn shop with the aid of Signor Benedetto, a lovely old Italian, to whom she had told her pitiful tale. The pawnbroker plied the heartbroken actress with homemade wine and showed her various pistols with which one could settle a *debito d'onore*, as he referred to it. Signor Benedetto was most encouraging. Julia finally selected a derringer. Small and ladylike, the gun fit snugly into her handbag. Signor Benedetto approved heartily. He would have purchased the identical *pistole* for his granddaughter, should she ever be seduced and abandoned like *la bella signorina*.

It was almost dark by the time Julia returned to Penn Station resolved as to her course of action. The derringer ticked away in her bag like a lethal alarm clock unheard by mere mortals. One expected it to go off on its own at any second. Making her way across the rotunda towards the ticket windows, Julia observed a great many young people in fancy dress. Perhaps, they were en route to early Hallowe'en parties. When the young Englishwoman finally reached the window, she asked for a ticket to New Jersey.

"Round trip or one way?" asked the ticket agent, without looking up at the girl in the black hooded cloak.

"One way," intoned Julia, in an unconscious tribute to her father's Sydney Carton climbing the steps of the guillotine.

"Okay. What town in New Jersey?"

Julia removed the envelope in her bag and read the postmarked stamp. "Grover's Mill." She had no idea that Orson Welles a few hours earlier had put the sleepy little town on the map with his soon-to-be legendary *War of the Worlds* broadcast.

"Oh, you poor kid!" said the ticket agent.

"Is something wrong?"

"On the radio. Just now. The whole town's been destroyed by Martians. The National Guard's been called out."

Julia screamed and collapsed unconscious onto the marble floor.

$10,000 WILL KEEP US QUIET

Flavia removed the photographs from the manila envelope for the hundredth time. What was she going to do? She couldn't tell her father. Something like this would destroy his career. They would have to leave America. Move to Rhodesia or New Zealand. She couldn't inform the police. They would contact Hedda or Louella straightaway. Hollywood was like a country village back in England. Everyone obsessed with everyone else's dirty laundry. Surely there had to be someone. What about that gangster Wendy Barrie was seeing? Ben-something-Jewish. Quite attractive, too. Did she have Wendy's number? No. Then she remembered: Set a thief to catch a thief. Sorry, Uncle Jas.

The telephone rang at the tiny cottage on North Doheny.

"Well," said Eunice Radford. "To what do we owe the honor, Princess Flavia?"

"Hello, Aunt Eunice." Flavia could barely get the words out. She loathed her uncle's wife and couldn't bear the woman using Jasper's affectionate term for her. "Is Uncle Jasper there?"

"How's your campaign going?" asked Eunice, ignoring Flavia's question. "For Scarlett."

"One can only wait and see."

"That's not going to get you anywhere, my dear. Proactive is the only way. Jasper is going to play Gerald O'Hara."

"What!?!"

"The role is his, if he will take it."

"Does David Selznick know this?"

"Next to Our Lord, I cannot think of another being, who has suffered as your Uncle Jasper has. All the ignominious lies he could not defend in court. The deceit of his partner. And, worse, his ex-wife heinously taking advantage of his shame to divorce him in favor of her long-time lover. His own beloved children will have nothing to do with him."

"May I please speak to Jasper?" Flavia asked briskly, not wishing to hear another word of her uncle's wife's prattle.

"Through all his travails," said Eunice, "he has had me and, indirectly, the teachings of Dr. Buchman to keep his spiritual craft afloat. The Oxford Group has shown the light to the world. The power of Moral Rearmament and divine intervention is stronger than any force on the planet. Why else should Herr Hitler fear it so? Trust me. Jasper will win the Academy Award."

"Perhaps, I should phone back later-"

"Moral Rearmament can rescue you, Flavia, from the tragic flaw in the Radford character. I've seen it hamper you on the path to true greatness. Strict adherence to the five C's— Confidence, Confession, Conviction, Conversion, and Continuance— could turn your life around, my dear."

"Sorry, Eunice, but Mrs. Roosevelt is coming to tea today and I promised to help Willi polish the silver."

Flavia replaced the receiver and shook her head. How could Jas put up with such a demented creature? Willi! That's the ticket. The housekeeper had mentioned a solicitor, who lived across the street. Flavia put on a scarlet cashmere sweater, black bell bottoms and open-toed shoes. Finger and toenails matched in flaming red lacquer. The ensemble was finished off by a pair of red Bakelite sunglasses her Great Aunt Arlette had sent her from the south of France. 'Ravishing' was the only word she could use to describe herself. Tucking the manila envelope under her arm, Flavia strode purposefully across Tower Road to meet what's-his-name, the solicitor.

* * *

Paul Merlin answered the doorbell clad only in a bathing suit with a towel draped around his neck. Flavia clinically eyed the blond Adonis standing before her from head to toe.

"Had a good look?" asked Merlin, after Flavia had failed to say anything.

Her inspection finally complete, she asked: "Are you the solicitor?"

"Where are you from?

"Across the road. And you?"

"Rochester. New York. Ever been?"

"The experience has eluded me."

"'Eluded'? Chet! Get in here."

"I'm not moving!" Lowenthal shouted from the pool area where he was stretched out on a chaise sunbathing in the raw.

"Would he be the solicitor?" Flavia tracked Lowenthal's voice through the living room and out to the pool area.

Not sharing an iota of Merlin's exhibitionism, Lowenthal rose abruptly and hurriedly put on his striped bathrobe.

"Don't dress on my account," said Flavia, not the least embarrassed by the lawyer's lack of formal— or any— attire.

"Do I know you from somewhere?" asked Lowenthal. Her face looked vaguely familiar.

"Claims she lives across the street," said Merlin.

"I do! That's my Packard in the driveway."

"The one that almost ran me over!" Lowenthal pointed his right index finger at her. "Two weeks ago."

"Would you mind awfully removing that finger from my face?" Flavia shoved his hand away. "It's rude. Where did this alleged offense occur?"

"In front of my house. Just after midnight. I was walking my dog."

Marlene trotted out onto the patio at that moment and begged to be lifted onto her master's lap.

"Who's this?" asked Flavia. Her eyes lit up with delight, as Lowenthal stroked the Dachshund.

"Marlene."

"She's divine."

Flavia reached out a hand to pet the dog. Marlene growled, leapt off her master's lap and hid behind a rose bush where she might observe the female intruding on her territory.

"A little possessive," shrugged Lowenthal. "So! What exactly do you want?"

"A solicitor!" exclaimed Flavia, with an isn't-it-obvious-tone to her voice.

"Ohh, an attorney," said Lowenthal, who turned to Merlin and said: "Did you hear that, Paul? Lady wants an attorney."

"Not me," said Merlin, who had a strong aversion to aggressive women. "I'm just a tennis player. That there's the lawyer. Reads books, too. With big words." Merlin quickly glanced at his watch. "Wonder what time the grunion are running. Nice almost meeting you."

"A most peculiar fellow," said Flavia, watching Merlin retreat inside the house. "Shall we get down to business?"

"Sure. What's your name, by the way?"

"Flavia Radford."

"Sir Osmond's daughter?"

"Do you know Daddy?"

"We met at an Anti-Nazi dinner the other week."

"Auntie Nancy? Who is she?"

"You're kidding, right?" Lowenthal couldn't decide if Flavia was dim or ditzy.

"Who was that half-naked man?"

"Paul Merlin. My partner."

"Partner? Ah! Yes." Pity, thought Flavia, who had found Lowenthal quite attractive. However, if he and Paul Merlin were an item, she certainly wasn't going to expend any further energy trying to get him into bed.

"Miss Radford, what is your husband's name?"

"Husband?"

"I assume you use Radford for professional reasons."

"And personal. It's my name."

"But when you got married—?"

"I'm not married."

"Then why do you want a divorce?"

"I don't." Flavia wrinkled her nose and pursed her lips, convinced that Willi had tricked her yet again. "Aren't you a criminal lawyer?"

"No. Have you committed a crime?"

"Possibly."

"You're not sure?"

"Is it true anything one tells you remains in confidence?" asked Flavia.

"That was in a film I did last year. At RKO."

"It's true. RKO or anywhere else. Before you reveal your dark secrets, may I suggest that a divorce attorney might not be the best—"

"You refuse to take the case?"

"Why would you want me to?"

"One feels badly almost running you down. What Mummy calls karma. Do you see?"

"No, I don't."

"Cockfosters! Are you intentionally being obtuse?"

"No. Just trying to figure out how your mind works."

"Complete waste of time," said Flavia. "Chucked out of three extremely posh boarding schools because the headmistresses couldn't comprehend my circuitry. What is your name, by the way? Our housekeeper told me, but I'm hopeless with details."

"Chester Lowenthal."

"German?"

"Jewish. Let's talk about the case. What have you got?" The lawyer pointed towards the manila envelope in her hand.

Flavia lifted the flap, removed an 8x10 glossy photograph, showing a man lying face down on the ground in front of her Packard. Flavia was standing above the man with her right fist clutched tightly to her mouth.

"Is this a movie still?" asked Lowenthal.

"Cockfosters!" Flavia said irritably. "Anyone can see it's real. That poor wretch on the ground is not a stunt man."

"And the woman is definitely you?" asked Lowenthal.

"Yes!"

"Who took this photograph?"

"Obviously the blackmailer."

"Whoa! Did I come in late to this picture? What blackmailer?"

Flavia thrust her hand into the manila envelope again and withdrew a note pasted together with letters cut out from different newspapers and magazines:

WE HAVE MORE. WOULD YOU LIKE THE POLICE TO SEE THEM?

$10,000 WILL KEEP US QUIET

BRING IT TO UNION STATION

TOMORROW NIGHT AT TEN. NO COPS!!

"What's all this about?" asked Lowenthal. "Start from the beginning, Miss Radford. If there is a beginning."

Flavia glared at him and said: "It was right after Marlene cut me to the quick."

"My dog?"

Flavia erupted into paroxysms of laughter and tumbled out of her chair onto the grass.

"Y'okay?" asked Lowenthal, extending his hand to help her back into her chair.

"Not your dog," replied Flavia, once she'd managed to catch her breath.

"Her namesake."

"Marlene Dietrich? What does she have to do with this?"

"Nothing really. I'd met her at a party at Charlie Feldman's. My father's agent. Fancied her like mad. She's very sexy. I was certain we'd shared a moment. Clearly not. Made a fool of myself. I'm versatile. It's not uncommon. Boarding school does have that effect on people. May I?" Flavia reached forward and took a cigarette from the silver box on the table.

"Not sure I understand." Lowenthal reached forward and lit her Camel with his gold Ronson lighter.

Flavia whipped off her Bakelite sunglasses for the first time since her arrival and stared at the lawyer. "I like boys and girls."

"Oh."

"Are you shocked?"

"None of my business."

"Under the circumstances, I completely concur." Flavia batted her eyelashes still convinced Lowenthal and Merlin were lovers. "I had an encounter with her at Cafe Gala. Made a complete fool of myself. Then I popped along to the Troc, hoping Violet and Consuela would be there. They're two delightful tarts of my acquaintance and an excellent source of reefer. My entire outlook on life had changed when I left the nightclub. As well as my sense of direction. I was zipping up Laurel instead of Benedict. Whereupon I executed a death-defying U-turn in the middle of the canyon. That's when I ran the man down with my car."

"Are you serious?"

"I swear on the King James. Why would one joke about a thing like that?" Flavia gave Lowenthal a summary of what happened after that right up to the events of that morning. "I checked the newspapers every day for an account of the accident. When nothing appeared after a week, I was relieved. Then I found the photos on the front seat of the Packard this morning. With the note." Flavia uncharacteristically burst into tears. "What am I to do, Mr. Lowenthal? I don't have $10,000."

PROPER DING-DONG

Searchlights were blazing through the night skies above Hollywood Boulevard. All the stars in the heavens— at least the ones under contract to Warner Brothers— were trouping down the red carpet. This ceremonial progress was interrupted by unctuous CBS announcer, Nolan Van Cleef, interviewing them on coast-to-coast radio.

"It is a star-studded night here for the premiere of *The Dawn Patrol* at the Chinese Theatre. And who do we have coming down the red carpet? He's a handsome devil and she's a beautiful angel."

Overhearing this inane introduction, David Niven turned to his date, Flavia Radford, and whispered: "I can't go through with it, Flaves. Being interviewed by the village idiot. Won't be able to keep a straight face."

"What would Aubrey say, Niv? 'Letting down the side, what?' This is your night, darling."

"Don't be daft. It's Errol's night."

"Errol's had many nights already. This is your innings, Niv."

"Promise you'll stick a pin in my head if it swells up?"

"Yes, indeed," Van Cleef boomed into the microphone. "It's Errol Flynn's good friend and co-star, David Niven. With the glamorous Flavia Radford on his arm."

Fans with autograph books struggled to get past the velvet rope barriers on either side of the red carpet. Uniformed police struggled to keep them back.

"David! David! Please sign my book!"

Niven dashed over to the rope to give the teenage girls his autograph, while his date was being grilled by Van Cleef.

"You look ravishing tonight, Flavia. If you don't mind my saying so."

"Say anything you want, Nolan. One is simply thrilled to be here."

"You and David looked pretty cozy coming up the red carpet together. Any chance of wedding bells?"

"Certainly not. Mr. Niven is a dear friend of the family."

"And what a family! CBS radio listeners know your dad, Sir Oswald Radford, as the host of *My Favorite Story*."

"Osmond. His name is Osmond Radford."

"That's what I said."

"I beg to differ, but you didn't."

"At least I didn't call him Oswald Rabbit." Van Cleef followed up that *bon mot* with a robust laugh.

"What an imbecilic thing to say," replied Flavia.

Niven arrived in front of the microphone at that moment and asked: "What did I miss?"

"Don't worry, David," said Van Cleef, grinding his molars following Flavia's tongue lashing. "Movie hasn't started yet. The whole town's buzzing with praise for *The Dawn Patrol*."

"I'm not sure who's tighter," said Niven, running his index finger between his neck and his dress shirt. "My collar or me."

"Edmund Goulding says you're headed for long overdue movie stardom. What is the secret to success in Hollywood? Perseverance? Luck?"

"One owes it all to clean living and Errol Flynn. Is that an oxymoron? Oops!" Niven winked impishly and glanced from side to side. "Errol's not around, is he?"

"He's already inside."

Pausing on the red carpet for their eldest daughter and Niven to enter the theater, a dyspeptic-looking Radford confided to his wife: "Why do they need to interview me? It's Errol and David's film. And Basil's." Radford could barely bring himself to mention Rathbone's name following the mountains of publicity the younger actor was receiving for *The Hound of the Baskervilles*.

"Haven't you forgotten someone?" asked Hyacinth.

"Donald Crisp?"

"Alec. Our son."

"Of course!" Sir Osmond rapped his forehead with his knuckles. "Top of my list. The others followed." The actor-knight removed a Hignett from his silver cigarette case, lit it and blew out a skein of smoke. "Where the devil is he? Trust Alec to be late for his premiere. Does he have a date for the event?"

"I don't know. Alec's very secretive about his love life."

Not with me, thought Radford, remembering his son's scratched-up face following his weekend sojourn in Tijuana.

"We don't entertain enough," said Hyacinth, bringing her husband back from his reverie.

"Entertain?"

"Ouida Rathbone's always throwing lavish parties and inviting all the poobahs like Goldwyn, Mayer and Zanuck. Very political is our Ouida. And very clever."

"Need I remind you, Lady Radford, that I was a big star in London and New York for many years without the aid of high-priced caterers or Chinese lanterns?"

"This is Hollywood," Hyacinth said emphatically. "One must adapt to survive."

"Darwinian cinema?"

"It's a game, Ozzie, and you're not very good at it. If you want to get back into the movies—"

"Not with this bum ticker," said Radford, tapping his chest. Dickie had instructed him to remind his wife— whenever the opportunity presented itself— of his health problems. Thus, the possibility of his real activities being discovered would be minimized.

"It wasn't giving you any trouble last night," said Hyacinth, touching her husband's cheek fondly. "Quite spirited, you were."

A Warner Brothers publicist stepped forward and led the Radfords over to the microphone. Van Cleef was double checking his script and repeating 'Osmond, Osmond, Osmond' under his breath.

"Here is Sir Osmond Radford, star of CBS's hit series, *My Favorite Story*. And with him is Lady Radford, who happens to be one of the best interior decorators in Hollywood. Tell me, Lady Radford, do your clients have to curtsy when you enter a room?"

"What a marvelous sense of humor you have, Nolan! So refreshing."

"Chaperoning your daughter tonight?"

"Not at all." Hyacinth laughed gaily. "We're here to support our son."

"Your son?"

"Alec Radford. He's in the movie."

"Of course, he is," said Van Cleef, checking his publicity handout. There was no mention of Alec Radford in the production notes. "And who do we have next?"

"Here we are!" chirped Eunice Radford, dragging an embarrassed Jasper towards the microphone.

"And you are?" Van Clef hadn't the slightest idea who the buxom redhead was breathing so heavily with her eyes aglow.

"I am Mrs. Jasper Radford. He is Sir Osmond's brother."

"Of course," boomed Van Cleef, enthusiastically blinded momentarily by the light bouncing off Jasper's bald pate. "You're in pictures, too. What a family! Just like the Barrymores. You look very familiar. Remind the radio audience what movies they'd have seen you in, Jasper. Are you Sir Jasper, as well?"

"No. Simply Jasper Radford, Esquire."

Eunice's bosom swelled to heroic proportions as she proceeded to halloo Jasper's name to the reverberate hills: "My husband has portrayed many butlers in some very prestigious films. Most recently with Fred Astaire and Ginger—"

"One butler he won't be playing," interrupted Van Cleef, "is Rhett Butler. Clark Gable has a lock on that role."

"Yes," said Eunice smugly. "But Jasper is going to be playing Gerald O'Hara in *Gone With The Wind*."

"Really! Has that been announced?"

"Only a matter of time," answered Eunice, with the assurance that comes from having God on one's side. Jasper was otherwise occupied ogling the long-legged usherette guiding the myriad celebrity guests inside the theater.

* * *

The lobby of Grauman's Chinese was packed with wall-to-wall Warner stars. Errol Flynn and director Edmund Goulding were chatting with David O. Selznick, who was taking a few hours off from his marathon preparation for *Gone With The Wind*.

"Sorry the loan-out didn't happen." Flynn's Tasmanian accent was always thicker off screen. The swashbuckling actor's gaze was fixated on an underage starlet purchasing popcorn at the refreshment stand. The nubile teenager was energetically scratching her epidermis six inches south of her navel. "Reckon she has crabs?"

"Loan-out?" asked Selznick, hoping he had a supply of Benzedrine in his pocket to stay awake during the premiere. The boisterous producer was going cold turkey as the sweat poured down his face. To make matters worse, his bladder was about to burst.

"Gone With The Wind." replied Flynn. "J.L. says you wanted to borrow me, Bette and Olivia. That would have been a proper ding-dong. Not that I'd

have made a fuckin' cent out of it. Is your father-in-law going to lend you Gable?" Louis B. Mayer, whose daughter was married to the hyperactive Selznick, was demanding 50 per cent of the gross in exchange for the services of his biggest male star.

"Excuse me, Errol," gasped Selznick. "I must go to the men's room. Nerves."

"Wouldn't have to drain the dragon if you'd cast me, sport."

Selznick was descending the carpeted steps two at a time to the basement lavatory when a beaming Flavia came up the stairs towards him in full Southern mode.

"Why, David Selznick! I do declare you grow more handsome every time I see you."

"For Chrissake, get outta my way!" roared the producer, shoving her rudely to one side.

Selznick made it through the men's room door just in time and stepped up to the urinal. He had unzipped his fly when the door to a cubicle opened, and a familiar English voice called out with buoyant bonhomie.

"Hello, old boy!"

A furious Selznick whipped around and almost peed on Jasper's leg. "Don't give me that old boy horse shit, Radford. What's all this about you playing Gerald O'Hara?"

"That was entirely Eunice's idea. Not mine. Then I got to thinking, it might not be such a bad idea. I still owe you that four thousand dollars from poker--"

"Five!"

"Was it five? Doesn't ring a bell. Let's call it five. For friendship's sake. I'm prepared to play the part for nothing. My side of the ledger will be clean, and you'll have made out like a bandit."

"Does insanity run in your family?" Selznick was washing his hands at the sink by this time. "Your niece is crazy as a shit house rat. Calling me day and night reciting whole chunks of the book. Her brother's been barred from every lot in town because of his temper. Now, you tell me you want to give Lionel Barrymore a run for his money. You're a barrel of monkeys, Jasper. Love having you around. But you can't act. Got any spare change?"

Selznick left a crestfallen Jasper behind in the men's room. Armed with two dimes and four nickels the would-be actor had given him, the mogul dialed his publicist, Russell Birdwell: "Find out if one of the books the Nazis set on fire in last week's *Kristellnacht* was *Gone With The Wind*. We might be able to get some publicity out of it."

* * *

Edmund Goulding was about to take his seat in the auditorium when he spotted Alec Radford entering the lobby. Clearly, the boy was a glutton for punishment. Who was the girl on his arm? A dyed blonde with a half-moon scar on her left cheek. She looked familiar.

"Hello, Eddie!" Alec strode towards the director, every inch a Sandhurst man (despite his short tenure at the military academy before he was expelled). "Grand evening, what?" The dyed blonde pinched the younger Radford's bicep. "Frightfully, sorry. You remember Violet, don't you?"

"So nice to see you again, Mr. Goulding. Thanks for inviting me." Violet wrinkled her nose and stuck her tongue out.

It was the tongue that jogged Goulding's memory. How dare the cheeky sod bring her to an event like this? A seasoned actor before turning to writing and directing, no hint of outrage marred Goulding's countenance. "Best hurry up, kids. Film's about to start."

Alec grabbed hold of Violet's elbow and briskly steered her inside the auditorium. They stepped across Flavia and Niven to get to their seats. Flavia did not show a glimmer of recognition for her reefer chum, even when Alec introduced Violet to his parents.

Radford had just finished nodding politely when Basil Rathbone leaned forward from the row behind the actor-knight and whispered: "Did my damnedest to get you the role of Watson. But the studio said you were too handsome. They went with Willie Bruce. How would you feel about playing Moriarity if it turns into a series?"

"You're far too kind," replied Radford. "Let's cross that bridge when we come to it."

Rathbone squeezed his fellow actor's arm affectionately and intoned: "First, last, and always a gentleman. Sorry about your son."

Radford had no idea what Rathbone was talking about. Moments later, the curtain parted, and the Warner Brothers shield appeared on the screen to tumultuous applause from the faithful. After the opening aerial dogfight, the vintage planes landed in France where Flynn and Niven exhibited an instant movie chemistry together. Watching their unique camaraderie on screen, Radford couldn't help but think of himself and Dickie in their place so many years before.

Flynn and Niven zipped across the airfield to check on Hollister, a younger pilot, who was in a bad way after his best friend had been shot down by the Germans. Alec sat upright in his seat and stared straight ahead at the screen. His first line was coming. An enthralled Violet squeezed his arm. With flying goggles and grease on the rest of his face, it was difficult to make out Hollister's face clearly. Alec emitted a peculiar animal sound and gripped the arms of his seat. Something was wrong.

Flynn chased after Hollister as he ran up the stairs of the barracks and into his room. Infuriated, Alec cursed under his breath, grabbed Violet by the wrist and yanked her out of her seat.

"Oww!" protested Violet. "I like this movie. Why are we leaving?"

Alec didn't answer as he dragged a reluctant Violet up the aisle towards the lobby.

Flavia stared at Hollister having a nervous breakdown on the screen. The actor was young, blonde, and English. But he wasn't her brother.

"What happened to Alec?" she whispered to Niven.

"We'll talk later," said Niven, thoroughly enjoying the movie up on the screen and the success it was going to bring him.

In the lobby afterwards, the cast and crew were bombarded with praise. Everyone agreed that *The Dawn Patrol* was Eddie Goulding's best picture since *Grand Hotel*. To many of his previous detractors, who could only describe Errol Flynn as 'athletic', they were forced to eat crow and admit the Tasmanian Devil could act. As the tortured martinet, Basil Rathbone was highly sympathetic. David Niven, as predicted, had been elevated into a new category.

Flavia and her bewildered parents stood off to one side wondering how it was possible Alec had disappeared from the movie when he had been hired to play Hollister.

"He quit," said Niven, uncomfortable as the bearer of bad tidings. "Or fired himself. It was most unfortunate."

"But why?" asked Hyacinth. "He was thrilled when he got the part."

"He didn't get along with Eddie Goulding. Or anyone. Kept telling us it was all wrong."

"What was?" asked Radford.

"Little details about the Flying Corps. Claimed to be an expert. Kept citing you as a reference. And he refused to cry. Said it wasn't manly. He and Goulding had words. Alec stormed off the set. Next day they hired Peter Willes. Alec's scenes were reshot."

"Why didn't you tell us, Niv?" asked Flavia.

"Frankly, it wasn't my place, Flaves."

"Quite right," said Radford. "How could Alec not know he'd been re- placed? Why go through the ritual of attending the premiere?"

"Don't fret, Ozzie." Hyacinth patted her husband's hand. "It was all an unfortunate experience. Alec must be suffering terribly."

"Who was that young woman with him?" asked Radford.

"I don't know," lied Flavia.

UP THE KHYBER PASS

Alec walked five paces ahead of Violet in stony silence. He had no destination in mind, but instinctively knew if he wasn't in motion his brain would erupt.

"Hey!" shouted Violet. "I can't keep up in these heels. Could you stop a second? What the hell did you invite me for if you can't treat me decently?"

Why, indeed? For the tenth time that evening, Alec wondered what his motive had been for inviting the prostitute to the event. Shock his father? That hadn't worked. Violet knew how to behave properly in public and had a decent wardrobe for such occasions. Perhaps, he had wanted to unnerve Eddie Goulding by bringing one of his "secret" stars to the premiere. But the director retained his charming veneer, as always.

The multi-talented Goulding was notorious for his "movie parties". He loved watching people having sex. Young, attractive people, whom he would photograph with a 16-millimeter camera. Home porno. There was no shortage of talent in Hollywood willing to do his bidding on camera in the off chance the *metteur en scene* might give them the opportunity to appear in one of his studio pictures.

Goulding first noticed Alec's bottom high in the saddle when the younger Radford was playing polo for Darryl Zanuck. The director decided on the spot that he had to see that fine bit of British rump on full display. He took the lad out for a drink afterwards. Several gins and tonic later, he asked Alec how he felt about having sexual relations on film.

"How much does it pay?" asked young Radford, always with a keen eye for found money.

"It doesn't," replied Goulding, "but there might be a nice role for you in *The Dawn Patrol*. If you can take direction."

Alec turned up at Goulding's house a week later. The Chinese-themed sitting room was filled with a dozen attractive young people drinking martinis and smoking the hand-rolled cigarettes scattered liberally about the room. The younger Radford tried one of the cigarettes and soon found himself chatting away to a pretty blond with a half-moon scar on her cheek. Her name was Violet Purdy and when she said something he didn't quite understand, he burst into uncontrollable laughter.

"Did I say something funny?" asked Violet.

"Sounded purdy damned funny to me," replied Alec, who tumbled to the carpet in paroxysms of mirth.

"Sweet mother of Jesus! You're higher than a kite,"

"Nonsense. I only had one drink."

"Not the drink. It's the reefer! Eddie gets the best Maryjane."

"I don't think I've met Mary Jane," Alec said solemnly.

It was now Violet's turn to laugh herself silly.

"Everyone having a good time?" asked Goulding in plummy English tones. He had made a dramatic entrance into the room wearing a black Chinese robe replete with orange and yellow dragons breathing red flames. "Ready for some movie magic?" The master of the revels clapped his hands together twice. Two men in masks appeared carrying a 16-millimeter movie camera and a clapper board. "Change into your costumes, children."

"Don't have a costume," said Alec, feeling five-years-old.

"Oh, yes, you do!" sang Violet, undoing his belt and threading it out of the loops of his trousers.

"Don't be so keen, Violet," said Goulding. "Mr. Radford's a big boy. He can remove his clothes without female assistance."

In a marijuana haze, Alec's condom-encased erection glided inside of Miss Purdy. He had a jolly good rhythm going when a palm slapped down sharply on his bare buttock. Goulding's scolding voice rang out from behind the camera: "No, no, no, dear boy. Ram her! Really hard. And let's see that lovely bottom swing back and forth like a pendulum. There! Much better. You *do* know how to take direction."

Unfortunately, that was not the case some weeks later at the Warner lot in Burbank. Alec was rigid and unemotional where Hollister needed to be shrill and semi-hysterical.

Goulding drew him off to one side and spoke intently in a hushed voice: "What's wrong, dear boy? You fucked that little tart the other week exactly the way I wanted you to. And with considerable panache. Why can't you do what I want now?"

"It's not manly."

"And a cock up your backside is?"

"What are you talking about?"

"The threesome you participated in. Surely that wasn't your first outing up the Khyber Pass. Shall we have a private screening for your father?"

"How dare you!" shrieked Alec. "I'd kill you first."

"Yes, yes! That's the tone I want. There's the moral outrage. The girlish hysteria Hollister needs."

"Then find another actor!" bellowed Alec, who promptly stomped off the set.

Shouting. Someone was shouting at him and pounding on his chest. "What the hell is wrong with you?"

Alec stared down at Violet hammering away at his chest.

"I'm freezing my tits off. Where did you park the car? Why are you just standing there like a dummy?"

You fucked that little tart exactly the way I wanted you to.

"Just drop me off at the Trop, okay?" Violet's hands were on her hips. She'd had enough of young Radford's unpredictable moods. "Can you do that for me?"

Surely that wasn't your first outing up the Khyber Pass.

"Know what? I'm taking a cab. You are one queer character."

A Yellow Cab pulled up at the curb. Violet climbed into the back seat, and called out: "Do me a favor? Forget my fucking phone number!"

"I'm not queer!" roared Alec, as her taxi sped west.

* * *

The beautiful redhead with the long shapely legs stared across the round cafe table at the fat, balding, mustached man sipping his third martini. It was a mistake to have come here, she thought to herself. Not just the Beverly Hills Hotel but Los Angeles itself. Why hadn't she been warned about these movie moguls? They wouldn't even look at her film, let alone distribute it. *Olympiad.* Her masterpiece. From the first images panning across the colosseum ruins to the naked gods and goddesses. Sheer genius. No one knew how to move a camera the way she did. The problem? *Juden! Immer Juden!* None of the scum had shown her the courtesy of an invitation to their dream factories. Only the genius in Burbank— with his divine little mouse— had rolled out the red carpet and treated her with respect. As an equal. He had no love for the Jews either. Or the Communist scum trying to unionize his studio.

She raised her left hand and snapped her fingers: *"Herr Kellner!"*

The nearby waiter froze, uncertain if the beautiful redhead wanted him. She looked like a movie star, but he couldn't place her.

"Was wollen Sie?" asked her overweight escort. Pointing to her whiskey sour, he asked: *"Einander?"*

Surprisingly, the redhead replied in English: "No. I want an Oscar." Georg Gyssling, the German Consul, threw his head back and laughed.

"Sehr gut, gnädige Fräulein." He spoke to the waiter in accented English: "Another round, please."

Leni Riefenstahl desired more than an Academy Award. Like her champion and supreme patron, Adolf Hitler, she wanted the world at her feet. It had not been enough to be a movie star eight years earlier; theirs was a brief season like the butterfly. The true artists of the twentieth century were the filmmakers. *Der Führer* realized that and recognized her genius. That was why he had given Leni carte blanche to make *Triumph of the Will*, her first masterpiece. She and the Reich's Chancellor were a great team despite the absence of sexual congress. Not that the vulgar American press believed it. "Hitler's honey" was how the tabloids referred to her. The Reich's Chancellor had never laid a hand on her. Now, in America, and treated like a social outcast, what Leni Riefenstahl really needed was a man. Not the overweight, fawning Gyssling, who kept suggesting she come back to his residence on Curson Avenue for some *deutsche Kuchen* and decent *schnaps*. The notion of the naked Consul made her stomach turn. No! What Leni desperately desired was a violent, passionate lover, who could erase the humiliation she had suffered since arriving in Hollywood.

Her wish was granted a moment later. He stood in the entranceway: young, blond, fit and ferocious. Rudely ignoring the *maitre d's* polite inquiry, the new arrival prowled the room like a dangerous young lion seeking its prey. The way he carries himself, thought the director, he must be German. She had grown moist between her legs thinking what the young lion would look like disrobed. Tearing her clothes off. Ravaging her. This was the only *deutsche Kuche* Leni Riefenstahl wanted that night.

Raising a bejeweled hand, she beckoned the ferocious blond to draw near.

"Wie heissen Sie?" Her voice was almost girlish. The young man did not reply. *"Setzen Sie, bitte. Sie sind Deutsch, nicht wahr?"* She patted the chair next to her.

"Actually, I'm English."

"But you speak German?"

"*Ein bisschen.*"

"Perhaps, you need a governess. Is that the right word?"

"Who are you?"

"My name is Leni Riefenstahl."

"You directed *Triumph of the Will!*"

"Have you seen it?"

"Half a dozen times. It's the greatest film ever made."

"You have excellent taste." Leni laughed at her little joke, then reached out and squeezed the young man's arm. "And so strong. He should be on a poster for the Fatherland. Don't you think, Georg?"

Fifteen minutes later, Alec Radford and Leni Riefenstahl were ensconced in her bungalow screwing like rabbits. Violent rabbits.

THEY'LL KILL MARLENE

Gladys McNutt was tapping away at her Underwood when a highly agitated Flavia Radford burst through the front door of the law offices.

"Is he here?" asked Flavia.

"Which 'he' did you want?" asked Gladys. "And who are you?"

The Pirate Queen looked around to insure sure no one was listening, then lowered her voice to a conspiratorial whisper: "Flavia Radford."

"Ohhhh!" said the red-haired, freckle-faced, five-foot nothing secretary, without looking up from her typing. "Now, I understand."

"Understand what?"

"What all the fuss is about." Gladys pushed a button on the intercom and announced: "Your neighbor is here."

Lowenthal emerged from his office and informed Flavia: "It's customary to phone and make an appointment before—"

Flavia moved past Lowenthal into his private office. He followed her and shut the door behind himself. It had been two weeks since Sir Osmond's daughter had crossed the street to engage his services. The blackmailers had sent two more notes with drop-off points in Griffith Park and the La Brea Tar Pits. Each missive was more desperate and threatening than the first. The lawyer instructed Flavia to ignore their demands. "Wait and see who blinks first."

"You're not going to believe this!" said Flavia, barely able to control her excitement. She paced up and down the office like a long-distance runner waiting for the starter's pistol to go off.

"Have you heard from them again?'

Flavia shook her head. "I came directly from Columbia. Lucky no one stopped me for speeding. I ran into Harry Cohn, whom everyone is terrified of, but I think is an absolute poppet. He asked if I wanted to make some money. Well, who doesn't? 'Strictly off the books', said Harry. Then he asked if I could scream. The girl they hired to scream sounds like a mouse in a paper bag. She opens her mouth, and nothing comes out. Huge closeup. No noise."

"Flavia, I really have to—"

"Harry whipped out a roll of ill-gotten gains and peeled off a fifty-dollar bill. He must have had a good day at the track. Or he just wants to get into my knickers. But gift horses are always welcome. I went over to the stage where they were doing the post. I put the headphones on and looked up at the screen. Waiting for my big moment. A sedan was speeding along a city street when it hit a pedestrian. The man went flying up in the air. When he came down, his face was plastered on the windscreen. And I screamed. 'Too early,' said the sound recorder. 'We haven't seen the girl yet.' But I'd seen what I needed to see."

"Which was?"

"The blackmailer! Or his partner. That man up on the screen was the supposed corpse from Laurel Canyon. *Mea culpa*, Chet. Clearly, he *is* a stunt man. Specializing in automobile accidents. Can we have him arrested?"

"Are you certain it's the same guy?"

"Cockfosters! One doesn't forget a face like that. Nose all mushed up. Must have been a prizefighter once upon a when."

Lowenthal opened his office door and called out: "Doherty! Get in here!" Francis X. Doherty, a moon-faced man with wispy, plastered down hair and an unlit cigar wedged permanently in his mouth, sauntered into the room a moment later. The lawyer introduced Flavia to his investigator.

"What do you think?" asked Lowenthal after Flavia had exhausted them with her tale.

"Got a name?" asked Doherty, picking bits of loose tobacco off the end of his cigar.

"Flavia Radford."

"You're cute," Doherty pointed a finger at Flavia. "The stunt man. Has he got a name?"

"Clyde Atcheson." Flavia removed a folded piece of paper from her purse and handed it to the investigator. "His address is on there, as well. Did I do the right thing?"

"She's cute," repeated Doherty, walking out of the office with the folded piece of paper.

"What happens next?" Flavia asked breathlessly. "Doherty makes a few calls."

"And?"

"We wait. But not here," said Lowenthal, steering Flavia towards the door. "I've got work to do."

"We haven't discussed your fee. Will fifty dollars suffice?"

"Your Harry Cohn money?"

"I scream well."

"I'll bet." Lowenthal smiled at her. Flavia regretted once again that he didn't dance on her side of the ballroom. What a pity!

* * *

Flavia pulled the Packard into the driveway and walked towards the front door. She spotted an envelope sticking out under the Welcome mat. Her name was scrawled across it. Tearing it open, she read another pasted together note:

WE GAVE YOU THREE CHANCES TO MAKE GOOD.

YOU DON'T GET ANOTHER.

WE TOOK YOUR LITTLE DOG.

IF YOU WANT TO SEE IT ALIVE AGAIN,

BRING THE MONEY TO THE SANTA MONICA

PIER TONIGHT AT 10 O'CLOCK.

COME ALONE. WE'LL FIND YOU.

REMEMBER…NO COPS!

Bursting into the house, she called out for the two Dromios. The twin Great Danes bounded out from the library and leapt up and down adoringly. The note made no sense. The dogs were hale and hearty, and anything but little.

"Willi?"

The tall German housekeeper emerged from the kitchen wiping flour off her apron. "Something is wrong?"

Flavia held the envelope aloft. "Someone left this envelope under the front door mat. Did you notice a suspicious type snooping around the grounds?"

"Only the woman who took the Dachshund."

"What woman?"

"Perhaps she works for the attorneys. She comes here all the time."

"The woman comes here?"

"*Nein, nein.* Marlene. The *kleine* Dachshund. She comes to play with the Dromios. She is lonely. The doggies adore her."

"Cockfosters! They took Chet's dog."

"She does not work for the men?"

"Can you describe what she looks like?"

"Not much. She had a big floppy hat and sunglasses. But she limped. That is the word, yes? Dragging the foot."

"Was she short? Tall?" By this time, Flavia was in the kitchen dialing Lowenthal's office number on the wall phone.

"Not so tall as me."

"No one is as tall as you, Willi… Hello? Miss McVey? Flavia Radford here. It's rather urgent… Thank you." Flavia took a deep breath and wondered how to break the news to the lawyer. Men of that ilk were unusually close to their dogs. Pray God he doesn't start weeping. "Hello?… Oh, hello, Chester. How are you?" Why was she being so formal at a time like this?

"About an hour older since you left. Doherty did his homework. Your Mr. Atcheson has quite a checkered past. And several aliases. Not to mention multiple outstanding warrants in five states. The company you keep, lady!"

"He left me another note. Rather his associate did. A woman."

"Probably Doris Runkle. Former model, who turned photographer after a bus hit her. Mostly pinups. Until now."

"Does she walk with a limp?" asked Flavia.

"Hey! Do you tell fortunes, too?"

"They've kidnapped Marlene."

"Dietrich?"

"No, your dog. Probably thought she was mine."

"How do you know that?" asked Lowenthal.

"It's in the note. Willi saw Doris take her. She said the woman limped. They want the ten thousand tonight or they'll kill Marlene. I'm so sorry, Chet."

"Where's the exchange to take place?"

"Santa Monica Pier. Ten o'clock tonight. No police."

"We won't need the police," Lowenthal said grimly.

* * *

Flavia stood in front of the full-length mirror of her bedroom debating what to wear that evening. Business suit? On the pier at that hour? Hardly. A dress? Nothing too formal. Cockfosters! It wasn't going to make the papers. Although the publicity wouldn't be such a bad thing to remind certain producers that she was still alive and looked bloody good for 26. The polka dot might not make a bad— No! Think, woman! What if they try and pull a fast one? Take the money and keep the dog. Flavia felt honor bound to give chase. Slacks and tennis shoes. Scarlet turtleneck and blazer. Practical and photogenic.

The door opened. Hyacinth stepped into her daughter's room and asked:

"Can you spare a moment?"

"Going out shortly. Can't it wait?"

"Not really."

Flavia watched her mother pick at the varnish on her right thumbnail with her index finger. Always a dead giveaway when something was troubling the usually unflappable Lady Radford. "Sit down, Mummy. What's amiss?"

"What isn't is more like it. There is a strange energy pervading this house."

"You're not going to go all Theosophical on me, are you? Krishna's divine and wildly attractive but one really doesn't want to swallow the wafer. I barely tolerate the Church of England."

"Is Alec in love?" asked Hyacinth.

"*Can* Alec love?" countered Flavia.

"What a horrible thing to say! Alec is troubled and we all need to support him as best we can."

"I shan't give him a penny."

"Emotionally, darling. He feels so unloved and unwanted."

"Very astute of him."

"Flavia, I'm serious. He's been seeing someone for over a week now. Doesn't come home till dawn."

"Oh, Mummy! You don't wait up for him, do you?"

"Can't help it. He's my son and he's paying some sort of karmic penalty for his present incarnation."

"Do you and Daddy talk about this sort of thing in bed?"

"I beg your pardon? In my day one never spoke—"

"In your day, Victoria was still the queen."

"I do wish you'd get married and become someone else's problem. He sings in the shower."

"Who does?"

"Alec. One can hear his robust baritone all over the house. He's never sung in the shower before. Your father's doubled over with laughter most mornings."

"What does he sing? Alec?"

"The Eton Boating Song."

"Perhaps she's a rower." Flavia sang: 'And they all pull together'."

"Daddy's been on my mind, as well."

"Has he gotten over his Sherlock disappointment?"

"Over? One would never think there'd been a crisis. He and Boggs are down in the cellar day and night repairing the wine racks. Or so they say. All that banging and sawing."

"What else could they be doing, Mummy? Installing a dungeon?"

"He's very happy to have Boggs back in his life. I suppose it reminds him of a more successful time. Not just the theatre but the war. He loved being a prisoner. Does that sound peculiar? Said it reminded him of school. Without the numbing pressure of competition. They were all equals in that POW camp— officers and noncoms— with one common goal: to survive and support each other."

"Quite heroic."

"Your father felt fulfilled then. That's not happening now. But Daddy's not my real concern. It's Julia."

"Has something happened to Ju-Ju?"

"I pray that it hasn't. We have no idea where she is. Daddy never talks about it, which worries me no end. Julia's not like you. The Pirate Queen ready to repel all boarders. Fearless and quite fabulous. Don't you dare curtsy! Julia is a spring flower with no one to tend to her in a world crawling with overwhelming weeds."

"You should hire a detective. I know a very good one. He must have associates in New York. They could track Ju-Ju down."

"Forgive me, Flavia, but you've appeared in far too many B-movies. If only the child would phone us. Or send a postcard…. Who is this detective?"

"He works for Chet. Chester Lowenthal. The attorney who lives across the street." Flavia tried to sound casual when mentioning his name.

"Does Chet always bring that twinkle to your eye?"

"Probably just a cinder. Chet doesn't like girls."

"He's never met one like you before, I'm certain. Is he good husband material? One could always lash it to a toothbrush every few years."

"Mummy!"

"Noel Coward said it to me ages ago. I was shocked then. Not now. Where are you going, by the way? In trousers. Your grandmother would have fallen on her lorgnette."

"Going out. With… Chet."

"Ah! Chet." A Cheshire cat smile appeared on Lady Radford's face. She touched her daughter's cheek and asked: "Does he play bridge?"

"Never asked."

"I'll wager he does. Bring him round some evening for a rubber. We can talk about detectives then."

EXTREMELY AGITATED MIDGET

The two Dromios were barking loudly in the hallway. Appearing on the upstairs landing, Flavia stared down in time to observe the Great Danes dashing away from the front door and into the sitting room. She hastily descended the stairs in pursuit of them. Arriving in the sitting room, Flavia caught sight of a shadowy figure treading on the rose bushes while trying to peek through the windows. The Pirate Queen went into operational mode and rushed into the library. Searching frantically through the bottom drawer of her father's desk, she located an object wrapped in a piece of black velvet. She unfolded the material and expertly examined a Webley Mark VI revolver, which had been her father's sidearm in the Royal Flying Corps over twenty years earlier.

Bullets were encased in all the chambers. Excellent!

The shadow flitted by the windows once again heading towards the front door. Flavia followed suit. Flinging the front door open, she stepped outside and planted the Webley squarely in the intruder's back.

"Turn around… very slowly."

Fully expecting to confront Clyde Atcheson, Flavia discovered Paul Merlin scowling at her.

"Is that a gun in your hand or are you just glad to see me?" asked the blond Adonis from Rochester. "Do you even know how to use that thing?"

"Most certainly. I'm a crack shot."

"Great. Bring it along. We may need it."

"You're going with us?" asked Flavia, unable to hide the disapproval in her voice.

"Marlene's my dog, too."

"Where's … Mr. Lowenthal?" She had no right to keep the partners apart in a moment of mutual tragedy.

"Waiting for us in Santa Monica. He went ahead with Doherty. They're on a reconnaissance mission. We'll meet them there. Hey, Calamity Jane!"

"Are you addressing me?" Flavia was thrown by this turn of events. Chet and Paul, joined at the hip, going to rescue their dog. Why was she even bothering? "What is it?"

"Put the goddam thing in your pocket. This isn't Dodge City."

"No need to be rude, Mr. Merlin. You have nothing to fear from me."

"Fear?"

"I'm not a poacher."

Merlin stared at her, totally mystified. "Did they drop you on your head when you were little?"

"No need for any further hostility. I'd like us all to be friends."

"Okay! One big happy family. Now, let's vamoose to the ocean."

* * *

Lowenthal was waiting for them outside the carousel on the Santa Monica Pier. He bought three tickets and led them inside to a gaudily painted chariot nestled between the plaster horses. The Wurlitzer music started up once more and the carousel began revolving. Lowenthal reached inside his pocket and handed Flavia a bulky, folded manila envelope.

"Is this the money?" she asked.

"No. We're not giving them any money. It's shredded newspaper."

"Careful, Chet. She's armed and dangerous." Flavia glared at Merlin, then turned back to Lowenthal. "What about Marlene? Aren't we putting her at risk?"

"Relax, kiddo." Merlin tapped her arm playfully. "That little girl will come running to Papa the minute she sees me. Or sniffs me."

"Then what are we actually doing out here?" asked Flavia.

"Getting our dog back," answered Lowenthal, "And snapping Clyde Atcheson's photo."

"Whatever for?"

"To prove he's alive and you didn't kill him. Exhibit A."

"You are a clever biscuit." Flavia beamed approvingly at Lowenthal.

"Where is Mr. Doherty? One assumes he's the picture snatcher."

"Best in the business," said Merlin. "Nobody ever sees him till he says 'Gotcha!' He's out there on the pier somewhere."

"What if Atcheson doesn't come and sends Limping Doris instead?"

"Clyde's the muscle. In case anything goes wrong." Lowenthal reached out his hand and touched her sleeve. "Nothing will go wrong."

The music had stopped a moment earlier and the chariot eased to a halt. Children dashed towards their waiting parents and exited the carousel. Merlin pointed towards a uniformed nurse aimlessly pushing a perambulator along the boardwalk. The woman walked with a pronounced limp. "At least Marlene's traveling in style."

"Think they stuffed her in the pram?" asked Flavia.

"Only by drugging her first," replied Lowenthal. "Another score to settle."

"Take it easy, tiger." Merlin glanced at his watch and stepped out of the chariot. "Ten o'clock. You need to make contact. We'll be two steps behind you or beside you." He pointed towards Flavia's pocket. "Try not to use that cannon except as a last resort."

"What cannon?" asked Lowenthal.

"I brought Daddy's old service revolver. Webley Mark VI. Has marvelous heft."

"You know about guns?"

"Hemingway invited me to go on safari with him."

"How do you know Hemingway?"

"Chet! Please!" Merlin gestured impatiently for them to get moving. "We don't want to lose her."

The trio moved towards the exit, then dispersed into the crowd. Flavia came up behind the limping nurse. In her most formal tones, she said: "Miss Runkle, I believe?"

Doris Runkle froze. This wasn't the plan. She was supposed to make contact with the Englishwoman. Not the other way around. Something was wrong. She turned and stared at Flavia.

"Were you addressing me?"

"Please, Miss Runkle. Drop the pretense. I find all of this extremely distasteful."

"How'd you know my name?"

"Have you got Marlene in there?" Flavia pointed inside the pram. "You got the money?"

Flavia opened her bag and pointed to the hefty envelope: "Show me the dog first."

Doris's eyes darted back and forth between the actress and the pram. Finally, Flavia reached her hand inside to pull back the blanket covering the Dachshund.

"Give me the money!" A hideous baby/midget spoke in a stilted East European accent. His wrinkled face was framed by an adorable sun bonnet as he aimed a Colt Service Ace up at her. "Make it fast."

Flavia looked around to see where Lowenthal and Merlin had planted themselves. They were nowhere in sight.

"Where is Marlene?"

"Give me the fucking money," growled the midget, "or I will use this."

"And I shall use this," replied Flavia withdrawing the Webley from her overcoat pocket and aiming it at the 'baby' in the pram.

"What the hell is going on here, Doris?" The extremely agitated midget sat up in the pram. The nurse limped over attempting to break the stale-mate. "This was not the plan."

"Calm down, Ferka. We can still make this work. Wanna see the dog, Miss Radford? C'mere."

"This was not the plan!" Ferka the midget shouted shrilly. By this time several passersby had stopped to stare at the baby wildly waving a firearm in the air. Doris shoved him rudely back into the pram and steered it towards the boardwalk railing. The limping nurse pointed down below towards the sand where Flavia saw Clyde Atchison squeezing Marlene far too tightly in his arms.

"Throw him the money," said Doris, "and he'll let the dog go free."

"No, Doris!" Ferka was standing up in the pram waving the Colt once again. "Clyde will have the money and we will have nothing."

"Clyde won't double-cross us," said Doris, then turned back to Flavia:

"Throw him the money!"

Ferka leapt out of the pram and ran over to Flavia. He aimed his gun at her knee cap.

"Change of plans. Give me the money or you will be crippled for life!"

But it's only shredded newspaper, thought Flavia. Cockfosters! She tossed the envelope down towards the sand. Atchison released Marlene, who promptly raced towards the stairs. The stuntman raced forward with arms outstretched to catch the money.

"Gotcha!" shouted Doherty, emerging from his hiding place under the boardwalk. He snapped Aitchison's picture as the hapless stuntman's hands clapped shut on the folded manila envelope.

"What the hell!" Atchison stared dumbfounded at Doherty. When the moon-faced investigator made no move to pull out a gun or cuffs, the stunt-man started running along the beach.

"He took the money!" shrieked Ferka. "I knew we could not trust him." The midget whipped off his nightgown, revealing a natty three-piece suit. Ferka was running towards the stairs when Flavia's voice rang out: "Stop at once or I'll shoot!"

The midget turned around and saw Flavia aiming the Webley at him. He cursed her in his native tongue and released the safety on his gun.

"Noooo!" Lowenthal appeared out of nowhere and tackled Flavia to the ground.

"But he's going to get away!" wailed Flavia, watching Doris and Ferka flee towards Ocean Avenue while Lowenthal lay stretched out atop her.

"What does it matter? Paul's got Marlene. Doherty's got the picture. And…"

"Yes?" asked Flavia, all too aware of the hardness she felt pressing against her leg from underneath the lawyer's trousers. What have you got there, Mr. Lowenthal? What on earth was going on?

Their eyes locked. Their lips met. The kiss seemed to last forever. When they finally came up for air, Flavia said in bewildered wonder:

"You're not a homosexual."

"Never said I was. Are you disappointed?"

"Not at all." Then returning to her tough girl persona, she asked: "Do you play bridge?"

"Yes."

"Mummy will be thrilled."

HELLIONS AND ROGUES

During his brief stay at Best of Times, Richard Ives-Curtis had made a thorough examination of the premises. The wine cellar in the basement proved a godsend. A week after his departure, Dickie sent Radford a coded message instructing the actor-knight to build a wireless room off the wine cellar in which a shortwave radio might be housed. The 'key' book for breaking the code was sent under separate cover to Boggs at his tiny apartment in the flats of Beverly Hills. Using the code, Dickie and Radford could transmit secret messages back and forth. The key book was Conan Doyle's *A Study in Scarlet*. If Dickie had meant the Sherlock Holmes mystery to be a joke, the actor-knight was not amused.

Several weeks transpired with no contact from the spymaster. Radford wondered if Dickie had lost faith in his old comrade-at-arms. After the initial shock of being dragooned into the Secret Service, the actor-knight had warmed to the idea and was looking forward to playing his new role. If his services were no longer required by His Majesty's government, what was Sir Osmond to do? Was there any hope of resurrecting his moribund screen career? Perhaps he could return to the stage. Find a vehicle he might perform in with Julia. Of course, one would have to find Julia first.

Then a transmission came through from London. It took Radford several hours to decode it. Finally, he put on his spectacles and read:

YOU AND HY SHOULD GIVE A WELL-PUBLICIZED COCKTAIL PARTY WELCOMING LAURENCE OLIVIER BEFORE THE END OF THE MONTH. HE IS THERE FILMING WUTHERING HEIGHTS FOR GOLDWYN. ISN'T FRANCES GOLDWYN A

CLIENT OF HY'S? TRY AND INVITE AS MANY FOREIGN ARTISTS AS POSSIBLE. SERVE PLENTY OF LIQUOR. KEEP ALL RECEIPTS FOR REIMBURSEMENT. BOGGS CAN SERVE AS WAITER CUM EAVESDROPPER. IS LENI RIEFENSTAHL STILL IN YOUR PART OF THE WORLD? SHE IS QUITE A PROVOCATIVE CHARACTER AND MIGHT PROVE A VALUABLE GUEST. ANY WAY OF FINDING HER?

Poor Sir Osmond! It was merely a matter of flipping his son and heir onto his back to make the *Fräulein* in question magically appear. But how could the actor-knight possibly know that? Or be aware that Alec was squiring the *Führer's* favorite filmmaker to events at the German Consulate in Hancock Park and the restricted California Club where portions of *Olympiad* had been screened to a tumultuous reception? Clearly, father and son did not travel in the same Teutonic circles. Otherwise potentially invaluable data might have been procured and forwarded to Whitehall.

Radford's current dilemma was of a far more humdrum nature. Coping with food, beverages and a guest list was the thirteenth labor of Hercules for the actor-knight.

"I owe you an apology," Radford said as he lay in bed with his wife.

"Anything particular reason?" asked Hyacinth.

"You were correct. As always. I'm just a stubborn farm boy from Kent. We *don't* entertain enough. Something must be done about it."

"Perhaps in the New Year we could—"

"No! This weekend. A cocktail party. For young Olivier."

"Do you know him?"

"Not really. But he plays cricket. And Aubrey approves of him."

"Rather short notice, don't you think?"

"You wouldn't have to do anything, darling. I shall take full responsibility for the event."

"Nonsense!" Hyacinth began to chuckle. "You wouldn't know where to begin. How many people were you thinking of?"

"Fifty."

"Gracious! Have you come into a legacy, Osmond?"

"Only cocktails."

"And food. Americans will expect little things on toothpicks."

"Pigs in a blanket? That sort of tosh? Can't Willi do it?"

"Willi can do anything if pointed in the right direction. What about staff? Charleston is an excellent bartender, but we'll need two butlers to keep the drinks properly circulating."

"Boggs can do that."

"Aren't you afraid he might pick one of the guests' pockets?"

"Youthful indiscretion, my dear. Boggs has matured."

"His Majesty's Prisons make excellent finishing schools, I'm told. Be it on your head, husband. But we will need a second—Ah! Temple Brown."

"Charleston's brother?" Radford was appalled by the notion. "Now, there's a villain, who I'm sure has been up the river. Besides, Temple is far too familiar with the guests."

"Only the women."

"Isn't that enough? We don't want a lynching in the garden."

"What about the guest list?" Hyacinth reached over to her nightstand and retrieved a small leather notebook and pen. "Who do we want? Aubrey, of course. Gwen and Hugh. Niven—"

"That will mean Flynn, as well. Those two are inseparable these days. Best invite a few unattached women so those two hellions aren't challenged to a duel by some cuckolded husband."

"What about Wendy Barrie? She's great fun. Oh, but she's seeing that sportsman. Something Siegel. Ben Siegel."

"Invite them both," said Radford. "Good to have some foreign types."

"Foreign? Mr. Siegel is from Brooklyn. What about the Goldwyns?"

"Quite right. Can't have a party for Olivier without inviting his producer," replied Radford. "Of course, Sam never thinks of himself as foreign. One hundred per cent American. We'll have to ask Merle, as well."

"She won't come if Larry's here. He spat on her the other day. She hasn't forgiven him."

"In public?"

"On the set."

"How do you know this?"

"Frances told me. She knows far more than Louella or Hedda."

"What about the newer arrivals?" asked Radford. "Martin Kohlinger, for instance. You said you wanted to have him for dinner. Let's have Kohlinger. And some Italians. Do we know any Italians?"

"Osmond, what's gotten into you? The prospect of this party has made you positively giddy. We could invite Ito. He's certainly foreign."

"Capital suggestion. And, er… we should ask Jasper."

"Jasper Radford? Really! Were you visited by three Christmas ghosts last night?"

"Please, Hy. He's been complaining bitterly that we never invite him."

"Because he turns up every time looking like Banquo's Ghost, all baleful and oozing resentment. With Mrs. Banquo on his arm."

"I shall introduce Jas to Temple. Those two rogues will get along like a house afire."

CRIMINAL TRANSACTION

Somehow, the guest list had swollen and almost a hundred were in attendance at Best of Times that Sunday afternoon. Radford was dreading the bill (despite Dickie's promise that expenses would be reimbursed). After a few of Charleston's Sazeracs (a blend of cognac, absinthe, Peychaud's Bitters and sugar), Sir Osmond was feeling no pain. All worries about being recompensed had vanished as he regaled actress Joan Fontaine and her fiancé, Brian Aherne, with a bit of impromptu autobiography.

"I had a dreadful stammer as a child," said Radford. "Positively paralytic. When I was eight, my sainted mother brought me up to London to see a Harley Street specialist. He, in turn, suggested Mama take me to the theatre to hear beautiful speech. The play was *Cymbeline* and Henry Irving was playing Iachimo. The result was mesmeric. At the first intermission I informed my mother that I was going to become an actor. My stammer had vanished on the spot, as if by magic."

"Never to return?" asked Aherne.

"Occasionally. In moments of stress. Ironically, the word that gives me the greatest trouble is 'I'. Most humbling."

In another corner of the room, the guest of honor had Flavia pinned against a wall while he ran an anxious hand through his long hair and passionately attempted to explain his bad reputation.

"You've worked in the theatre," said Laurence Olivier. "A bit of spittle is bound to fly across the stage in the heat of the moment. It's *de rigeur* in our profession. Try explaining that to Korda's kept woman. Oh, God! It's so humiliating. I'm an actor not a mannequin. Did you know she pretends her mother is her maid?"

"Who?" asked Flavia.

"Merle-bloody-Oberon. Her mother's too dark for white society. Not that there's any society to speak of out here. Notwithstanding you and your family, of course. Did you know your father was a great influence on me? Saw him as a child in *Kismet*. He owned that stage. Everyone else was renting. Never forgot his swagger. Forgive my staring. You so remind me of Viv."

"Who?" asked Flavia, beginning to feel more and more like an owl.

"Vivien Leigh. We're to be married."

"Congratulations."

"Once we're divorced."

"We? Both of you?"

"Alas, we both have partners. Very difficult. And children."

"You and Vivien have children?"

"By our partners."

"What does Vivien do?"

"She's a bloody brilliant actress. Come now, Flavia! You're teasing me, aren't you? Vivien's a big star in England. She's also the most beautiful and enchanting woman in the world."

"Is she working now?"

"She just did a film with Charles Laughton and Rex Harrison. But she's waiting for David to come to his senses and cast her as Scarlett O'Hara."

"David Selznick will never cast an Englishwoman as Scarlett," said Flavia, parroting Leslie Howard. "The American public would never tolerate it."

"You don't know Viv. Once she puts her mind to something, it's uncanny. Always gets what she wants. Trust me. She'll find some way to get the part. There's a demon lives inside her."

Flavia wanted to tell Olivier she felt the same way about the role. But he wasn't much of a listener. She looked around the room for Chet. Why wasn't he there? Too much traffic crossing the street? Why hadn't they slept together yet? Where? Clearly not at either of their homes.

"When is your birthday?" asked Olivier.

"My birthday? November 6th."

"The day after Viv's. That's why you seem so alike. Don't suppose you were born in India, too?"

"No. But my mother grew up there."

"She can't suffer fools either."

"My mother?"

"Viv. I'm afraid I'm behaving like a fool."

"Not so very much."

"I miss her desperately. Ohhh! Why didn't she play Cathy instead of that dreadful half caste? Goldwyn's not here, is he? That man drives me to distraction. Always popping up out of nowhere from behind the set, ruining my concentration. Don't know if I can take much more of it."

Temple Brown walked by at that moment wearing a white mess jacket and carrying a tray of drinks. Flavia grabbed a Sazerac and handed it over to the lovelorn Olivier. Temple was returning to the bar when his progress was interrupted by a tiny man with bulging eyes and horrible teeth.

"Excuse me." The tiny man spoke with an Austro-Hungarian accent.

"How can I help you?" asked Temple, flashing his most ingratiating smile. He was a foot shorter than his younger brother, stocky, with large nostrils. Temple Brown's eyes were always darting about, afraid of missing any opportunity.

The tiny man lowered his voice: "Do you know where I might get some heroin?"

"Sir! I am shocked," said Temple. A beat later, he lowered his voice and said: "Meet me round the side of the house in fifteen minutes."

"Don't know if I can wait that long." The tiny Austro-Hungarian was perspiring profusely.

"Here, brother. Have a Sazerac. It'll help pass the time."

Temple made his way back to the bar where Charleston was pouring a glass of Châteauneuf-du-Pape for Martin Kohlinger.

"Who's that funny little dude with the pop eyes?" asked Temple.

"Him?" asked Charleston. "That's Mr. Moto. The Japanese detective."

"He ain't no Jap."

"His name is Peter Lorre," said Kohlinger, shaking his head sadly. "And he was the greatest actor in Bertolt Brecht's company in Berlin."

"Zat so?" said Temple. "Well, he got himself one helluva jones."

A distraught Willi stepped nervously into the sitting room on the verge of tears. Standing on tiptoes, the six-foot-four German housekeeper searched the room for Hyacinth, whom she finally spotted chatting with Gwen Harcourt.

"Ouida Rathbone just mistook me for your sister-in-law," said Gwen. "I've never been so humiliated. Not since the last sighting. Do I really look that much like Eunice? Must be the red hair. Perhaps, I should become a brunette. No, damn it. Let her have the dye job. They're not here, are they? Jasper and Eunice?"

"We had to invite them. He *is* Ozzie's brother. But I haven't seen them yet." Hyacinth became aware of Willi hovering mournfully over her. "Has there been an accident?"

"The pigs in a blanket," answered Willi, unable to meet Lady Radford's kindly gaze. "They... they..."

"Yes?"

"They are no longer in the blanket."

"Did they escape?" asked Hyacinth, dreading the worst.

"There was sawdust in the chipolatas," replied the housekeeper, unable to meet her employer's gaze. "One could not possibly serve them to the guests."

"Did you telephone the butcher?"

"Impossible. They are closed on Sundays."

"Is the bacon alright?"

"*Ja.*"

"Do we have any prunes?"

"*Ja.*"

"Then wrap the bacon round the prunes and serve them up as Devils on Horseback."

"*Danke*, Lady Radford. You are so clever."

"Think she's tall enough?" asked Gwendolyn, after the outsize housekeeper scurried back to the kitchen.

"The woman's an absolute treasure but sometimes she's thick as a brush." Gwendolyn turned her head and saw the beloved Ito enchanting Wendy Barrie and Ida Lupino with one of his folk tales.

"When I was a tiny child," said Ito, "my mother told me about two spirits— male and female— called *Izanagi* and *Izanami*. They stirred up the water in the Great Void with a spear. When they lifted the spear, the water that dripped off the end of it created a perfect island. *Izanagi* and *Izanami* settled on the island in a palace. Later they created more islands with the spear until there were eight. They called this blessed paradise Japan."

Miss Barrie and Miss Lupino applauded the recitation; Ito bowed deeply. Wendy Barrie looked up towards the hallway where a handsome rake with slicked black hair and wearing a hound's tooth sports jacket stood chewing gum and casing the place.

"It's Ben!" Wendy gushed with unbridled delight. "He did come. Oh, Ida! You must meet him."

Ben Siegel grabbed the arm of a baleful-looking, bald-headed man in a cutaway coat and growled: "Hey, pal! Grab me a Scotch and soda, willya?"

"Fetch it yourself," said Jasper Radford. "I'm not a butler."

"Then what the hell you dressed like one for?" asked Siegel.

"This is proper attire for a cocktail reception." Sir Osmond's older brother snapped his fingers and called out: "Boggs!"

Boggs took his leave of Aubrey Smith, Basil Rathbone and Boris Karloff, who were all deep in cricket controversy.

"Yes, Mr. Jasper?"

"Be a good fellow and fetch this man a whisky." Jasper turned back to Siegel and informed the Brooklynite: "He is a servant. I am a guest."

Siegel rammed his hand into Jasper's crotch, grabbed his testicles, and asked: "Howdja like to be a corpse? Open your mouth to me again, pal, and I phone Forest Lawn." Leaving a stunned Jasper reeling, Siegel stepped down into the sitting room.

Jasper stumbled blindly out the front door writhing in pain. Sir Osmond's older brother made his way round the side of the house where his blurred vision caught sight of Peter Lorre and Temple Brown engaged in what he instinctively recognized as a criminal transaction.

"Are you actively engaged in the narcotics trade?" Jasper asked Temple, after the diminutive Lorre passed by the bald Englishman muttering something about having misplaced his automobile.

"You Scotland Yard?" asked Temple, hoping to call the Englishman's bluff.

"Hardly. Do you, by any chance, own a Bentley or a twenty-foot sailboat?" Temple snorted and rolled his eyes. "Would you like to?"

SOME BIG NAZI

Errol Flynn and David Niven sauntered into Best of Times in a state of benign intoxication. Heralding all the guests and subsequently exploding with laughter, they serpentined their way through the sitting room. Determined to restore decorum, Aubrey Smith approached the duo. The venerable actor cleared his throat and suggested they withdraw to the kitchen as quickly as possible where they should consume large amounts of coffee.

"Spanish coffee?" asked Flynn. The question convulsed Niven into paroxysms of laughter. Taking it upon himself to sober up the two hellions, Hugh Harcourt stepped forward and ushered them into the kitchen.

It was a fortunate exit for Niven. His boss, Sam Goldwyn, arrived shortly afterwards with his wife Frances.

"Quite a house you got here, Redfield." No matter how often Frances corrected her husband, the Polish-born mogul with the high-pitched voice could never get Radford's name right. "Lot of people. Radio pays that well? We should sell the studio tomorrow, Frances, and go into radio. Is that Larry over there hiding?"

Olivier held his glass aloft in greeting to his producer. "Hello, Sam."

"Now, he likes me! So stubborn. For the first week, he stank. Why did I hire him as Heathwell? He was so dirty looking. And filthy. But he cleaned up nice and he's pretty good in the picture now. Hello, Aubrey. See, Larry? An Englishman, who's a good actor. You could learn a lot from him."

Inside the kitchen, Harcourt refilled Niven's mug with black coffee, as a look of panic swept across the younger actor's face.

"Do I hear Sam Goldwyn?" asked Niven. "He mustn't see me like this."

"We could hide." Flynn covered his eyes with his hands. "It's quite easy."

"No, no, no, Errol. You don't understand. Sam's been like a father to me. If he thought for a moment that I was a reprobate—"

"Why don't we sneak out the back?" asked Flynn. "We could go up the road and visit Barrymore. Have a nightcap with Jack."

"It's four in the afternoon," said Harcourt.

"Not in Australia, Hughie. You and Ozzie were Down Under together, weren't you?"

"Before you were born, Errol."

"What's that noise?" asked Niven.

"I didn't hear anything," said Harcourt.

"That's what I mean," replied Niven. "It's gone awfully quiet out there."

Best of Times had gone incredibly silent when Alec Radford came through the front door with Leni Riefenstahl on his arm. One could almost hear a swastika drop.

Leslie Howard, his body vibrating like a tuning fork, broke the silence demanding his host expel the woman from the house.

"But who is she?" asked Radford, staring at his son's companion bedecked in black leather.

By the time Howard had listed the litany of Hitler's honey's offenses, Radford was secretly over the moon. Dickie would be most impressed. This was the very woman Ives-Curtis had hoped would attend the soiree.

All eyes were trained on Alec as he led the *Führer's* favorite filmmaker across the floor of the sitting room where Hyacinth was chatting with Frances Goldwyn.

"Mother, I'd like you to meet my friend, Miss Riefenstahl. She makes movies."

"Ask her about *Kristellnacht*," snapped Leslie Howard. "Ask her about the Jews who were slaughtered, and the synagogues set ablaze."

"*Bitte?*" asked Leni, feigning complete ignorance of the Nazis horrific rampage against the Jews of Germany only a few weeks earlier. "*Ich kann night verstehen.*"

"Who is this broad?" asked Siegel, appraising *Fräulein* Riefenstahl's gams.

"No idea" said Flynn, who was supporting himself on Siegel's right shoulder. "But she certainly gets my pecker up."

"Hitler's girlfriend," said Niven, propping himself up on Siegel's left shoulder. "A Nazi pin-up."

"Nazi, huh?" Siegel rotated his shoulders upon hearing her political affiliation, dispatching the two drunken film stars from their perch. "I gotta friend, Countess Dorothy Di Frasso. You guys know Dottie, dontcha? We were travelin' through Europe together earlier this year. She got this big villa outside Rome called *Casa Madama*. And she tells me *Il Duce* is comin' to dinner. I thought she meant Eddie Duchin. But she was referrin' to Mussolini. The head goombah. Know what I mean? And he's bringin' this guy Joe Goebbels, who I don't know from a hole in the ground. Some big Nazi. What do I know from Nazis? I grew up in Hell's Kitchen with George Raft. So, while I'm puttin' on my tux, Dottie mentions that these Nazis aren't fond of Jews. Matter of fact, they want to exterminate 'em. Now, I'm a Jew. Anybody got a problem with that?" Flynn and Niven shook their heads, totally transfixed by Siegel's story. "So, I grab my rod and tell Dottie I'm gonna plug a hole in this fuckin' Kraut. She begs me not to. What'll the neighbors think? What the fuck do I care about the neighbors? Know what I mean?"

"Actually, we were just leaving," said Niven, who had noticed the bulge under the left arm of Siegel's hounds tooth jacket. "Errol?"

"Pleasure meeting you, sport," said Flynn, now transfixed by the bulge, as well. "Watch out for those *goombahs*."

"I can handle myself," said Siegel, patting the bulge where his rod was safely nestled.

Niven and Flynn slipped out the front door just as Chester Lowenthal entered the foyer. Flavia's face lit up when she saw the lawyer.

"Where have you been?" asked Flavia, abandoning her usual *sang-froid*. "I was sure you weren't coming."

"Is there somewhere we can talk?"

"The library."

Once inside Sir Osmond's sanctum, the two stared awkwardly at each other once again. Finally, Flavia broke the silence: "What did you want to say?"

"Have I lost my marbles, or did I just see Bugsy Siegel in your living room?"

"No one by that name. There's *Ben* Siegel, Wendy Barrie's friend. He's a gambler, I believe."

"Bugsy Siegel is a cold-blooded killer. He's Meyer Lansky's partner."

"Is that what you wanted to tell me?"

"No," replied the lawyer, drawing the Pirate Queen towards himself. He kissed her. A long, slow kiss that built in its intensity. Flavia began fumbling with his belt buckle.

"Heyyy!" protested Lowenthal. "Not here."

"Where? When?"

"Paul's gone out of town for the weekend. We can go back to my place."

"What have you done to me?" asked Flavia, shaking her head in disbelief.

"I'm the one who's disheveled," replied Lowenthal, refastening his belt buckle.

"Where did you learn to kiss like that?"

Flavia lifted her lips up towards his, hungry for more. Her passion was dampened by her mother's voice calling out: "Flavia! Come quickly." It was an almost plaintive cry, so unlike Hyacinth. Was something wrong? Had Daddy suffered another attack?

Stepping out of the library, Flavia stared in astonishment at the sight of her mother and father comforting a sobbing Julia. Her little sister was wearing a black cloak and clutching her suitcase like the original orphan of the storm.

"Ju-Ju!" Flavia rushed towards Julia, tore the suitcase loose from her grasp and took her sister in her arms. "What's happened?"

"Oh, Flaves! I've made such a terrible mess of things."

"Shh-shh! You're home now." Flavia looked over her shoulder and saw Lowenthal standing behind her. "Chet, this is my sister."

Julia collapsed to the floor. No one knew what to do next. Boggs pushed his way through the crowd and knelt beside the stricken girl.

"Boggsie, is that you?" Julia's eyes lit up when she saw her childhood protector.

"Yes, miss."

"Remember when you took me to the Regent Park Zoo? We laughed at the penguins. They were so funny. That was such a lovely day. Wasn't it, Boggsie?" Julia sighed deeply and lost consciousness.

Boggs tenderly lifted her body up from the floor and looked inquiringly at Hyacinth.

"Take her to her room, please, Boggs."

"Yes, Your Ladyship."

Boggs carried her up the stairs to the second floor while the other Radfords looked on in stunned silence.

Sir Osmond finally overcame his emotions and said: "Our little girl's home now."

HONEYCHILE

The night sky was ablaze as Chester Lowenthal showed his driver's license to the security guard at the entrance to the Selznick Studios. The guard had no problem with the ID. He did do a double take, however, as he stared at the beautiful woman in the passenger seat with a scarf tied around her eyes.

"This a gag?" asked the guard.

"No," replied Lowenthal. "It's a blindfold."

"A gag is to keep one from speaking," said Flavia, who had no idea where she was nor the identity of the interrogator. "The other is to keep one from seeing. I am most definitely the latter."

"Should she be allowed out?" asked the guard.

"It's alright, Warden," Lowenthal solemnly replied. "I'm her physician."

"Okay, Doc. Know where you're going?"

Lowenthal nodded and gunned his Lincoln-Zephyr towards the flames.

"Warden?" asked Flavia. "Have you brought me to a prison?"

"No. That was a red herring."

"I hate herring. Where are we? Is this what they mean by a blind date? Do you smell smoke? This is the strangest— You are a very peculiar man, Chester Lowenthal. May I take this thing off now?"

"Not yet," replied Lowenthal, executing a sharp left turn. "Almost there."

"It's getting very warm. What's all that noise? Oh, Chet, please! A girl can only take so much Kraft-Ebbing. You are torturing me."

Lowenthal put on the brakes, hopped out of the Lincoln, and ran around to the driver's side. He opened the door and helped Flavia out. Finally, he removed the blindfold.

Flavia opened her eyes and saw the night sky over Culver City ablaze with yellow, orange, and red flames. At first, she thought Lowenthal had driven her to the Angelus National Forest where they were trapped amid a natural disaster. Then she saw the sidewalk beneath her feet and the low-rise buildings. It was a movie studio. But which one? Night shooting. He's brought me to watch night shooting. As if I've never seen-

"Have you guessed yet?" asked Lowenthal.

"It isn't Columbia. Or Paramount. Or RKO. They're in the middle of town. The Los Angeles fire department would never permit a blaze like this. We must be in Culver City. MGM?"

"Stop being so goddamn analytical. Come on!" He took her hand and pulled her towards the area of the fire. Zigzagging through a few more alley-ways, they arrived at a railway yard engulfed in the largest, most intense fire Flavia had ever witnessed. Hearing a horse whinnying with fright, she turned her head and beheld the animal pulling a flatbed wagon alongside the flames. The man holding the reins was dressed in a white suit with a plantation hat on his head. Despite the extreme heat, Flavia felt a cold chill run down her spine. It wasn't possible. This only existed on paper.

"Where are we, Chet? Where have you brought me?"

"The Burning of Atlanta. Can't you tell?"

Flavia heard a familiar voice calling out through a megaphone. "Where the hell is my brother? I can't keep this blaze going all night, you know. The fire department will close me down. Has anyone seen Myron?"

Standing up on her toes, Flavia caught sight of David Selznick and George Cukor surrounded by production staff, seven different Technicolor cameras, and several hundred people in overcoats, who appeared to have nothing to do but gawk. Jewish, overweight, possessed of identical wavy hair and glasses, the producer and director were often mistaken for brothers.

"Is this really *Gone With The Wind*?" asked Flavia. "Or am I tucked up in my bed dreaming?"

"This is it. Selznick couldn't afford to wait any longer. They had to start shooting something. He got all the old sets from *King Kong* and *King of Kings* and set them on fire."

"How do you know this? How did we get invited?"

"Thank your pal Merlin the Magician. He's the one made it happen. Russell Birdwell is Paul's publicist as well as David O's. The pride of Rochester thought it would make you happy."

"Happy? What about delirious? Over the moon? I haven't felt like this since Daddy came back from the war. And to think I once hated Paul Merlin.

He is the dearest, most thoughtful man in the— Who's that?" Flavia pointed towards the wagon racing along the edge of the inferno. There was now a woman seated on the buckboard next to the man in the white suit.

"Is that Scarlett? Have they finally cast Scarlett? Who is she? Tell me, so I can go home and put my head in the oven."

"Relax," laughed Lowenthal, wrapping a loving arm around Flavia's shoulders. "It's a stuntwoman. You aren't out of the running yet."

"Oh, Chet! Do you really think there's still a chance? How can David have started shooting without the role being cast?"

"According to Birdwell, they haven't got a shooting script."

"Is there a church nearby?" asked Flavia. "Perhaps a prayer is in order."

Loud honking was heard. A limousine pulled up. Myron Selznick, the film industry's most notorious agent, emerged feeling no pain. A notorious lush, Selznick's older brother was also the toughest negotiator in town. A young couple emerged from the back seat of the vehicle a few seconds later.

"It's Larry Olivier!" said Flavia, waving to the actor to get his attention. "Who's the girl with him? Is it Merle? No. Not exotic enough. Geraldine Fitzgerald?"

The mystery girl was wearing a mink coat. Myron Selznick took her elbow and steered her towards his brother, who was shouting orders to Ray Klune, his production manager.

"Hey, genius!" Myron called out to his kid brother. "I want you to meet Scarlett O'Hara."

No! No! That can't be right. Flavia thought she was going to be ill. She observed the girl's exquisite face illuminated by the flames and was dazzled by her incredible green eyes. This must be Viv. Larry was right. The part *would* be hers. Flavia knew it to be true as well as she knew herself. Staring at her almost twin, Flavia knew in her heart of hearts that Viv possessed a certain magic she most certainly lacked.

"Please take me home, Chet."

"Something wrong?" asked Lowenthal.

Flavia shook her head, unable to speak. She couldn't think about it any longer. If she did, she'd go crazy. Tomorrow. She'd think about it tomorrow.

Glancing over her shoulder one last time, Flavia saw David Selznick's head nod up and down as he engaged in conversation with the luminous Vivien Leigh.

Tomorrow is another day, thought Flavia.

* * *

Christmas Day at Best of Times was filled with a number of surprises. Beginning early that morning when the hot water abruptly turned cold. This calamity caused the female Radfords, who were engaged in various stages of bathing, to wail as one. Guests were expected for lunch at noon. What if the water stopped completely? Twenty minutes later, it did. As it was December 25th, there wasn't a plumber to be had in all of Los Angeles. Lady Radford suggested they send for Temple Brown, the resident handyman. His baby brother, Charleston, had departed for West Adams Boulevard at the crack of dawn to spend the day with his family. Sir Osmond dreaded what ransom his chauffeur's brother would demand in exchange for his never satisfactory services. The actor-knight bit the bullet. The prospect of Aubrey Smith not being able to wash his hands before dining was unimaginable. The thought of dealing with Temple was so daunting that Radford's stammer returned in full force. Thus, it fell upon Lady Radford to make the urgent phone call to the Brown Household.

"Hello," a smoky, female voice from far south of the Mason-Dixon line answered at the other end.

"Good morning. This is Hyacinth Radford. I'm frightfully sorry to ring you up on Christmas Day. But I was wondering if—"

"Lady Radford? That really you?" The woman's chuckle started low, then moved into an upper register. "My boys do nothin' but talk about you day and night. Oh, honeychile, they are bewitched. How's that man of yours doin'? Don't let him stray too far from home. He's in season, if you get my drift."

"Forgive me," said Hyacinth, slightly confused and more than a trifle embarrassed. "Is this the Brown Residence?"

"Sure is. And I'm their Mama. But you can call me Florabelle."

"Thank you, Florabelle. Your sons are divine."

"Hmmm. They a little more earthbound than you think, Lady Radford."

"Please call me Hyacinth."

"My favorite flower."

"Really? You must come and see my garden sometime."

"The one Ito planted?"

"How do you know about our gardener?"

"Oh, honeychile. That little Japanese boy ain't just a gardener. He's an artist, a holy man, and a saint. Charleston tells me Ito makes animals out of little pieces of paper. His is a soul to be cherished."

There was the longest silence on the line until Hyacinth finally spoke: "Florabelle, I telephoned to see if your son Temple could possibly find it in his heart to come here today and repair our plumbing. But I would like you to come, as well. As my guest. I feel we are kindred spirits."

"Lemme see if I can rouse that good-for-nothin'."

One hour later, an uncomfortable Charleston Brown found himself seated opposite Sir Osmond in the sitting room. Both men were staring up at the giant Christmas tree drenched in tinsel and antique decorations with a moat of gaily wrapped presents surrounding it. Willi emerged from the kitchen bearing two cups of egg nog. Employer and employee toasted each other.

"Frightfully nice of your brother to drive all the way up here like this."

"He didn't want to," said Charleston. "But Mama said she'd been invited by Lady Radford herself and we was all to put on our best Sunday go-to-meetin' clothes."

"Your mother is a beautiful woman, Mr. Brown. We only ever met that one time through the screen door."

"'The most beautiful gal in Tupelo'. Or so they said."

"Lady Radford seems quite keen on her."

"And vice versa," said Charleston. "What can they be doin' in the garden all this time?"

Florabelle Brown was having the rudiments of yoga explained to her by her newfound friend, Hyacinth Radford.

"Of course, you're not wearing the proper clothes, Florabelle. But the next time, I will show you how to perform Downward Facing Dog—"

"Honeychile, I think I done that more than once."

Lady Radford didn't know what to make of the ribald remark until Charleston's mother exploded with laughter and Hyacinth went along for the ride. She was totally in the thrall of Florabelle Brown.

Julia came down to the sitting room and sat cross-legged on the floor between the two adoring Dromios. Sir Osmond's youngest child was slowly coming out of the mysterious, emotional trauma she had suffered back east. She was thinking more and more about a return to London and resuming her West End career. Not wanting his fragile daughter to depart again so quickly, Sir Osmond proposed to his producer at CBS that Julia appear in an episode of *My Favorite Story.*

Such an idea would normally have sent Alec into a petulant tailspin. But nothing could penetrate the chainmail of his depression following Leni Riefenstahl's departure to Berlin, a Teutonic Robert E. Lee taking her leave after Appomattox. Alec, in a moment of impassioned bravado, had offered to accompany his beloved mistress and make a life together back in the Fatherland. Leni gave him an enigmatic smile and a chaste kiss on the lips.

* * *

Temple Brown was wrestling with the water tank in the garage when the Harcourts came up the front walkway bearing holiday gifts.

"Hey, boss!" said Temple, calling out to Harcourt. "Gimme a hand here, willya?"

"Is he addressing you in that manner?" asked Gwen. "What impertinence! Don't you dare respond."

"We know him," replied a conciliatory Harcourt. "He's Charleston's brother."

Gwen stared in amazement as her husband set his gift-wrapped packages down on the front step and walked briskly towards the garage.

"Put your finger there for a minute." Temple pointed to a brass coupling emerging from the wall. "I only got but two hands."

"Delighted!" Harcourt dropped his voice to a stage whisper and asked: "Do you know where one might purchase some reefer?"

Harcourt had promised Toby he would be at her place right after the early service at St. Mary of the Angels. Gwen sang in the choir of the venerable Anglican church in Los Feliz. Vic Pomfrett had insisted they come round to his house for a cup of cheer afterwards. It was almost midnight before the Harcourts miraculously made their way home to Locksley Place. Toby was heartbroken at her lover's failure to appear and told him through tears that she never wanted to see him again. The little Brooklyn hood ornament would brood for days unless the florid-faced Englishman could find a way to appease her. Toby loved marijuana and she loved loving Harcourt when she was under the influence. Merry Christmas, indeed!

"Ain't cheap," answered Temple, wrapping some electrical tape around the brass coupling. "Bunco squad's been workin' overtime lately." Temple turned his attention to Gwen tapping her toe impatiently on the front step. Hmm. Nice bit of trim for a woman her age. "You and the missus meetin' up under the mistletoe?"

"Yes," lied Harcourt. He turned to his wife and held up a finger. "Almost done, darling! Go on ahead. Ring the bell." He turned his attention back to Temple. "How much?"

"A ten spot for some Maryjane will put a permanent wave in your privates."

"What about hers?"

"She gonna be like a magic carpet."

Harcourt cleared his throat, took out his wallet and handed a ten-dollar bill over to Temple.

"How's it going?" Paul Merlin called out to the repair squad, as he crossed Tower Road carrying a stack of presents. Chester Lowenthal walked behind him holding Marlene on a leash; the little Dachshund wore a sprig of mistletoe attached to her collar and a red woolen jacket to ward off the cold.

"Gotta get it from the car," Temple hissed to Harcourt. "Catch up with you later."

Harcourt entered the house. Temple started down the driveway to the street when he encountered Boggs walking the other way. They passed each other, until Temple scampered back and pointed a finger at the Cockney.

"I know you!"

"Don't think so," replied Boggs, without breaking stride.

"Santa Anita! Right?"

"Shh!" Boggs held a finger to his lips.

HARDLY SHOWING

The two Dromios ardently chased little Marlene from room to room. Rather like a canine version of the Tarleton twins pursuing Scarlett in the opening chapter of *Gone with the Wind*. If Flavia had considered the allusion, she did not express it. Chastened by the Burning of Atlanta, the eldest Radford daughter had switched her literary allegiance from Margaret Mitchell to Daphne du Maurier.

"Have you read *Rebecca*?" she whispered to Lowenthal. He shook his head. "It's Selznick's next movie. I'm perfect for the lead."

Paul Merlin had never met Julia Radford before and was totally beguiled by the petite blond. He even fantasized what their children might look like. Rare behavior for the perennial bachelor.

"Have you read *Rebecca*?" asked the youngest Radford daughter. The blond Adonis shook his head. "It's Selznick's next movie. Orson Welles wanted me to perform it on the radio. But I wasn't available."

Marlene ran up to Merlin and desperately scratched at his slacks. The Dachshund was weary of the Great Danes' attentions. Merlin scooped her up from the floor and cradled the little dog in his arms.

"Seems a strange pet for a large man like you," said Julia.

"I'm surprisingly gentle with small creatures," replied Merlin.

Marlene gazed adoringly at her master. If she could have stuck her tongue out at Julia, she would have.

On the other side of the room, next to a large window overlooking the front lawn, Hyacinth and Gwen exchanged presents.

"It's so very dear of you to include us every year," said Gwen, with an uncharacteristic display of vulnerability.

"Don't be ridiculous, Gwen. You and Hugh are family. We've known each other through three monarchs."

"That's a most sobering thought," said Gwen, lighting up a Pall Mall. "Speaking of family, will we have the favor of your in-laws' company?"

"Unfortunately, no."

"You are a saint, Hy. There's not the slightest trace of tongue in your cheek. Where are they dining? The Save-a-Soul Mission?"

"No. They're down in Long Beach. With someone called Bijou Destino. A Buchmanite."

"And where's Alec? Sulking in his room again? Didn't Father Christmas bring him what he wanted?"

"He's taken the departure of his German lady badly," replied Hyacinth. "Wanted to be by himself today. Which led to another row with Osmond last night with Alec storming off to places unknown. If he'd only come up to Ojai with me and spend some time with Krishna."

Gwen missed the last part of what her friend said due to something that caught her attention outside the window. "Who on earth is that? You certainly have the most colorful guests."

Ito, splendidly dressed in the ceremonial robes of a Shinto priest, was proceeding up the driveway carrying several tiny boxes in his hands,

Hyacinth opened the front door and stared adoringly at her 'other son'. Ito bowed deeply to her, presented the boxes, and explained his attire. "This is a holy day, is it not? I trust I have dressed appropriately."

Lady Radford bowed in turn to Admiral Hashimuro's son and ushered him inside Best of Times.

* * *

At half past one, Willi carried a huge roast goose out of the kitchen and placed it on the dining table.

"Think Ronnie Colman has a proper Christmas goose like this one?" boomed Hugh Harcourt. "Hardly. Dickens himself would have approved of this bird."

"Where might one wash up?" asked Aubrey, who'd been flirting outrageously with Florabelle Brown in the sunken sitting room. His wife, Isobel, had patiently endured his behavior for forty years.

Radford looked anxiously at Charleston Brown, who crossed both his fingers. Temple was nowhere in sight.

Aubrey disappeared into the guest bathroom. Two minutes later, he emerged scowling: "Want to do something about that hot water, Ozzie. Nearly scalded myself in there. Waiting for me, are you?" Crisis averted, Sir Osmond and Charleston breathed a sigh of relief.

Under Willi's supervision, Boggs had added another leaf to the dining table to accommodate the last-minute Browns, in addition to all the Radfords, Harcourts, Smiths, Lowenthal, Merlin, Boggs, and Ito. The errant Alec had not returned after quarreling with his father the night before. Sir Osmond stood at the head of the table about to carve the goose when the doorbell rang.

"Who on earth can that be?" asked Radford poised for surgery with his Sheffield utensils.

"Perhaps it's Alec," said a hopeful Hyacinth. "I don't like the idea of his spending Christmas alone."

"Why doesn't he ring up that young woman he took to the premiere?" asked Radford. "She seemed pleasant enough."

Flavia choked on her water. The doorbell rang again.

"Got it," said Boggs. "Just like the old days backstage, innit?"

The former dresser gazed in awe at an immense, muscular man wearing white slacks and t-shirt, who all but filled the door frame.

"Is this the Radford residence?" The man was a male nurse and his tiny voice did not match his giant physique.

"Can I 'elp you?" asked Boggs, taking his role as the gatekeeper quite seriously.

"Does Sir Osmond Radford live here?"

"Occasionally." Boggs felt a degree of evasion evasion was called for under the circumstances. He was also suspicious of a big bloke sounding as tiddly as this one did.

"Didn't I tell you?" asked a distinctive voice sheltered behind the huge presence. Its owner finally peeked his head around the nurse.

"Mr. Barrymore! Cor! We 'aven't set eyes on you since—"

"Marie Antoinette was a chorus girl. Boggs, isn't it?" The Great Profile stared up defiantly at his mountainous minder. "See, Tiny? I can still remember the important things in life. Not the drivel Hollywood hacks churn out to numb the minds of popcorn munchers."

Everyone at the dining table stared at each other in astonishment upon hearing the legendary voice of the unexpected visitor. Radford put down his utensils and rushed towards the front door.

John Barrymore stood timidly in the hallway holding a small, gift-wrapped box.

"I remembered that we were neighbors," said the Great Profile, "and wanted to bring this little gift for you and your family. Merry Christmas, Ozzie."

"That's most kind of you, Jack, but highly unnecessary."

"I feel rather like Scrooge visiting his nephew, but don't tell anyone. That's encroaching on my brother Lionel's Yuletide employment. Come on, Tiny."

"Where do you think you're going, Jack?"

"Home. You have guests and—"

"You are the guest of honor. You and …?"

"This is Tiny," said Barrymore. "Don't worry! I only feed him once a day. He's a sort of bodyguard."

"Are you in danger?"

"Only from myself. And demon whisky." Barrymore's eyes darted wildly about the premises.

By this time, Hyacinth had arrived on the scene and warmly embraced the Great Profile.

"It's been a great many years," said Lady Radford. "The Haymarket. 1924."

Barrymore gasped and asked Sir Osmond: "Is this your child bride? How have you made the clock stop, dear lady?"

Hyacinth threaded her arm through the legendary Hamlet's and led him into the dining room. Barrymore's eyes lit up when he saw Aubrey and Isobel. He bowed deeply. "Most esteemed Lord and Lady Capulet." The two veteran actors had appeared together a few years earlier in MGM's *Romeo and Juliet.*

Aubrey roared with laughter. "What a wicked Mercutio you were, Jack. Best recitation of the Queen Mab speech I've ever heard. Come sit beside me."

"Why don't you sit here?" asked Florabelle Brown, her voice a languid purr as she patted the empty seat next to her.

Staring in delight at this unexpected female companion, Barrymore beamed and recited:

It was an Abyssinian maid,

And on her dulcimer she played,

Singing of Mount Abora.

Barrymore sat down next to the slender, dark-skinned beauty. Arching one eyebrow, he asked: "Have you ever been to Mount Abora?"

"What time's the next bus?" growled Florabelle.

"Does anyone know if I'm married at the present time?" asked the Great Profile. "If not, I have found myself a bride. What is thy name, goddess?"

Sir Osmond raised a Waterford tumbler and tapped it with his fork. Conversation ceased at the dining table.

"Thank you all for coming," said Radford. "To share our Christmas cheer. I'm always grateful on this day to be surrounded by family and friends. Both old and new. There were several years in my personal history when Christmas was not a joyous event, and one was never certain about ever sharing it with family again." The actor-knight took an interminable pause, one he would never have had the temerity to attempt on stage. Gazing helplessly towards his wife at the other end of the formal dining table, he asked: "Are you certain this is the best time?"

Hyacinth nodded and beamed adoringly at her husband.

"We have three grown children, as you all know," said Sir Osmond. "Sorry that Alec isn't here to join us, but… Alec is Alec. Strangely— miraculously— by next Christmas and, with the grace of God, there will be a fourth Radford child."

Flavia and Julia both stared in stupefaction at their mother. No one said a word until Gwen blurted out: "You're preggers!?!"

"Three months." Hyacinth blushed,. She nodded her head up and down repeatedly and finally exploded with laughter. Her two daughters leapt up from their seats, raced to their mother and embraced her.

"You're hardly showing," said Gwen.

"It's kicking," said Lady Radford. "In the middle of the night. Trust we're not embarrassing you, Isobel."

"I'm a mother myself," replied Mrs. Smith. "How courageous of you, my dear."

"You might have given me a hint," said Harcourt. "Your oldest friend."

"We didn't want to say anything," said Radford, "until we knew Hy was out of danger."

"When are you due?" asked Flavia.

"June."

"Sly dog!" said Aubrey. "Who started that rumor about a heart condition? Better sign him up for Charterhouse now."

"It might have the impertinence of being a girl, Aubrey," said Isobel.

Ito burst into tears and hastily explained: "I am so happy."

Florabelle grinned from ear to ear. Nodding at Sir Osmond, she told her hostess: "Didn't I tell you he was in season?"

Radford rose from his seat and walked down the length of the table to join his wife. He took her hand in his and murmured: "The best Christmas present I ever had."

"This calls for a toast," said Barrymore. His male nurse stepped forward and placed a restraining hand on the Great Profile's shoulder. "In spirit, Tiny. That's all I meant."

"May I make the toast, Jack?" asked Hyacinth. "I realize that a Hindu word is not appropriate for Christmas, but under the circumstances what I wish for us all— those living and not yet born— is *Shantih*. 'The peace that passeth understanding.' May we all be together again next year… in peace."

How was Lady Radford to know that, halfway around the world, *der Führer* and his fanatical followers were about to destroy any hope of her wish coming true?

MORE GRAVE THAN DEAD

The staff of the Reich Ministry of Public Enlightenment and Propaganda on Wilhelmplatz had grown used to Dr. Goebbels' daily hysterical tirades. That Tuesday morning was the worst explosion ever. The club-footed Minister was standing in front of a full-length mirror rehearsing a speech he was to give that evening when his aide, Bernhard Friedhoff, appeared in his private office with a cable from Consul Gyssling in Los Angeles.

HAVE DONE EVERYTHING POSSIBLE TO PREVENT

WARNER BROTHERS FROM FILMING CONFESSIONS

OF A NAZI SPY. PRODUCTION BEGINS NEXT WEEK

WITH EDWARD G. ROBINSON STARRING. BREEN

POWERLESS TO INTERVENE. PLEASE ADVISE.

"Advise? Advise? Blow up the fucking studio!" shrieked Goebbels, who stared with unbridled hatred at the unfortunate Friedhoff. "When the hell did this arrive?"

"Yesterday." Friedhoff clicked his heels together, more from desperation than discipline.

"Yesterday!?! And only now am I seeing it?"

"It was misplaced, Herr Doctor Goebbels."

"Get out of my sight, Friedhoff! Out, out, out! No! Get me Ambassador Kennedy in London."

It took half an hour to get a line through from Germany to Great Britain. During the wait, Goebbels stood in front of the mirror and rehearsed what he would say to Kennedy and, worse, to *der Führer*.

"Heads will roll for this." Goebbels placed a hand on his hip and scolded the *doppelgänger* in the mirror. "I can assure you. This level of incompetence will not be tolerated. Gyssling has been given far too much freedom with nothing to show for it."

A knock at the door. Goebbels spun around from the mirror and saw Friedhoff standing with his arm raised in salute.

"What is it now, Friedhoff?"

"Ambassador Kennedy is on the telephone. From London."

The Propaganda Minister limped across the room until he reached his desk, picked up the telephone and cooed into it. "Is that you, Joe?"

"Hello, Doctor Goebbels?" Kennedy's voice was as crisp as a walk on Boston Common. "What can I do for you today?"

"Why so formal, Joe? After the lovely evening we shared at the Berghof together. Surely there is no need—"

"Are you in your office, Doctor?"

"Naturally."

"And I am in mine. This is strictly business?"

"Of course, Herr Ambassador. But I have a small problem. Perhaps, it is your problem, as well."

"Keep talking."

"The Warner Brothers are starting a film next week with the outrageous title *Confessions of a Nazi Spy.* The title is libelous, yes?"

"Not if it's based on truth. Didn't the FBI arrest your spy ring in New York last spring and put them on trial? That's what the movie's based on, isn't it?"

"Lies! All lies!" shrieked Goebbels. "Made up by the Jews. You know how they are, Herr Ambassador. We made it clear to these moguls several years ago that we want no Jews on the screen. No Jewish writers, producers, or directors. And what do they do? They cast a Rumanian Jew to harass and trick the innocent citizens of the Fatherland. Outsmarting the Germans at every turn. This Goldenberg with his big Jew lips and his nyah-nyah."

"Who is Goldenberg?" asked Kennedy. "Never heard of him."

"Because they call him Robinson. Pawning him off as a gentile. Another devious trick of those Hollywood Jews to try and fool us. But we're on to them. If Harry Warner wants war, we'll give him war."

"The Jews run the movie business whether you like it or not," replied Kennedy. "The world is crazy about American movies. No one makes them like we do. There's nothing I can do for you."

"But they will listen to you. You were one of them. Another mogul. You speak their language."

"I now serve at the pleasure of the President of the United States. Plus, we have something in America called free enterprise."

"Please, Herr Ambassador. Your advice is like gold. *Der Führer* has sent for me. He'll want to know how we are going to retaliate. What can I tell him? You've seen his temper. There must be something that can be done to stop this film from moving forward. What about Breen? The censor. He is powerful. Have you no influence there? He is Irish. And a Catholic."

"Playing the harp card with me, Doctor? You must really be desperate."

"Tell them if they make anti-German movies like this, we will make anti-Semitic films like they have never seen. Those German actors in the movie? There will be grave repercussions against their families."

"More grave than dead? Haven't you killed all the Jews by now? Or are those concentration camps really holiday resorts? This is Gyssling's problem, Joe. Not yours. Let him take care of it."

"But he already lodged his complaints. With no results. Right up to the White House."

"It's not a diplomatic problem, Doctor. It's economic. Same sort of thing happened over here during Prohibition. There comes a time when talking doesn't help. You people haven't been shy about using a little muscle up till now. Let Gyssling handle it. Plenty of Silver Shirts in Los Angeles, who'd be pleased to—"

"Cowboys!" Goebbels spat out the word.

"Cowboys settled the West. They could certainly handle some puffed-up Hebes in Hollywood. Take a long, deep breath, Joe. Accidents are expensive. Too many accidents, the studio will scrap the movie."

"Brilliant! Thank you, Herr Ambassador. I will take your words to heart."

LIKE READING THE BIBLE

January had been a hectic month for Osmond Radford. Starting on New Year's Day when he received an hysterical phone call from a female with an unintelligible accent.

"He told me to call you," sobbed the woman. "He said you was discreet."

"This isn't about my brother, is it?" asked the actor-knight. "What's he done now? Where is he?"

Hyacinth was busy in the garden with Ito planning a reception for his father. Admiral Hashimuro was stopping in Los Angeles on his way to a conference in Washington the following month. Radford didn't bother saying goodbye to his wife.

The address was on Hayvenhurst just south of Sunset. Spanish style apartments surrounding a common courtyard.

A tiny creature with an exquisite body and perfect legs on display under a skimpy negligee opened the door. She was weaving from side to side and her pupils were dilated. A peculiar odor in the room reminded Radford of long-ago days on tour in India.

"Thanks for comin', Your Knightship." She had calmed down since their telephone conversation. Sir Osmond recognized her accent as straight out of Brooklyn.

"Where is he?"

"In the bedroom. He gonna be alright?"

"I'm not a physician," replied Radford. The actor-knight entered the girl's boudoir fully expecting to see his older brother lying on the floor with his skull bashed in. What he hadn't anticipated was a bloated and naked Hugh Harcourt sprawled across the bed like a beached, pink whale.

"Ozzie? Is that you?"

"Hell's bells!" Harcourt's pupils were dilated as well. "What happened, Hughie?"

"Reefer. Catnip to her."

"You're not making sense."

"My ticker, old boy. Main spring's shot."

"He's not going to die, is he?" The tiny creature was biting her lip.

"Could you fetch some water, please, Miss …?"

"Toby. Toby Winslow."

"Rather suspected that," murmured Radford.

The half-clad cigarette girl disappeared into the kitchen, then called out: "I know your daughter. Flavia. She's been improvin' my mind. She's a great gal."

"Er, yes. Do you know where his clothes are, Miss Winslow? Ah! Found them."

"Has he told you about me?" asked Toby, returning with a glass of water which she held up to Harcourt's lips. "What did he say?"

"Only nice things," said Radford, who was helping Harcourt step into his trousers.

"Really? Cause he can be a real stinker y'know."

"I worship the ground you walk on," gasped Harcourt, causing the water to dribble down his chin.

"Honest?" asked Toby, tears welling up in her eyes. "Cross yer heart? You shouldn't not have done it that third time. Was that bad English?"

Harcourt stroked her arm fondly. "If Ozzie can have a baby, so can I."

"Ohhhh!" Toby squealed with delight. "Let's get married."

Harcourt sang the last line of a popular old music hall standard: "My wife won't let me." The little cigarette girl threw her arms around her portly lover and showered him with kisses.

Radford plied her loose from Harcourt. "Now, now. Mustn't get him stimulated again." He steered his longtime friend out the front door, wishing Toby a happy new year as he did so. The scene was reminiscent of an Aldwych farce. Except no one on that stage had suffered a heart attack during the third act.

"Just like the good old days Down Under," said Harcourt. "You always pulling me out of some Sheila's bed in time for the matinee. Remember the publican's daughter in Sydney?"

"How does a cigarette girl afford an apartment like that?" asked Radford, helping an unsteady Harcourt into the passenger seat. "Not on tips."

"Toby's on a Hugh Harcourt Bursary."

"Gwen will kill you when she finds out. If that little girl isn't the death of you first." Radford drove his Rolls-Royce east on Sunset towards Los Feliz.

"Not a bad way to go," replied Harcourt, taking deep breaths of fresh air. "When I was younger, I dreamt of dying on stage. When I turned forty, I decided to meet my Maker playing cricket. But this might be a far preferable exit."

"What about Gwen?"

"I love Gwen. But I adore my little Brooklyn hood ornament."

* * *

Harcourt was his usual buoyant self the next day. As an act of loyalty and friendship, Radford proposed that they appear together on the following week's *My Favorite Story* episode as Holmes and Watson in Sir Osmond's own adaptation of *A Scandal in Bohemia*. To make it more of a family affair, he offered the role of Irene Adler to Flavia.

The actor-knight was taken aback when his eldest daughter declined the role. She claimed to have gone off the idea of acting altogether. She had read *Out of Africa* over the weekend and decided it would be fun to run a farm in Kenya like the heroine of Karen Blixen's novel. Radford never pretended to comprehend the wild spirit that dwelt within his daughter, the girl he had dubbed the Pirate Queen when she was three years old and had chased the neighbor's sons away with a wooden sword.

What Sir Osmond failed to realize was that his eldest daughter was heartsick. She had fallen ass-over-teakettle in love with Chet Lowenthal. For one incredibly romantic week, the lawyer and the actress had been inseparable. Then he vanished. No explanation, no phone call, no note. After two days of pretending she didn't care, a devastated Flavia walked across the road one night and banged at the bachelors' front door. Merlin came down the stairs fumbling with the sash on his bathrobe. Flavia could see a pair of naked, female legs hopping up and down at the top of the stairs.

"Where is he?" demanded Flavia.

"Nice to see you, as well," said Merlin. "I'd invite you in but…" The blond Adonis gestured vaguely towards the legs at the top of the stairs.

"I phoned the office every day. Gladys said he's out of town."

"He is."

"Where?"

"Chet doesn't tell me everything."

"Is it another woman?"

"Not his style."

"Oh, Paul…." Flavia stared at the blond Adonis, doing her best to fight back tears.

"He'll be back. You got to have faith, kid."

Flavia jumped into the Packard and drove herself straight to Violet Purdy's apartment on Franklin. She rang the bell downstairs using their secret code. No answer. Not my day, thought the Pirate Queen, as she crossed the street once again. She was about to pull the Packard away from the curb when a large man with short, cropped hair and a walrus mustache emerged from the building. He looked familiar. Where did she know him from?

Raising her eyes, Flavia caught sight of Violet pressing her naked body against the window and blowing kisses to her.

Ten minutes later, the two women were pleasuring each other in Violet's bed.

"At least we won't get pregnant," said Violet, as they lay sated next to each other.

"Is that why we do it?" asked Flavia.

"Maybe. That and the fact no man gets me off like you do." Violet made a cursory examination of her body. "Sweet mother of Jesus! Think that Kraut left enough bruises? Should have asked for risk pay. I left a farm in Wisconsin for this?"

"Who was he? A wrestler?"

"Says he's a director. In pictures. Never heard of him. Krauts are all lousy tippers."

"Martin Kohlinger! I thought he looked familiar. A refugee. Family was murdered by the Nazis. He was at Larry's party the other week."

"Larry who?"

"Another self-absorbed English actor."

"How's your brother?" asked Violet, with studied casualness. After the incident at the premiere, she feared Alec and prayed he'd never contact her again.

"Heartbroken. Like his sisters."

"Somebody got to you?" asked Violet.

"Is that so strange, Vi?"

"Hey, don't go deep dish on me, Limey."

"How do you know my brother?"

"We met at a party."

"Whose party?"

"Can't remember. What the hell does it matter? You Radfords are all fucking moody."

"How many of us have you had, Vi?"

"Don't go there, Limey. I'm a working girl. You know that."

Flavia swung her legs off the bed and grabbed her dress from the floor.

"I'm leaving now."

"Always have to call the shots, don't you?" said Violet. "What if I asked you to stay?"

"I'm leaving." Flavia was on her feet now and stepping into her high heels.

"Do me a favor. Don't come back. Okay?"

By the time Flavia turned her car off Benedict onto Tower Road, she had reconsidered her father's offer. Kenya was a pipe dream. She was a Radford. Acting was in her blood. Chester Lowenthal had merely been an aberration.

"Daddy!" she said, bursting into the library where Sir Osmond was going over his script with a red pencil. "I've reconsidered."

"How's that?" asked the actor-knight without looking up.

"Irene Adler. We'll be marvelous together."

"Sorry, Pirate Queen. When you turned me down so definitively, I made an offer to your sister. She said yes. In lieu of a going away present."

"Who's going away?"

"Julia. She's been offered a play in the West End. Sails for England in two weeks."

* * *

Alec sat in the overstuffed leather chair remembering the many evenings he had shared with Leni in that same room. Watching her cross and uncross those fabulous legs.

Georg Gyssling appeared from the kitchen carrying two large steins filled with pilsener. "*Prosit.*" The German Consul and Alec clinked their steins together.

"Does it seem strange to you that I feel more comfortable here than in my parents' home?" asked Alec.

"Do you feel guilty about it?" asked Gyssling.

"Not at all. I was adrift for so long. Until I read *Mein Kampf.*"

The Consul nodded: "It is like reading the Bible. Except there are no Jews. It meant a great deal to me when you joined us here on Christmas Day, Alec."

"Being with you reminds me of my time … with her."

Kirsten Flagstad's voice could be heard on the gramophone performing Brunhilde's Immolation scene from *Götterdämmerung*. Gyssling closed his eyes and listened in a state of rapture. "She is almost German," said the Consul, bestowing the highest compliment he could afford the Norwegian soprano.

Unable to stand it any longer, the young Englishman asked: "Have you heard anything from Leni?"

"Alec, Alec." Gyssling shook his head in despair. "Forget about her. She is married."

"No!"

"To her work. Like all of us, we are committed to a new world order. You have suffered terribly, my boy. What those Warner Brothers did to you. Stripping you of your manhood. Artistically castrating you. It should have been you up on that screen in *The Dawn Patrol*. You must despise them."

"I do."

"As does *der Führer*. What he would not give to have his revenge on them. Even as we speak, the Warner Brothers rub his face in the dirt with their filthy propaganda." Alec stared curiously at the Consul. "What! You do not know about the pornography they are shooting next week with Edward Jew Robinson? If only one could drop a bomb from the air and blow up their studio."

"Why not on the ground?" asked Alec. "How difficult could it be with a few sticks of carefully planted dynamite? Might not destroy the place, but certainly put them out of commission for a few weeks."

Gyssling's eyes were dancing with delight as he stared at Alec's almost demented face as he debated aloud the best building to target. The Consul could hardly wait to cable Goebbels and tell him his plan was working beyond their wildest expectations.

"But where could one find a man brave enough to attempt such an almost suicidal mission?"

"I'll do it," said Alec with religious fervor. "If I could only get on the lot. Not exactly persona grata there these days."

"Truly? You would commit to this undertaking?"

"For the Fatherland," said Alec, "I would risk my life."

Gyssling pulled the young Englishman to his feet and embraced him. "The *Führer* shall know of this," said Gyssling. The Consul had already formed a plan in his mind to smuggle the idiot Englishman onto the Warners lot.

UNINVITED SUITOR

WHAT A COUP! AREN'T YOU THE SLY BOOTS? YOU'VE TAKEN TO YOUR NEW LIFE LIKE A DUCK TO QUACKING. THIS EVENT WILL PROVE THE OPPORTUNITY OF A LIFETIME. GLEAN WHATEVER YOU CAN FROM YOUR NIPPONESE GUEST. THE SLIGHTEST BIT OF TRIVIA WILL BE PANNED LIKE GOLD ON OUR END. WHAT DOES HE LIKE TO EAT? DOES HE PREFER A CERTAIN SCENT OVER ANOTHER? WHAT IS HIS SEXUAL PREDILECTION? WE ALSO NEED TO KNOW EVERYTHING ABOUT ERROL FLYNN.

Sitting in his radio room off the wine cellar, Sir Osmond had been awake since dawn laboriously transcribing the latest coded message from Richard Ives-Curtis. *Full reimbursement*? Hell's bells! The actor-knight still hadn't seen a farthing for the Olivier party. Best of British luck trying to get Hyacinth to betray a confidence. As for Hashimuro's sexual predilection, how in hell was that to be determined? Even after a lifetime in the navy, one couldn't exactly ask the Admiral if he 'liked it rough' occasionally. Besides, the man spoke no English. His son would be translating for him. And what was all this rot about Errol Flynn? Hell's bells, Dickie! If a secretary in Whitehall wants an autographed photo of the Tasmanian Devil, just come out and say it.

"Darling?"

Hyacinth's voice startled him. Radford gauged his wife was calling down to him from the top of the stairs. He dreaded her stumbling onto his secret. He also feared her literally falling down the rickety steps in her present condition.

"Shan't be a moment!"

"Barbara and Bob are here!" The couple she referred to were Barbara Stanwyck and her fiancé, Robert Taylor. The former Ruby Stevens was the one movie star that Admiral Hashimuro had expressed any desire to meet.

Barbara and Sir Osmond were old friends from their days on Broadway fifteen years earlier. Radford had watched helplessly as she was mentally and verbally abused through the years by her then husband, Frank Fay. The actor-knight couldn't have been more delighted when Barbara finally divorced the drunken lout. Although he wasn't quite sure what to make of Bob Taylor. The rising MGM leading man was four years Barbara's junior, much prettier and unnaturally devoted to his mother. But the former Spangler Arlington Brugh adored Barbara to distraction.

"And the Admiral?"

"Not yet."

"He'd bloody well better show! Or we'll be eating raw fish right up to your due date."

"Which is not a good idea."

"Your due date? Or the sashimi?"

"Come up here, please, Ozzie! We have guests."

Sir Osmond had spared no expense to entertain Tamon Hashimuro. With Ito's assistance, the dutiful (albeit secret) civil servant and Lady Radford had traveled to Little Tokyo (with Charleston and Boggs in tow) where they engaged the services of a Japanese chef and a phalanx of kimono clad waitresses to attend 'the esteemed nautical personage', as Radford described Hashimuro when only Hyacinth was around.

Ito suggested the reception be restricted to a small gathering. His father did not like large crowds (something he had in common with Miss Stanwyck). Who would comprise the limited guest list? The Japanese Consul, of course. Despite the fact the Admiral's visit was an unofficial stopover, the Japanese government must not be slighted in any way. Who else? Hyacinth suggested Aldous Huxley, a dear friend from her Bloomsbury days and her frequent companion at Arya Vihara. Hyacinth said that Aldous had the gift of engaging any one from any culture in a verbal exchange. Krishna, despite his pacifist commitment, promised he would drive down from Ojai to meet the Admiral. Aubrey, of course, would be in attendance as the unofficial leader of the Raj. Very few other actors would be invited. Certainly not the Harcourts. Since the mission of mercy on New Year's Day, Radford had felt most uncomfortable in any social situations involving Hugh and Gwen. The actor-knight hadn't breathed a word to Hyacinth about Harcourt's cigarette girl mistress. And, in her fourth month of pregnancy, Sir Osmond certainly wouldn't do or say anything that might upset his beloved wife.

"Where the devil is this foreigner?" asked Aubrey, who'd been cooling his heels in the sitting room for almost an hour. "Does he think he's the Mikado?"

Flavia giggled and gently slapped the back of the old Carthusian's hand. "This is a diplomatic event, Mr. Smith. Don't embarrass us."

"Pot calling the kettle black," retorted Aubrey. "Your madcap behavior has not gone unnoticed, my dear. As your godfather, I have a—"

"You're Julia's godfather. Not mine."

"What's that? Of course, I am. Where is the little poppet?"

"Gone back to England. Three weeks ago. She's doing a play in the West End."

"Leaving your mother in the lurch. Difficult things, these change-of-life babies."

"Have you had one?"

"Good thing you're supposed to be female," said Aubrey, "or I'd cuff you."

"If one more man promises me that!"

A kimono-clad waitress approached Aubrey with a tray of sushi, which she held up to him. The elderly actor began to hum 'Three Little Maids from School' until Flavia glared at him. "What have we got here?"

"*Uni,*" replied the waitress.

"Sea urchin," said Flavia.

"Take it away!" said Aubrey. "I don't dine on barnacles. What's become of your lawyer chap? Quite agreeable sort for an American."

"He travels a great deal." Flavia couldn't bear to think about Chet, let alone discuss him. She had been greatly relieved the day before when Paul Merlin told her that Chet had been at Warners when the mysterious explosion occurred. Lowenthal had returned home safely and unscathed.

"They've arrived!" Hyacinth took her husband's hand and led him out the front door where a limousine had just pulled up in the driveway. She was curious as to how the Admiral might be dressed. In military uniform or ceremonial robes? What she was not prepared for was elegant mufti; Tamon Hashimuro emerged from the back seat wearing a grey double-breasted Savile Row suit that might have been borrowed from her husband's upstairs closet. The Admiral was also much taller than she had imagined. Quite handsome, his mustache gave him the look of a Japanese Clark Gable.

Forgotten in the footnotes of the Great War was a treaty between Great Britain and Japan. In 1917 a special force of Japanese destroyers was dispatched to the Mediterranean to protect Allied shipping from German submarines. Hashimuro commanded the destroyer, *Kusonoki*, that defended shipping lanes between France and Egypt until the end of the war.

Commander Hashimuro returned to Japan convinced the nation that controlled the seas controlled the world. For almost sixty years, the flame of revenge had burned in the Japanese ruling class: a desire to avenge the humiliation of the treaties imposed on them by foreign powers in the 19th Century. By 1920, Japan had built the third most powerful navy behind Great Britain and the United States. Hashimuro and his fellow officers had sworn an oath to make Japan the most powerful navy on the planet. The English and Americans had foolishly sent their ships for the Japanese to study. "Copy, improve, innovate." This was the credo of Hashimuro and his friends. By 1938, through an almost religious dedication of purpose, they had become the dominant naval power in the world.

Ito Hashimuro, carrying a beautiful rosewood case under his arm, dashed forward in blue blazer and flannels to introduce his father to the Radfords. The Admiral and the actor-knight exchanged bows. The senior Hashimuro said something in a deep, guttural growl. Hyacinth looked to Ito for a translation until Sir Osmond realized the Admiral had quoted from Shakespeare. The Scottish play, no less. *"This castle hath a pleasant seat."*

"You speak English?" asked Radford in a mix of amazement and delight.

"Not so very much," replied the Admiral haltingly, "but I spent some pleasant time in England during the last war. We were on the same side."

Hashimuro followed this last sentence with a sustained guttural laugh. "I went often to the theatre. But never had the privilege of seeing you."

"You're far too kind," said Radford. "Unfortunately, I spent much of the war as a guest of the Germans."

"But you fought with honor."

"One would like to think so." Radford found himself totally in the thrall of the urbane and charming Admiral. "Please, come and meet our guests. Your guests."

The Admiral grunted, bowed again, and followed his host and hostess inside Best of Times. Stepping down into the living room, Hashimuro's eye was caught immediately by the framed Russell Flint portrait of Lady Radford hanging over the fireplace. He moved slowly and reverently towards it as one would a holy shrine. Then he turned his gaze to Hyacinth, who was standing nearby.

"This is you," said the Admiral in bewilderment.

"Many years ago," replied Hyacinth.

"No. Like it was yesterday. This hung in the National Portrait Gallery in London."

"Until my husband purchased it."

The Admiral grunted. "The mystery of its disappearance is solved. Many times I would visit you there. Your uninvited suitor." He emitted his guttural laugh, then turned to Sir Osmond and bowed low. "Please to forgive my youthful reminiscence. Hopefully, it has not given offense, honorable knight. But you are a particularly blessed man. Your exquisite wife has never changed."

"You're far too kind."

"She has given you children. And still more to come." Hashimuro turned to Ito and spoke rapidly in Japanese. His son blushed and did not translate. The Admiral grunted and stared sternly at his son.

"My father envies you, your … virility." Ito barely whispered the last word.

The possibility of any subsequent embarrassment was alleviated by the Admiral gasping audibly at the sight of Barbara Stanwyck clinging to the arm of Robert Taylor. Hashimuro strode towards the movie star, bowed deeply and said: "*The Miracle Woman*."

Stanwyck was so startled by this pronouncement that she lapsed back into her basic Brooklyn. "You've seen my pictures?"

The Admiral did not respond but continued in a litany of her films: "*The Bitter Tea of General Yen*. A Japanese would not have treated you this way. *Stella Dallas*. What sacrifice! And, of course, *Annie Oakley*. You are a great shot." Hashimuro snapped his fingers. Ito stepped forward and handed his father the rosewood case he had been carrying under his arm. The Admiral, in turn, presented it to the movie star.

Stanwyck opened the case containing two antique *tanegashima* matchlock pistols.

"They are two hundred years old," said Hashimuro.

"For me?" The movie star laughed self-consciously, then asked: "Do you like horses? Would you like to visit my ranch?"

"I live next door," said Taylor in his flat Nebraska accent.

Hashimuro ignored her fiancé and replied: "It would be my great honor. Unfortunately, I must begin my long journey to Washington in the morning. And I have had no time alone with my son."

"Maybe on the way back?"

"Regretfully, I will be returning home the long way." The Admiral employed his finger to encompass an imaginary globe from west to east. He had purposely not mentioned the most important detail: Hashimuro would be stopping off in Berlin to secretly confer with the German High Command.

MUMMIFIED

Special Agent Floyd Hightower stared mournfully at the sandwich he had removed from its wax paper enclosure. Before taking off to visit her mother in Bakersfield, his wife Ethel had prepared seven days' worth of sandwiches. The Hightowers had been going through a rough patch and the maternal visit was to be somewhat of a trial separation. Ethel's ill-will was blatantly reflected by the different choices of fillings she had coated between the slices of Wonder Bread. Cucumber, liverwurst and five other ingredients that Hightower could not stomach.

"Agent Hightower?" Marjorie, an overweight secretary, stood over his desk licking her lips repeatedly. The tall, pockmarked FBI agent couldn't decide whether she wanted his liverwurst sandwich or was attracted to him. He didn't think either choice was likely. Probably chapped lips.

"Director Kirby would like to see you."

"Okay," growled Hightower in his forty miles of bad road voice. His Cherokee ancestry had afforded him a hawk nose and great cheekbones, but a genetic intolerance for alcohol, which the tall Federal agent refused to acknowledge. The unpleasant affect excessive drinking had on him was one of many reasons Ethel had gone to visit her mother in Bakersfield. "Would you like my sandwich?"

"I hate liverwurst," said Marjorie, licking her lips once again.

"Me, too. You married?"

"Aren't you?"

"Meaning?"

"Bet you need a good meal."

"Got that straight."

"Like home cooking?"

"Is that an invitation?"

Marjorie arched her left eyebrow enigmatically and finally remembered the purpose of her visit. "Director Kirby's waiting."

Hightower walked behind her down the hall. He'd never noticed before that Marjorie had great legs. Ethel's were like piano rolls. Skinny and straight. No shape at all.

Dixon Kirby was a sawed-off runt with dyed black hair and a night school. law degree. But Kirby knew how to play the game. It was rumored he was a distant cousin of J. Edgar Hoover. The framed photograph of the legendary lawman contained the fond, if not slightly provocative, autograph: "For Dix, the one that got away. As ever, John."

"How's bachelor life?" asked Kirby, as Hightower sauntered into his boss's office. "Did she leave you sandwiches?"

"Yeah. Want one?"

"Never eat lunch," replied Kirby, slapping his flat belly. "Big breakfast. That's my secret. Still working on the Anti-Nazi League?"

"Yeah." Hightower wondered for whose benefit Kirby was putting this act on. Then he noticed the large man with a walrus mustache, who had been sitting silently on the sofa against the wall. Hightower knew him. One of the thousand faces he and Matt Corcoran had spent hours photographing through their telephoto lens.

"Agent Hightower, I'd like you to meet Martin Kohlinger. He's a movie director at Warner Brothers."

"Believe you had a little disturbance out there recently," said Hightower. A mysterious explosion had rocked the Warner Brothers lot the week before. As a movie studio wasn't federal property, the botched fire/bomb/whatever incident didn't fall under FBI jurisdiction. The Burbank Police Force was handling the investigation. As Edward G. Robinson and the rest of the Hebes were the obvious targets, Hightower couldn't get too worked up about it.

"Mr. Kohlinger has a very interesting story he wants to tell us, Floyd."

"Really? Is it about Nazis? Or Commies? We're not really in the Nazi business, Dix." Hightower had enough brains to keep his support of Hitler's avowed anti-Semitism to himself.

"Hear him out, Floyd."

"Promise me, gentlemen, that you can protect me." Kohlinger's hands were shaking. "They lied to me about my family. They forced me to do things that I am ashamed of. I love this country. It has been good to me." The director burst into tears.

Kirby poured Kohlinger a glass of water and carried it over to him. "Tell us your story. From the beginning. Take your time."

* * *

Ito Hashimuro watched as his father packed each item of carefully folded clothing into his suitcase. The Admiral had told Barbara Stanwyck how he wished to spend time with his son. But not a single word of conversation had transpired between the two men during the journey from Beverly Hills to the Biltmore Hotel in downtown Los Angeles.

The Admiral removed several sheets of fine stationery from an elegant leather binder and held them up to the light. He grunted approval at something he saw that was otherwise invisible to the naked eye. The elder Hashimuro broke his silence and spoke in Japanese: "These people are very fond of you."

"They have been like family."

"You have only one family," snapped his father. "But it is good that they hold you in such high regard. It will make your work so much easier."

"My work? What do you mean, Father?"

"Your mother treated you like a girl. By the time she died, the damage was irreparable. What dreams I had of a great naval dynasty would never come to pass. But you possess a fine mind, and no one would ever suspect you of being more than a harmless poet."

"What is it you want of me, father?"

"Not I, my son. What we do is in the service of the Chrysanthemum Throne. The time for the fulfillment of our destiny is now. The people you are so devoted to are children. With no tradition. They are mongrels, drawn from the exiles and undesirables from every corner of the planet."

"Hyacinth Radford is a great lady. From an honorable family."

"You are besotted by her beauty, as I was. This can serve our purpose. Continue to be her favorite. Learn her most intimate secrets. She has many powerful friends. As does her husband. Travel with them. Suggest a trip to Santa Barbara. Take photographs of the coastline. This would be very helpful to us. The Emperor will be grateful."

"How can you ask me to betray their trust? Such action is not honorable. I will not do it."

The Admiral closed the clasps on his briefcase and looked about the bedroom of the suite. "Where is my walking stick? Have you seen it?"

Ito saw the walking stick leaning against a writing table beside the window. He retrieved it and passed it to his father.

"This belonged to your grandfather," said Hashimuro, admiring the craftsmanship as he held the walking stick out in front of himself like a sword.

"He was a great man, Ito. I worshipped him. Kneel down."

"Father?"

"On your knees. Kneel!"

The younger Hashimuro did as his father commanded.

"That was not difficult, was it?" asked the Admiral. He raised the walking stick over his head and brought it down with a powerful blow across his son's shoulder blades. "You will obey my commands." The next blow was across Ito's back. "Do you understand? ... Do you?"

Ito nodded his head, dreading where the next blow might fall.

* * *

"You're in a talkative mood tonight," said Violet Purdy, lighting up a Lucky Strike. "And generous." She had planned on meeting Consuela at Ciro's that evening and seeing what kind of trouble the two could get into. Then her client phoned and asked if she liked champagne. He sounded quite playful, which was not like him at all. When he arrived at her apartment on Franklin Avenue, his face was quite flushed. He dangled two bottles of Moet Chandon aloft in his hands.

"What are we celebrating?" asked Violet as she shoved double the usual payment into the drawer of her vanity.

Martin Kohlinger laughed. He had much cause for jubilation, but no one with whom he dared confide. As of that afternoon, he was a double agent working for both the Nazis and the FBI. When it became obvious to him that the G-Men were America Firsters with no axe to grind with the Third Reich, Kohlinger deftly switched his trump card to suspected Communist infiltration of the studio labor unions. Thus, he would prove himself indispensable to the FBI should Gyssling grow disenchanted with the emigre director's efforts and attempt to have him deported. Should the Third Reich carry through its plans for world domination, Kohlinger would be rewarded for his secret activities as a member of the advanced guard. For now, the new double agent's only interest lay between the legs of the pretty blond with the half-moon scar on her cheek.

"You are a beautiful girl," said Kohlinger, filling two Mason jars with champagne as he watched Violet pull her slip over her head. "Have you never thought of acting in pictures?"

"Who says I haven't?" Violet took the glass jar from Kohlinger and chug-a-lugged the champagne. "Know Eddie Goulding?"

"Slowly, *liebchen*. That's not ginger ale from the drug store. Where did you work for Eddie? Metro or Warners?"

"Private pictures. Artsy stuff."

Kohlinger knew all about Goulding's home porno, which only made him more desirous of the young prostitute. He switched the subject abruptly: "Remind me to buy you some proper flutes for my next visit."

"Gonna be a regular?"

"Maybe even exclusive. Move you to a nice apartment in Beverly Hills. With a maid. Would you like that?"

"Oooh! You're making me wet, Mr. Kohlinger."

"Call me Marty."

"C'mere, Marty. And show me that big torpedo bobbin' up and down in your shorts. Sweet Mother of Jesus! I don't know if I got room enough for that. Maybe I *will* have to get a bigger place."

An hour later Violet lay next to Kohlinger, who was snoring loudly with a grin plastered on his face. She wondered if the big Kraut had been serious about setting her up in Beverly Hills. He wasn't such a bad guy. Maybe after a little while they might get hitched. She wouldn't be the first hooker in Hollywood to hang up her douche bag and go ritzy. Mrs. Martin Kohlinger. Didn't have to be a pipe dream.

The doorbell rang from downstairs. Who the hell was that? The bell rang again. Kohlinger began to stir. She stroked his furry chest and told him to go back to sleep. The downstairs bell rang again. She grabbed her wrapper and walked over to the window.

She stared down at a man of indeterminate age standing below on the sidewalk gesticulating wildly. He looked mummified with his face and hands swathed in bandages. Violet walked back towards the bed.

Then a familiar voice bellowed out from the street: "Tart! Fucking tart!"

It was Alec.

SOUR CREAM OR APPLE SAUCE

He walked briskly along Brooklyn Avenue past the kosher meat market and the tiny shop selling *menorahs* and *tallisim*. The neon sign above the brightly lit delicatessen in the working-class Jewish enclave east of Los Angeles read ALTER'S. A string of salamis was drying in the window. The seductive aroma of pastrami and sour dill pickles immediately overwhelmed him. Sitting down on a stool at the counter, he stared up at the wall adorned with framed vintage photographs of unfamiliar actors from a bygone era.

An elderly man in an apron shuffled along behind the counter proffering a well-thumbed, grease-stained menu. He looked like a clean-shaven biblical prophet.

"I'm not eating," said Chester Lowenthal, who had driven to Boyle Heights for another of his 'secret missions'.

"Just dropped by to look at the pictures?"

"I have an appointment with Rose. Rose Alter."

"You a new boyfriend?"

"Is Miss Alter here?"

"Rose! A *shaygetz* out here wants to see you."

A pretty, olive-skinned woman in her late twenties with masses of curly dark hair entered from the kitchen wiping her hands on her apron.

"Yes?" she asked. "Can I help you?"

"I'm Chester Lowenthal."

The young woman turned to the elderly man behind the counter: "He's Jewish, Uncle Lazer!" She turned back to the lawyer and gestured towards a well-worn red leather booth. "Come and sit down."

"Are you Rose Alter?"

"Who else? Katherine Hepburn? You don't look Jewish. Want a soda? Sit, sit." Rose slid into the booth across from Lowenthal. "Where are your people from?"

"Germany," replied the lawyer. "It was still Prussia in 1848."

"That's ninety years ago! Your family's been here almost a century. No wonder Lazer thought you were a *goy*. Why are you doing this?"

"Doing what?"

Rose leaned her face in to his and whispered: "Smuggling Jews."

Lowenthal burst out laughing. "You're very funny."

"Yeah," replied Rose wryly. "A regular Baby Snooks. Fanny Brice won't sleep nights knowing I'm around. So? What's your story?"

Lowenthal shifted gears and pointed to the framed photographs over the counter. "Who are they?"

"My father's idols. The great stars of the Yiddish Theatre. We had a deli back in New York. On Second Avenue. Before my father got sick. All the great legends were customers. Before the show. After the show. And during intermission."

"Wait a minute!" Lowenthal rose from the booth and walked over to the counter. There was a photograph on the far end he hadn't noticed earlier. A handsome man in his late thirties wearing dinner clothes. His eyebrows looked like inverted parentheses. No way he was Jewish.

"Is that Sir Osmond Radford?" The inscription on the photo was too far away for Lowenthal to decipher.

"You know him?" asked Rose.

"He's my neighbor. We live across the street from each other."

"Then you know Lady Radford? And the girls? Flavia and Julia." She said the names with an affectionate intimacy.

"How do you know them?"

"Never had the pleasure," replied Rose. "But Sir Osmond I've known since I was a kid. He comes in here regularly."

"Osmond Radford eats here?" Lowenthal was unable to disguise his amazement.

"He's crazy about pastrami. My father made him a convert."

"You're going to leave it like that?"

"It's not much of a story," Rose replied coyly.

"Come on, Scheherezade. You're dying to tell me."

"Okay!"

Uncle Lazer shuffled out of the kitchen bearing a plate stacked high with potato pancakes. He deposited them on the table while intoning: "He looks hungry." The old man turned to walk away, then spun round with a dexterity that belied his years. "Sour cream or apple sauce?"

"For the latkes," said Rose.

"I know," replied Lowenthal. "Sour cream, please."

"Might be a Jew after all," said Uncle Lazer shuffling back to the kitchen.

"Do you know the Lower East Side of New York?" asked Rose, not waiting for a response. "That's where I was born and raised. Until six years ago. We lived on Hester Street. It was 1926. I was fourteen. Now you know how old I am. My father, Moishe Alter, was very devout. *Davvened* in the morning and the evening. Prayed."

"I know what *davven* means," said Lowenthal. "Where does Sir Osmond fit into—?"

"*Sha*! Let a girl tell a story." Rose slapped his hand playfully, then she continued: "My father and his cronies prayed at a tiny little *shul* on Rivington Street. One of the regulars, Herschel Zuckerman, contracted whooping cough. Touch and go for a while there. With Zuckerman sick, they didn't have enough for a *minyan*. You know what that is?"

"A quorum," replied Lowenthal, who was plowing through the *latkes* on his plate. "You need ten men to have a prayer service. These are delicious."

"They're much better with the sour cream. Uncle Lazer! Did you fall in? Zuckerman's whooping cough was a potential catastrophe. Where was a tenth man to be found? In desperation, my father stepped out onto Rivington Street hoping against hope he'd spot somebody. But no one was in sight. And it came to pass that the Almighty performed a miracle. Whatever a gentleman like Sir Osmond was doing on the Lower East Side, I will never know. But there he was. My father grabbed him by the arm and dragged him inside the synagogue. What a kafuffle that caused. 'Are you crazy, Moishe? A *shaygetz*!' 'He's a man, isn't he?' asked my father. 'We need a tenth man for the *minyan*!'"

"Sir Osmond *davenned* with them!?!"

"Of course not. But he stood with them while they prayed. What a *mensch*! He had only one stipulation. They had to finish in time for him to get uptown for his performance that evening. My father said he and his friends never *davenned* so fast in their lives."

Uncle Lazer reappeared with a bowl of sour cream and plunked it down in front of Lowenthal. "I'm not eating." He shrugged his shoulders above his ears and returned to the kitchen.

"My father and Sir Osmond became friends. Whenever he came over from England, his first stop was Second Avenue. When my father got sick, we moved out west. Settled here in Boyle Heights. Deli is deli, right? Jews have to eat. My father died two years ago. Sir Osmond came to the funeral. What a *mensch*! Haven't seen him now for six months. How is he?"

"He's going to be a father again."

"*Oy vey!*" Rose shook her head in disbelief. "Tell him *mazel tov* for me."

"I will. Now, we really need to talk about—"

"Yeah, yeah. Business. It's my mother's family. They made their way from Rumania to Mexico, but they can't get visas."

Lowenthal sighed sympathetically. "It's four months into 1939 and the quotas are filled already."

"How much is this gonna cost?"

"Expenses. I don't take money for this."

"What! You own a bank?"

"Used to. How many family members are there?"

Rose stared at the handsome lawyer and asked: "Why do you do this?"

"If my great-grandfather hadn't come here all those years ago, I might be stranded in Mexico, too."

"Another *mensch*." Rose reached her arm across the table and squeezed Lowenthal's hand. "You married?"

COLD BLOODED KILLER

Osmond Radford's mind was filled with a myriad of thoughts as he walked along Canon Drive in Beverly Hills. Hyacinth had expressed a desire to move up to Ojai. She wished the peace and serenity Aya Vihara offered her for the duration of her pregnancy. Julia had written that her play closed in Manchester during its pre-London tour. She would return to California by June to be at her mother's side when the baby arrived. Flavia's mood swings alternated between debilitating boredom and manic bursts of activity. Jasper was becoming a concern, as well. Not that the sometime movie butler had gotten himself into another scrape, but because he had been incommunicado for so long. The actor-knight was used to his older brother being short of cash monthly. So far that year, there had been no pleas for financial assistance. Whether this was a good thing or a bad, Sir Osmond could not decide.

On the professional front, his career continued apace. *My Favorite Story* held its spot in the ratings and CBS renewed the show for another year. Dickie sent him coded messages lamenting Czechoslovakia being the latest casualty in Hitler's march through Europe and Franco's fascist victory in the Spanish Civil War. Ives-Curtis felt like a Cassandra warning all within earshot that the world would be at war by the end of the year. Dickie also repeated his request for anything untoward regarding Errol Flynn.

As it had been for the past twenty years, Sir Osmond's main concern was Alec. No one had heard from him since Christmas. Radford assured his wife that all was well. They would undoubtedly receive a postcard from their errant son any day. In his heart, however, the actor-knight knew something was wrong.

Radford entered the reception area of Blaine, Merlin and Lowenthal and addressed the tiny woman pecking away at her typewriter. That voice! Gladys McVey stayed home every Saturday night and listened devotedly to *My Favorite Story* just to hear those dulcet tones. Now Sir Osmond Radford was standing in front of her. She tried to speak but no sound came out.

"Is something wrong?" asked Radford.

Gladys made a peculiar tweeting sound, pressed her fingers to her lips, then over her heart. Finally, she recovered the use of her voice box and said hello.

"Mr. Doherty is expecting me."

Gladys nodded her head up and down, floated up from her chair and led him towards the investigator's office. She knocked on the door, opened it and breathlessly announced: "Sir Oswald Rabbit."

"Do you have this effect on many women?" asked moon-faced Francis X. Doherty after the actor-knight had taken a seat.

"Not since Coolidge was president. Do you mind?" Radford removed a Hignett from his silver cigarette case.

"Not if you don't," said Doherty, lighting up a ten-cent cigar. "I know your daughter."

"Yes. She has spoken highly of you. Which is why I'm here."

"Wanna drink?" Doherty opened the bottom right-hand drawer of his desk and was ready to pull out a bottle of Dewar's. The actor-knight shook his head.

"How can I help you? The boys think the world of you."

"They're far too kind." Radford paused, took a deep breath, and dove in. "My son has disappeared."

"Okay." Doherty reached for a pad and pencil. "How long?"

"Since Christmas Eve." Radford reached inside his jacket pocket and removed a postcard sized head shot of Alec. The young actor's vital statistics were printed on the back along with his agent's phone number.

"Nice looking boy. Your kids all actors?"

"Something of a curse."

"Has he done this before? Disappeared?"

"Yes. But never for this length of time. My wife is quite distressed. She's expecting a child and I worry that the stress may—"

"This your second wife?"

"No. Lady Radford and I have been happily married for twenty—"

"Sorry. Just don't meet many people your age who have— who, uh— Congratulations."

"Thank you."

"Where did he go before? When he disappeared."

"Mexico."

"When was that?"

"October."

"Has he got a car?"

"We share automobiles. The MG is gone."

"License plate?"

Radford gave him the number. Doherty made a call to a friend at the DMV.

"Might take a day or two. In case it's been stolen or an accident. Tell me, Sir Osmond. Why didn't you just go to Missing Persons?"

"My son is troubled. Publicity is the last thing—"

"He got a rap sheet?" Radford stared blankly at the private investigator. "A criminal record."

"Speeding. Drunk driving." Radford was embarrassed by the long list of offenses. "He's been in a few fights, as well."

"Gotcha. Has he got a girlfriend?"

"There was a woman before Christmas. Older. Worldly. Alec was quite besotted with her. She was only visiting. He was desolate when she left."

"She got a name?"

Radford rubbed his eyes with his right hand, then ran the same hand though his hair and exhaled. "Leni Riefenstahl."

"Hitler's honey? That who we're talking about?"

Radford rocked back and forth in his chair. "His mother and I did not endorse their liaison. It's rather a long list of things we don't approve of vis a vis our son. Particularly his admiration of Hitler and the Nazis."

Doherty whistled, stared directly into Radford's eyes and asked: "What do you want him back for? Kid sounds like a pain-in-the-ass."

"He's my son. One hopes he'll have a change of heart."

"It's tough on these kids having famous parents. 'If Dad walks on water, why can't I?' Sorry. I don't bullshit people. His head's not screwed on right. Has he had any dealings with the Silver Shirts?"

"Who are they?"

"Home grown fascists. Their leader is a nut job named William Pelley. Idolizes Hitler. Ran for President three years ago. Didn't win."

"How would one find this man Pelley?"

"Hey!" Doherty grinned and ran a hand through his wispy, plastered down hair. "That's my job. You just pay the bills."

* * *

Unaware that Sir Osmond had already set the wheels in motion to locate her brother, Flavia took it upon herself to find Alec and give her father some peace of mind. At least until the baby was born.

Her first thought was Chet. With his brilliant mind, he'd have known in an instant how to solve the problem. But now Chet was the problem. Her outwardly invulnerable heart was shattered, and she didn't want him to see the broken pieces scattered about. She could ask Paul, but there was always the risk of running into Chet.

"Down in the dumps?" asked Toby, when she saw a sorrowful Flavia enter the Trocadero that night.

"Is it that obvious?"

Toby nodded and asked: "Man trouble?"

"Sort of. My brother. Did you ever know him?"

"No, but—" Toby realized she was on the verge of breaking a confidence. She pursed her lips together and said: "No."

"This is important, Toby. My brother has vanished and—"

"Hey, Limey! How you been?"

Flavia turned her eyes away from the tiny cigarette girl and gazed at the voluptuous Consuela Gonzalez draped on the arm of the slit-eyed band leader, Chico Rodriguez. Introductions were made and Gonzalez excused himself to go to the *bagno*.

"Coming up in the world, Consuela." Flavia nodded towards the band leader heading for the men's room.

"Hey, if that *puta* from Wisconsin can hook herself a director, I can get myself a band leader. Chico wants me to sing. Says I got big talent."

"Violet is getting married?" Flavia tried to remain calm and collected, but her heart was pounding. Losing Chet and Violet was unbearable.

"I dunno about gettin' hitched, but this big German moved her into a fancy apartment on Charleville. In the hills of Beverly."

"What's his name?"

Before Consuela could reply, Chico Rodriguez raced over to her side and began nibbling on her ear.

"You make me so hot, baby."

"Heyyy!" she squealed. "You made my neck wet."

Rodriguez wiped his nose, snorted up the residue of cocaine dripping from it and hustled Consuela out of the nightclub.

As Flavia watched the voluptuous Mexican prostitute disappear with her latest patron, she heard a man's voice behind her ask: "Where you from?"

"Flatbush." Toby Winslow's Brooklyn accent was unmistakable. "And you?"

 "Williamsburg."

"No kiddin'! Small world. You look familiar. Y'in pictures?"

"Nah!"

"Yer handsome enough. What's yer name?"

"Ben Siegel."

Flavia's head snapped round like a whippet racing at White City. Was there a church in the neighborhood? She would give thanks for this. "Hello," said Flavia thrusting out her hand to the man Lowenthal had described as a cold-blooded killer. She still refused to believe it. But if Siegel did have underworld connections, he might be able to locate her missing brother. A criminal is always more help in solving a crime than a policeman. Flavia wasn't sure if she'd read that somewhere or just made it up. Whatever the source, she liked the sound of it. "Do you remember me? Flavia Radford."

"Oh, yeah." Siegel gave her the once over and liked what he saw. He was crazy about Englishwomen. And Wendy Barrie was shooting late at RKO that night. "Comin' or goin'?"

"I was going," replied Flavia, "but I think I'll come now. Could you take care of my friend?" She nodded in Toby's direction.

"Sure. We Brooklynites gotta stick together." Siegel pinched Toby's chin and slipped her a twenty-dollar bill.

Flavia offered Siegel her arm. He led her across the floor towards a table marked 'Reserved'. En route, several people called out: "Hello, Flavia". Her stock was decidedly on an upward trajectory that night.

Twenty minutes later Flavia was roaring at Siegel's off-color jokes, while his right index finger performed a mad fandango under her dress.

The Pirate Queen's pulse was racing when a waiter arrived at the table carrying a telephone.

"For you, Mr. Siegel. He says it's urgent."

"Who is it?" Siegel's index finger continued its rotating rhythm.

"Mr. Cohen."

"Plug it in." Siegel removed his hand from its nesting place and lifted the receiver.

"Yeah, Mick. What's up?… When the hell was this?… Yeah?… Yeah?… Does this shine have a name?… Don't mean a thing to me. And the other guy?… Say it again?" Siegel stared curiously at Flavia: "You got a relative named Jasper Radford?"

"He's my uncle. My father's older brother. In point of fact, you met him. At our house."

"What's he look like?" asked Siegel.

"Bald head. Rather stocky."

"Mickey? What's this guy look like?… Uh-huh… Uh-huh… No… No!… Wait till I get there."

Siegel replaced the receiver on its cradle. He turned to Flavia flashing all his teeth at her.

"What was all that about?" she asked. "You look like the cat that ate the cream."

"I just saved your uncle's life." Siegel glided his hand back inside Flavia's dress. "Now, whatcha gonna do for me?"

SOME SORT OF HINDU THING

Sir Osmond was at CBS rehearsing for the next evening's show when he received an urgent phone call from Willi. His presence was required at Best of Times immediately.

Half an hour earlier, Hyacinth had been seated comfortably in the sitting room with her feet propped up on an ottoman. The doorbell rang. Willi made her way from the kitchen to answer it. Seconds later, the German housekeeper announced nervously that a man was at the door from the government.

"Whatever do you mean, Willi? What government?"

A tall man with a hawk nose, high cheekbones and a pock marked face appeared behind Willi flashing a badge. He spoke in a low, gravelly voice: "Federal Bureau of Investigation. Special Agent Floyd Hightower. Have you got a few minutes to answer some questions, ma'am?"

"In England one only refers to the Queen as 'ma'am'. I am Lady Radford. As we are in America, you may address me as Mrs. Radford."

Hightower was startled by Lady Radford's beauty and the fact she was visibly pregnant.

"Sorry about that, ma'am." Hightower came out of his reverie. "Did it again, huh? I'm from Oklahoma, you see and—"

"Really? Did you ever know Will Rogers?" asked Hyacinth. "He and my husband met in New York when Will worked for Ziegfeld. Our son Alec played polo with Will out here. Marvelous seat on a horse. Part Cherokee, you know."

"No, ma'am," replied Hightower. "Never had the privilege of meeting him. Every Oklahoman— man, woman and child— was proud of him. We're almost all part Cherokee."

"So sad when he died in that crash. I've never flown myself. We're not meant to be up in the sky like that."

"You mentioned your son Alec. Could I possibly have a word with him?"

"Alec isn't living here at the present time."

"Do you have another address for him?"

"Regrettably not. Is there a problem?"

"Not really. Do you know a young woman named Violet Purdy?"

"Purdy? I don't think so."

Hightower had been suspicious of Martin Kohlinger ever since the big Kraut had turned up at FBI headquarters offering his services as a double agent. The G-man had a hunch Kohlinger was really a Communist spy working every angle possible.

"That's funny. Beause I have several photographs of your son and Miss Purdy at the premiere of *The Dawn Patrol*. Didn't you meet her at that time?" Hightower was too in awe of Lady Radford to add that Violet had not only been Alec's date that evening but had co-starred with him in a stag movie that had recently been seized in an interstate commerce raid.

"Ohhh! Yes. The pretty girl with the half-moon scar on her cheek. I don't really remember if Alec ever told us her name. She was awfully sweet. Is she alright?"

"Do you know Martin Kohlinger?"

"He's a client of mine, which I suspect you already know. There's no need to be coy, Agent Hightower. I have nothing to hide from you."

"Does your son know Martin Kohlinger?"

"You'd have to ask him. Regrettably, I don't know where he is. So that brings us right back to the beginning again. Rather like *Alice Through the Looking Glass*."

The telephone rang. Willi picked it up in the kitchen and called out for Lady Radford.

"If you'll excuse me, Agent Hightower. I'm moving a little slowly these days."

Hyacinth went into the kitchen to answer the phone. Less than a minute later, Willi cried out for Hightower to come immediately.

The G-Man entered the kitchen and discovered Lady Radford lying on the floor. Willi knelt beside her holding a glass of water to her employer's lips. Hyacinth opened her eyes, sipped the water, and noticed a concerned Hightower staring down at her.

"I think the time has arrived for me to go to Ojai. Willi, could you please phone Sir Osmond at the radio station? Ask him to come home immediately.

I'm so frightfully sorry, Agent Hightower, but this baby seems determined to arrive ahead of schedule. Could we possibly reconvene at a future date?"

* * *

Radford rushed inside Best of Times where he was greeted by a radiant Hyacinth sitting on the bottom step with an overnight bag next to her.

"Are you alright, darling?"

"Yes, dearest Ozzie. The baby is coming."

"But it's early!"

"It happens."

"Is that all you're taking?"

"No. I have another suitcase upstairs. Please ask Charleston to fetch it for me, please? Could you do me a great favor?"

"Anything, my love."

"Drive me to Ojai. In the Rolls. Just you."

"Are you certain. Wouldn't you like me to sit in the back with you and rub your feet or whatever."

"Nooo. I want to ride up front with you. I've left a note for Flavia so she shouldn't worry when we're not here. What a time for her to disappear!"

Radford heaved a sigh: "Julia's going to be disappointed when she arrives and the baby's already here. She wanted so very much to be with you for the delivery."

"She'll be with me in spirit. Come, husband. It's a two-hour drive and we don't want the baby born en route."

The Rolls-Royce made its way down into the San Fernando Valley and accessed U.S. 101 going west towards Ventura. The Radfords drove along in silence for quite a while, exchanging occasional smiles and squeezing each other's hands. Sir Osmond was riddled with guilt. Francis X. Doherty had brought him several reports over five weeks concerning Alec's fate. The actor-knight had chosen not to share the information with Hyacinth. The MG had been sold in April to a car dealership in San Diego. The seller had been described as a young Englishman, who was heavily bandaged. He had told the dealer that a Coleman stove exploded on a recent camping trip in the Sierra Nevadas. Contacts at the border patrol remembered a bandaged man traveling by bus into Tijuana. He had an English accent and told the Mexican authorities he was a portrait painter heading towards San Miguel de Allende to recuperate following a freak explosion in his studio.

The combination of the words 'explosion' and 'studio' triggered something in the former LAPD detective's brain. Doherty contacted a buddy on the Burbank Police Force. Afterwards he asked Radford to meet him at a coffee shop on La Cienega.

"We don't have to go any further than this," said Doherty nursing a cup of black coffee. "Your son's alive and living south of the border."

"But?" The actor-knight had difficulty absorbing the reality of what was happening to him and his family. Would life have been better for them if he had never come to America? Senseless to think that way now. He had chosen to live like Harun al-Rashid and this was all part of the purchase price.

"He should stay there," said the moon-faced investigator, who gestured for the slouch shouldered waitress to give him a refill.

"And if he chooses to return?"

"You're a tough cookie, Sir Osmond. Okay. Taking off the gloves. Remember a mysterious explosion at Warner Brothers couple of months ago? It was in all the papers. Somebody smuggled a home-made bomb onto the lot. Blew up before it could do any real damage. Except to the dimwit who set it off."

"Alec?"

Doherty nodded: "They found the detonator. His prints were on it."

"How did they identify his fingerprints?"

"They didn't. I did. His LAPD rap sheet." Doherty removed an envelope from his jacket pocket. "You can burn that if you want."

"Can you get in trouble for this?"

"Nobody's really looking for him, Sir Osmond. And that should include you. I know he's your kid, but he'll drag you under with him."

* * *

The Rolls-Royce drove up the steep road leading to Aya Vahara. To Sir Osmond's amazement, his wife had no difficulty navigating the steps leading up to the house. Krishna was waiting for them at the front door.

"Is she alright?" asked Hyacinth entering the house. "The doctor thinks it could be any time today."

"Forgive me," said Sir Osmond, who was directly behind them. "But who are you talking about?"

To his amazement, Lady Radford reached under her maternity dress and began fumbling with some buttons. A minute later a fat suit with enough padding to stuff a Macy's Department Store Santa Claus tumbled onto the carpet. Hyacinth had just lost her 'baby'.

"Where is she?" asked Lady Radford, breathing a sigh of relief at the freedom her body was experiencing.

"In your room."

Hyacinth began to walk briskly, then turned back to her husband and asked: "Are you coming, Osmond?"

"What happened to the baby?" Radford was now the equivalent of a shell-shock victim. "What is that— that outsize waistcoat lying on the floor? What does this all mean?"

Hyacinth's hand was on the doorknob by then and she entered the guest bedroom. An extremely pregnant, extremely radiant Julia Radford was sitting up in bed beaming at her parents. Lady Radford sat down beside her daughter and took her hand. Sir Osmond's eyes ran back and forth uncomprehendingly between the two women.

"Oh, Daddy! I've missed you ever so much."

"How long have you been here?" Radford could hear his voice being lobbed back to him like a tennis ball. "In Ojai?"

"Just after New Year's."

"So … you never went to England? There was no play?"

"I'm sorry, Daddy. This wasn't the plan. The baby's almost a month early."

"I-I-I don't understand any of this. You're having a baby and Mummy pretended she was having one, too. Is it some sort of Hindu thing? Hell's bells! What am I failing to fathom, Hy?"

Lady Radford stared at her husband not knowing whether to laugh or cry. The morning after her dramatic return home, Julia was violently ill. Hyacinth heard retching sounds from inside her daughter's bathroom. She prayed it was something one could discuss in polite conversation like influenza. When Julia continued to be unwell the following morning, Lady Radford lovingly led her daughter outside to the garden for a heart to heart. Through an endless cascade of tears, Julia told her mother the story of her reckless affair with Lansing, right up to the point when she collapsed on the floor of Penn Station.

"When I discovered that the Martians hadn't invaded New Jersey and it was just a hoax perpetrated by Orson Welles, I was livid. I had made a complete fool of myself."

Hyacinth was silent for an eternity before she asked: "Do you love this Lansing person?"

"Yes," sobbed Julia. "But he's married. And he has children."

"Thank goodness for that!" said Hyacinth, heaving a sigh of relief. "We shan't be hearing from him again."

"I love him so much, Mummy!"

"You used to love Tipsy Laird Trifle as well, but you haven't eaten it in donkey's years. People change, Julia. Does anyone else know about your … condition?"

"I saw a doctor in New York, but I didn't give him my real name."

"Does this Lansing person know about the baby?" asked Hyacinth.

"Of course not."

"Nor shall he ever."

"What am I going to do, Mummy? My career! My reputation! It will ruin you and Daddy. We'll have to move to Rhodesia or New Zealand. What have I done to this family?"

"It's alright, dearest. Everything will be fine."

Hyacinth dreamt that night she was sitting on the beach under the shade of a large striped umbrella watching the waves lap up onto the shore. Was she in England or California? Ito ran towards her in a state of jubilation wearing a vintage striped bathing costume.

"The baby is coming, *Izanami*."

A procession of ecstatic celebrants in multi-colored Hindu garb walked along the sand playing sitars and pounding on dholaks. Radford was proudly leading the parade wearing a white robe with a red henna mark in the center of his forehead. Flavia and Julia danced barefoot ahead of him strewing flower petals in his path. The actor-knight cradled an infant in his arms, grinning from ear to ear with paternal pride. Jasper and Alec walked behind him beating on drums.

"Look, darling!" Radford walked over to where his wife was seated and displayed a beautiful baby girl. "It's Domini. Isn't she beautiful?"

Lady Radford woke from her dream knowing what must be done. It would have to remain a secret between her and Julia. No one else could know. Not even Osmond. It would require every bit of Julia's talents as an actress until she supposedly departed for England. The true star of the charade would be Hyacinth, who thought her role much more of a military exercise than a performance. She designed and manufactured the waistcoat herself. She invented a fake gynecologist, whom she visited regularly. Having given birth to three children, Hyacinth was able to simulate the symptoms of pregnancy and behaved by rote as the months progressed. Only one thing bothered her: deceiving her husband. Osmond had been so doting and vulnerable. How would he react when he discovered it had all been a hoax to protect the family honor?

What am I failing to fathom, Hy?

Hyacinth took her husband's hand and held it to her bosom as they walked the grounds of Arya Vahara together. She told him everything just as Julia had related it to her. Surprisingly, Osmond did not explode with paternal rage. Nor did he vow to track down Lansing and thrash the bounder within an inch of his life. Julia was well rid of him.

"Are we to raise the child as our own?" asked Radford.

"Yes."

"And Julia will be her sister?"

"Yes."

"Julia is agreeable to do this?"

"Very much so," replied Hyacinth. "She doesn't think she'd make a good mother."

"Flavia knows nothing of this?"

"No."

"The Pirate Queen won't take it lightly when she finds out."

"She need never find out. Only we three know the truth. And Krishna."

"Has he known about this from the beginning?" Radford was making a great effort to suppress his jealousy of the World Teacher.

"The plan wouldn't have worked without his assistance. Are you terribly upset with me, Ozzie?"

"One initially felt a degree of shock and a sense of masculine outrage. But you are the author of this libretto, Hy. You have astonished me throughout our marriage. This event is merely a variation on a theme. What does bother me is having absented myself from your bed these past five months when it wasn't at all necessary."

Hyacinth blushed and touched her husband's cheek. "'*No sooner met but they looked, no sooner looked but they loved.*' I shall scatter rose petals 'round the four poster the moment this baby is born. Honor bright." She brought her lips to his and kissed him fervently.

"Steady on," warned Radford. "You could have that change-of-life baby after all."

Julia cried out in pain. Krishna emerged from inside the house and called out: "We must fetch the doctor immediately."

MESSAGE IN A BOTTLE

ow much did Kate Smith weigh? Surely it was more than two hundred pounds. The rotund coloratura had won the actor-knight's heart when she confessed that she was his biggest fan even if they performed on rival networks. Sir Osmond knew he should be concentrating more on his upcoming performance than the possible tonnage of the popular radio star seated across from him in the East Room of the White House.

It had all begun a week earlier at dawn when a telegram from Lord Lothian, the Ambassador to Great Britain, arrived at Best of Times. Their Britannic Majesties, King George VI and Queen Elizabeth, had been crisscrossing Canada on their first official visit to the dominion. They were taking a break from the official itinerary to spend a brief five days in the eastern United States before resuming their tour in the Canadian Maritime provinces. Their impending side trip would mark an historic event: the first visit of a ruling British monarch to America. President and Mrs. Roosevelt would be receiving them at the White House for a state dinner and entertainment afterwards. Lord Lothian apologized for the lack of reasonable notice. Her Britannic Majesty had specifically requested that Sir Osmond also participate in the event. Could the actor-knight make his way to Washington with the greatest alacrity?

Her Britannic Majesty, the former Elizabeth Bowes-Lyon, was barely a teenager when her brother Michael was held prisoner in Germany with Radford and Ives-Curtis. By the time the actor-knight had made his successful return to Shaftesbury Avenue, Elizabeth and her girlfriends were haunting the stage door. Until Bertie Windsor wooed and won her. As the Duke and Duchess of York, they were a lovely young couple. Fate thrust them into a spotlight they neither dreamt of nor wanted but were now brilliantly playing their roles as Britain's monarchs.

Radford could just imagine the young Queen preparing for the journey and informing her husband: "My brother's old friend Osmond Radford lives in America. He must come and see us." Like most Britons, she couldn't fathom the enormity of their former colony. To travel from Los Angeles to Washington was probably on a par with taking the commuter train from Victoria to Brighton. But a Royal command is a Royal command, and Radford remained his sovereign's dutiful subject.

The way Hyacinth and her daughters reacted to Radford's summons, one would have thought the actor-knight had been elevated to the peerage. Lady Radford immediately inspected her husband's closet to make sure he had the proper attire for the occasion. Flavia and Julia both asked if he had a need of handmaidens. Even little Domini made happy sounds in the upstairs nursery until a loud crash reverberated through the house.

Radford took the stairs two at a time. Bursting into the nursery, he saw Domini lying happily in her crib pointing at something across the room. Boggs lay half on the window seat, half on the floor groaning in pain. He had been standing on the top rung of a ladder hanging a mobile when he'd lost his footing and come crashing down in a grotesque posture. Luckily the former dresser hadn't broken his neck— just his leg.

Sir Osmond was faced with a dilemma: how could he possibly travel to Washington without his trusted valet? Regretfully, he would have to decline the invitation. As always, Lady Radford solved the problem. Charleston Brown would make the journey cross country with the actor-knight serving as valet, chauffeur, bodyguard, and late-night companion.

It was in the latter function that Charleston knocked on the door of his and Sir Osmond's adjoining compartments one night outside of Kansas City. "Come in, Mr. Brown." Radford was plowing through assorted hard bound volumes debating what he would read to the Roosevelts and the Royals. "Care for a brandy?"

"Don't mind if I do."

Radford unzipped an alligator case, removed two pewter cups and a matching flask. He filled both cups and passed one to his chauffeur. The two men clinked cups.

"Thank you for bringin' me on this trip," said Charleston.

"Thank you, Mr. Brown. I always enjoy your company."

Charleston sipped the brandy and watched the darkened Mid-West roll by before he finally unburdened himself to his employer. "Do you know about my brother and your brother?"

"Temple and Jasper? Are they acquainted?"

"More than that. They in business together."

"What sort of business?" Radford feigned an amused tone but dreaded what the answer might be.

"Drugs."

"Illicit drugs?"

"Heroin, cocaine, and marijuana."

"Hell's bells! How long has this been going on? Where did this unholy alliance spring from?"

"It was that party you gave for Larry what's-his-name. When Mr. Alec showed up with that German woman. Remember Mr. Moto being there?"

"Moto? Do you mean Ito?"

"No, sir. Little man with bug eyes. Hungarian or somethin'."

"Peter Lorre."

"Yeah. That's the one. He got a real jones."

"Jones?"

"Bad drug habit. Real bad. He bought some H from Temple."

"H being… heroin?"

"Yes, sir."

"In my house?" Radford's blood was beginning to boil. "Drugs… were being sold in my house? Hell's bells!"

"More out on the driveway than inside."

"Did you know about this?"

"Nooo! But that's when your brother hooked up with Temple. Mr. Jasper saw the deal goin' down and wanted a piece of the action."

Radford buried his face in his hands and muttered: "This is all my fault. How far has this partnership progressed?"

"They got themselves in trouble."

"Trouble?"

"Big trouble. Do you know who Mickey Cohen is?"

"An agent?"

"No, sir. He works for Bugsy Siegel. Remember Miss Wendy Barrie's date at the same party?"

"The Countess De Frasso's friend? Wasn't his name Ben?"

"Bugsy's like a nickname. Mickey Cohen works for him. He even crazier than Bugsy. He'll kill you soon as look at you. Mickey handles all the drug trade in Los Angeles. Sometimes he turns a blind eye on some penny ante sale on Central Avenue. Says it's a *mitzvah*. But he weren't gonna tap no white cane where Temple and Mr. Jasper was concerned. They was definitely cuttin' in on his territory. He warned your brother. But you know how Mr. Jasper gets. Lookin' down his nose like the skunk did a job on his shoe. That didn't sit well with Mickey. No, sir. Not one bit. He drove the two partners down to Long Beach where he got a warehouse and he strung 'em up by their feet. After he stripped the clothes off 'em."

"Good Lord! Are they alive?"

"Mickey had a moment of sanity while he was heatin' up the brandin' iron. He called Bugsy and told him what he was plannin' to do. Bugsy asked what Mr. Jasper's name was and he figured out Jasper was related to Miss Flavia. So, Bugsy drove on down to Long Beach to have a powwow with the competition."

"And what was resolved?" asked Radford.

"Temple and Mr. Jasper ain't in the drug business no more. I'm glad to get that off my chest. Gonna sleep better tonight."

* * *

Kate Smith had just finished singing 'When the Moon Comes Over the Mountain' when a White House staff member tapped Radford's shoulder and whispered: "It's your turn, Sir Osmond."

The actor-knight rose, bowed to the King and Queen, and made his way to the podium. During the cross-country train journey, he had planned on reading something by Mark Twain. Radford was partial to the American humorist and had read his stories on the air several times. He was subsequently taken aback when proceeding through the reception line, Mrs. Roosevelt said: "I do hope you're reading something British. With all the Negro spirituals and square dancing, it would make a welcome change."

"Of course." Radford nodded politely to the First Lady. He stared at the Queen, who was beaming proudly and affectionately in his direction. Why were they really here? This visit wasn't on the original itinerary. He had radioed Dickie after receiving the telegram to notify him of his command performance. Ives-Curtis, in response, had stressed the importance of the King's meeting with Roosevelt. When war came, England was going to need all the friends it could muster to come to its defense. With this political background to inspire him, Radford thought of Matthew Arnold's poem

"Dover Beach." His voice rose to a stirring climax when he stared directly at the King and said:

And we are here as on a darkling plain

swept with confused alarms of struggle and flight,

Where ignorant armies clash by night.

The King was moved by what he called Radford's "little message in a bottle." Queen Elizabeth thanked him profusely for coming to Washington. His appearance amidst all these strangers reminded her of a happier, long-ago time. She and the King would be traveling north to New York City the next day, then on to the Roosevelts' summer home in Hyde Park. Would Sir Osmond care to accompany them? The train ride through the picturesque countryside would enable them to reminisce at leisure. Radford said he would be honored and delighted to join their party.

Unfortunately, the King was preoccupied with diplomatic cables for most of the trip to New York, but the Queen and Sir Osmond strolled happily down memory lane. She was especially pleased to hear that the former matinee idol had become a father again at fifty. Radford had become so accustomed to such constant enthusiastic congratulations, he was beginning to think Domini really was his child. Before they knew it, the train pulled into Grand Central Station where the Royal party was to make the connection to Hyde Park.

Stepping off onto the platform, Radford was startled to see a familiar face grinning at him.

"Sir Richard!" said the Queen. "What a surprise! How lovely to see you!"

Ives-Curtis bowed and replied: "The pleasure is entirely mine, Ma'am. And how are you, Osmond?"

"Of course," said the Queen. "I'd forgotten. You, Osmond and Michael were all incarcerated together. Will you be traveling up the Hudson with us, as well?"

"Sadly not. And I fear, ma'am, I shall have to deprive you of Sir Osmond's company. We have pressing matters to attend to."

A disappointed Radford bade both monarchs farewell. While Charleston went off to collect their luggage, Sir Osmond gave Ives-Curtis a withering glance and asked: "What's all this about?"

"There's really no place for you to stay at the Roosevelts, and I have several things to discuss with my most valuable West Coast asset. There's a suite waiting for you at the Waldorf, and we have tickets tonight to see *The Philadelphia Story*."

PRIMAL RAGE

The two old friends sat in a booth at Sardi's nursing their second martinis while waiting for their food to arrive.

"Perhaps Tony and Domini will marry someday," said Ives-Curtis, poking the olive in his glass with a fork. "Wouldn't it be nice to be related after all these years?"

"What are you up to, Richard?"

"Oh, dear. One has the distinct impression of being in trouble with the headmaster whenever you call me Richard. Aren't you the least bit happy to see me, Ozzie? You *were* reimbursed for those two parties, weren't you?"

"Eventually."

"I signed off on them the minute your receipts arrived. The tardiness of His Majesty's counting house cannot be laid at my door. How did you find FDR? And Eleanor? An *eminence cerise*, don't you think? One hears the New Deal was entirely *her* idea."

"Why do you keep pestering me about Errol Flynn?" asked Radford.

"Because of the company he keeps."

"Errol went to Spain two years ago and fought bravely on the side of the Loyalists."

"Master Flynn went to Spain and got the clap," replied Ives-Curtis. "At least that's what our 'researchers' tell us. He went with a chum, Dr. Hermann Erben, a charter member of the Nazi Party. Errol and the good doctor continue a rife correspondence in which the Tasmanian Devil regularly complains about 'slimy Jews' and how he wishes Hitler would come over and 'teach these Isaacs a lesson'. One seriously doubts they'll be hanging his autographed photo in Alter's Deli."

"How do you know about Alters?"

"One must regularly keep up to date on your activities, Ozzie."

"You have someone watching me?"

"What do you know about Martin Kohlinger? Ah! Here's our food."

The waiter placed two filets mignon in front of the Englishmen and departed.

"Classic Richard Ives-Curtis," said Radford, watching in awe as Dickie tucked into his blood rare steak. "Jolly one along with bonhomie and heart-warming reminiscence, then totally disarm the victim with a question out of left field."

"Do you think yourself a victim, Ozzie? And where exactly is left field?"

"It's a baseball term. Kohlinger is a client of Hyacinth's."

"Is there anyone in Hollywood who isn't? The tax boys must take a big bite out of her every spring."

"Fortunately, we file a joint return. My minuscule earnings drag her down to a reasonable rate."

"Rubbish! You make more money on the radio than you ever did on Broadway or in the West End."

"Why are you so interested in Kohlinger? His wife and children were murdered by the Nazis. His credentials are impeccable."

"They would be if one could find proof that there had ever been a wife or children. No, Ozzie. Herr Kohlinger is what we call 'a mole'. Planted deep and asleep in the unsuspecting earth waiting for the great come-and-get-it day. Hallelujah! But he's an ambitious mole, our Martin. Never quite sure if the Nasties were going to make a success over here. Hence the *faux* widower offered his services to the other side. Marty, as he longs to be called in America, has become an FBI informant. He also smuggled your Alec onto the Warner Brothers lot in the boot of his automobile."

"Yes, I know."

"Do you? Were you also aware of Alec's mission?"

"Yes," replied Radford. "I also know how he botched it."

"Ozzie, I am impressed. However did you learn about this?"

"I have my own 'researchers'. My son is lucky to be alive. Do you know where he is, Dickie?"

"We lost him in Mexico."

"'We?' Do you have people looking for him?

"For quite some time."

"What is your interest in Alec?"

"His father is a dear old friend of mine." Ives-Curtis stared with unabashed fondness at Radford. "One would hate to see something happen to the lad. Come on, Ozzie. Eat up, old boy. Don't want to miss the curtain."

* * *

"What is the next stop on our Cook's Tour?" asked Radford, as their cab sped south towards Greenwich Village after the curtain had come down on *The Philadelphia Story*.

"A charming nightclub called Cafe Society. Quite *avant garde*. Caters to whites and Negroes. It's been described as 'The Right Place for the Wrong People'."

The cab pulled up outside the controversial night spot. Charleston Brown was pacing up and down in front of the entrance.

"I took the liberty of inviting Mr. Brown," said Ives-Curtis. "Thought he'd appreciate the headliner."

The place was packed to the rafters. Radford had never seen a mixed race audience like that before. Charleston insisted on buying the first round of drinks at their ringside table. The lights dimmed. A beautiful black woman stepped out onto the stage. Radford was grateful that his wife had not accompanied him. He was totally entranced by this ebony female as she began to sing:

Southern trees bear a strange fruit,

Blood on the leaves and blood at the root

The audience was on its feet cheering when the song was over. Some people were weeping openly. Radford had never been so moved by a public performance in his life. He had no idea that a song could have such an effect on people. It was halfway through the ballad before the Englishman realized the song was about lynching. Radford was devastated. How was it possible that this barbaric act could be legal in the most democratic of nations? But that was undoubtedly why this extraordinary woman could sing the song so plaintively.

"Who is she?" asked Radford, his voice barely above a whisper.

"Billie Holiday," replied Charleston. "Did you like her?"

"She's the greatest artist I've ever seen."

"Wanna meet her?"

Unbeknownst to the trio seated at the ringside table, they were being observed from across the room by an eerily attractive young German. His short-cropped hair was white blonde and the chroma of his piercing blue eyes seemed to change with his moods. Klaus Erik Meinster was officially a low-level consular attaché. He had actually been trained by the *Sicherheitsdienst*, the intelligence division of the German SS. Arriving in New York from Berlin a few weeks earlier, his job was ostensibly to spy on Fritz Kuhn, the *Bundesführer* of the German American Bund, and to send back reports to the Fatherland.

Hitler was not the least bit enamored of the German-born Kuhn and had snubbed him when the self-styled American *Führer* turned up at the 1936 Olympics in Germany. Perversely, Kuhn returned to America claiming an even closer relationship with the real *Führer*. Resolutely determined that America remain neutral in the coming conflict, Hitler issued specific orders forbidding Kuhn to use the Reich Chancellor's image or any Nazi iconography in his rallies. When the Bund held its biggest rally ever earlier that year in Madison Square Garden, Kuhn dutifully replaced the image of the *Führer* with a gigantic blowup of George Washington.

The young German intelligence officer was not the only person following Kuhn's activities. Mayor Fiorello Laguardia had assigned his pit bull District Attorney, Thomas E. Dewey, to investigate the nefarious activities of Kuhn, suspected of embezzling thousands of dollars from the Bund's treasury.

But Meinster was not at Cafe Society in pursuit of the *Bundesführer* nor to impress the gauche secretary from the embassy typing pool whom he'd brought with as his cover. He had been hard on the heels of Richard Ives-Curtis, from the moment Berlin had informed him that the British spymaster had arrived in New York. Ives-Curtis was on the *Führer's* list of the first five Englishmen to be hanged once the Nazis conquered Great Britain.

But it was not the sight of the legendary British spymaster that caused a primal rage in Klaus Erik Meinster. Although he had not seen the man since he was seven years old, Meinster recognized him instantly. It was that same British flier, who had hidden in their barn over twenty years earlier. The same *Englischer*, who had seduced his mother, Willi Klarfeld, and forced her to betray the Fatherland. He had dreamt for years of finding this man again. Soon he would exact his revenge on Osmond Radford.

TRIPLE DIGIT HEAT

"If your pussy had air conditioning, I'd live in there."

Flavia opened one eye and saw Ben Siegel standing over the bed beaming down at her. Cockfosters! Not again! The man was positively insatiable. It was a miracle Wendy Barrie wasn't confined to a wheelchair.

"Ben, darling, couldn't I sleep just a wee bit more?"

"It's ten o'clock, babe. Gotta get some sunshine. Wanna play tennis?" Siegel was shaved and dressed. Hopefully, he wasn't feeling amorous again.

"I think I'd like a massage," said Flavia, wondering how on earth she could truncate this desert idyll and get back to Los Angeles. "From a professional."

Jasper certainly owed her one now. Big time, as her new gangster lover was wont to say. She had no desire to learn the sort of mischief her uncle had been involved in that would have aroused the wrath of Ben Siegel. (She refused to even think of him as 'Bugsy', let alone say it to his face. He'd probably knock out her front teeth.) Whatever foolish indiscretion Jas had committed, he was mercifully spared punishment by their familial bond. Flavia had put off paying the piper as long as she could. But Siegel was relentless in his pursuit of her, and her omnipresent danger jones was aroused by the intimate proximity to a man so violent and outside the law. Ironically, Flavia never did get around to asking his assistance in finding Alec. She knew indebtedness to Siegel for *two* Radford males would be sheer folly.

When Siegel proposed a weekend getaway to the desert, Flavia was in no position to refuse. She had always wanted to visit the notorious Dunes Club in remote Cathedral City. Illegal gambling was its main attraction, and the cordially corrupt Palms Springs police turned a blind eye to such goings-on in the middle of nowhere.

Flavia was impressed by the grandeur of their suite and the degree of deference the hotel staff paid to Siegel. One might have taken him for visiting royalty. By the end of her visit, she realized that he was King Ben in his circle. And she appeared to be his consort.

Flavia flopped down on the gigantic bed with her arms spread-eagled, ready to sleep. The two-hour drive from Beverly Hills in Siegel's convertible was made oppressive by the triple digit heat and her escort's insistence that they ride with the top down all the way. "This must be costing you a packet, Ben."

"Nah," said Siegel. "It's on the arm."

"Whose arm? I don't quite—"

"It's a freebie. Al and I go way back." Al Wertheimer, a former member of Detroit's infamous Purple Gang, had fallen in love with the desert a few years earlier, said goodbye to Michigan and opened a resort-casino. "He owes me. And so do you." Siegel shed his clothes and all but tore Flavia's dress from her body.

Eating, gambling, and screwing. Those were the handsome Brooklyn gangster's preferences. The day-to-day order shifted as easily as his moods. Don't wanna screw? We'll eat. Don't wanna eat? We'll shoot crap.

"Massage?" asked Siegel. "Call the front desk. Have 'em send a girl up. Make sure it's a girl. No guy touches that body but Benny. If you were only Jewish, I'd marry you in a flash."

"How would your wife feel about that?" Flavia asked with a smile in her voice.

Siegel was on her in a second, grabbing the back of her chestnut hair in a tight knot. "Never mention my wife. Never! She's a fuckin' saint."

Flavia wasn't sure if any Jewish women had ever been canonized but knew this wasn't the best time to discuss ecclesiastical matters. She put on a bathing suit, robe and slippers and bade the brooding Siegel ta-ta. Then she made a hasty exit downstairs to the hotel spa.

The masseuse was booked for the next half hour, so Flavia set off for the ladies steam room. Wrapped in a sheet, the Pirate Queen gingerly made her way through the billowing clouds of wet steam and sat down on the middle shelf. A tiny hand reached out and touched her on the knee. A familiar voice said: "Small world, ain't it? I mean isn't it?"

"Toby! What on earth are you doing here?"

"Oh, I'm just nuts about steam. My grandmother used to drag me with to Ladies Nights at the Turkish baths in Brooklyn. It's so good for your pores."

"I meant the resort. Rather pricey, isn't it? Or are you on the arm as well?"

"Get you with the gangster talk! No, my boyfriend brought me here. As a birthday present."

"Oh, Tobes! Happy Birthday! I shall get you an appropriate gift as soon as I escape from this den of iniquity. How did your grand pash manage to escape from his missus?"

"Told her he was going to San Francisco to audition for a play."

"He's an actor?" asked Flavia.

"Yeah. He's a friend of your Dad's. Oops! You didn't hear that. I could get in big trouble. And him and me is havin' such a good time." Toby lowered her voice to a whisper. "He wants to have a baby with me."

Flavia said nothing. Her mind was running rampant trying to imagine which of Sir Osmond's pals could have taken up with the little cigarette girl. Ronnie Colman? Bart Marshall? Cedric Hardwicke? Willie Bruce? Not Basil! How could he possibly escape from Ouida to have an assignation?

"Who ya here with?" asked Toby. "Didja kiss and make up with that lawyer? He was awful cute."

"How do you know about Chet?"

"You two came into the Troc one night. Dontcha remember? Listen to me! I forgot all the things you learned me. Oops! Taught me. Problem is my boyfriend loves the way I talk. So, who you with?"

"Just a girlfriend," lied Flavia. "Wendy Barrie."

"Oh, wow! I just saw her in the lobby. Did she break up with that nice Mr. Siegel what gave me such a big tip?"

"What!?!"

"'*Who* gave me such a big tip. *Who*.' Sorry."

"No, no, no. That's not what I mean, Toby. Are you certain that you saw Wendy Barrie?"

"Yeah. And she looked real mad. Maybe you should find out what's wrong."

"Yes. That's an excellent idea, Toby."

Flavia showered, put on her bathing suit and robe, and walked across the lobby. She was standing in front of the elevator when the door opened. Hugh Harcourt emerged. Both stared at each other in shock. Flavia had no idea what her father's oldest friend was thinking, but she had solved the mystery of Toby's secret lover.

"Are you stopping here?" asked Harcourt with fraudulent cheer.

"Yes. Came down with some girlfriends. You?"

"Yes?"

"No. You. Not Hugh."

"Perhaps we should get up a double act together. Tour the halls." Harcourt chuckled hollowly.

"Are you here with Gwen?" Flavia prayed the portly actor would say yes.

"Gwen?" Harcourt said the name as if he'd never heard it before. "Oh, Gwen! No. Poor love's not feeling well. She has migraines, you know. Can't bear to have anyone around her. So, I, uh… got in the car. Started driving. Suddenly I was in the desert. Fortunately, I had my tennis togs and racquet in the boot."

Before Harcourt could continue with his preposterous improvisation, a uniformed bellhop walked across the lobby calling out Flavia's name. When she identified herself, the bellhop said there was a telephone call for her. She stepped into a booth next to the elevator and picked up the receiver.

"I got a problem," said Siegel, his voice bristling with tension on the other end of the line. "Wendy's here."

"I know."

" Didja see her? Did she see you?"

"No."

"This is very embarrassing. You know how I get hard just lookin' at ya. But, uh, you know, Wendy got there first. So, you're gonna have to leave."

"In my bathing costume?"

"What are ya fuckin' nuts? I packed yer bag. Gave it to the bellhop."

"Aren't you the soul of efficiency! And how am I supposed to get back to Los Angeles?"

"Take a cab."

"A taxi from Palm Springs to Los Angeles? Cockfosters!"

"Don't bust a gut. I put a couple of C notes in your bag. That'll more than cover the ride. You can buy a new hat with the change. Thing is, we shouldn't see each other no more. Too complicated. But you're still the greatest lay I ever had. Take care of yourself."

Flavia exited the phone booth feeling a great sense of relief. She had barely escaped with her life. Is there a church nearby, she wondered. Perhaps a prayer was in order. She was en route to retrieve her suitcase from the concierge when she caught sight of Hugh Harcourt and Toby Winslow walking arm in arm towards the coffee shop. The Pirate Queen turned away abruptly and asked the concierge to order her a taxi while she changed in a cabana.

HOPELESSLY BESOTTED

Willi cursed to herself as she burned a second loaf of bread in the oven. What was happening to her concentration? Ever since the postcard had arrived from New York two weeks earlier.

Liebste Mutti:

It has been so long since we gazed upon each other. I am coming to see you soon.

Heil Hitler!

–Klaus Erik

On the reverse side of the card was a glossy color photograph of the Bavarian Alps. She tore up the card into little pieces. *Teufel!* He had always been a devil. She remembered how he had looked at her the first time she met him. The cruel piercing blue eyes, that could change intensity with his moods. Early in her employment Lady Radford had asked about her life in Germany. Hyacinth was not prepared for the housekeeper's modern take on the Brothers Grimm. She absorbed the tale with a mix of horror, shock, compassion, and occasional laughter.

"I was born in a forest," said Willi. "Which is how I came to be so tall. This was my mother's favorite joke for many years. My father was a woodcutter. We lived in Bavaria. It was very pretty. With mountains and goats. My father was not tall. My mother was not tall. My sisters were not tall. My mother said I got the height for all of them because of my coming out first. But they married when they were very young. Because I was too tall for the boys in the village, I grew to be a spinster. My parents were much ashamed and worried what would become of me when they would go to Heaven. When I had twenty years, Herr Meinster came to our cottage to speak with my father. Herr Meinster was a farmer— rich compared to my father. His wife had died. His older sons were in the navy. There was also a late-in-life boy, who badly needed a mother. Could I cook and sew? *Ja!* Did I fear the Lord? *Ja, ja!* Herr Meinster slapped the side of his leg and announced to my father that he would marry me. Romantic, *ja?* Nobody asked me."

"So you did marry him? And became a stepmother."

Willi nodded: "The boy's name was Klaus Erik. He was seven years old and very beautiful. Of the face. White-blond hair and blue eyes. He favored his mother. There was a shrine to her in his bedroom. When first I came to the farm, he hated me. He would not speak *einzige wort*— not one word. When I told Herr Meinster about this, he stared at me as if I was speaking a foreign language."

Willi did not tell Lady Radford about the time Klaus Erik came into the bathroom where she was soaking in the tub. The towel was too far for her to reach and cover her nakedness. Klaus Erik stared at his stepmother with hungry eyes. He tried to nurse from her breasts. Willi violently shoved him away. The boy cursed at her and ran out of the bathroom. That night he put a dead rat in her shoe.

There was no sense in telling her husband. His relationship with his new young wife had swiftly deteriorated into drunkenness, reading the Bible aloud and beating her.

"What was your husband's first name?" asked Hyacinth, wondering how their wonderful housekeeper had managed to escape from such a predicament.

"Gustav. But he insisted that I call him Herr Meinster. Only the first wife had been allowed to call him Gustav. He was very strict. And cruel."

Willi looked out the window to the garden where Hyacinth was playing with little Domini. How wonderful, thought Willi, that a woman older than me could have the strength and courage to have another child. Why is Klaus Erik writing to me? Why is he tormenting me?

The doorbell rang. Willi hurried out of the kitchen to answer it. A handsome, middle-aged man with thick eyebrows and a rakish mustache stood on the front step whistling a Strauss waltz. The man touched the brim of his fedora and nodded agreeably to her.

"*Sind Sie deutsch?*" he asked.

Ever since Klaus Erik's postcard had arrived, Willi was wary of any strangers who spoke German.

"Yes," replied Willi. "But I choose to speak only English in America."

"*Sehr gut.* I, too, will only speak English. Is Sir Osmond home?"

"No."

"Lady Radford, perhaps?"

"Do they know you?"

The stranger laughed and said: "The mother lioness protecting her pride. No pun intended. I'm an old friend of the family. My name is Jurgen Schiller."

"*Entschuldigen Sie mich, bitte!*" Willi's cheeks had turned flaming red. She remembered going to the cinema when she was first married to Herr Meinster. It was a love story and her husband groaned and made stupid jokes all through the movie. But Willi paid no attention to his juvenile behavior. She was transported to a happier, more romantic plane by the handsome young man up on the screen. He was like the prince in a fairy story. His name was Jurgen Schiller. Years later the same prince stood on her doorstep and no less handsome. "Forgive me, Herr Schiller. It has been many years since I saw *Röslein auf der Heiden.* You did not have a mustache then. Please, please, come in."

Julia descended languidly down the front staircase just as Willi led the attractive stranger into the library. The housekeeper rushed away excitedly to inform Lady Radford of the visitor's arrival.

It was almost two months since little Domini's arrival. Julia remained in Ojai for another week after the delivery. Then she traveled by train to Los Angeles, where she went through the charade of 'returning from New York' following her sojourn in England. Only Flavia thought that this had been her baby sister's real itinerary. During the drive to Best of Times, Julia gave another brilliant performance begging her mother's forgiveness for not being present at the birth. Flavia patted her sister's hand to let her know everyone understood.

Julia would lie in her bed at night, listening to her baby crying in the nursery. No! She would listen to her baby *sister* crying in the nursery. It was Mummy's baby now. She only prayed it wouldn't look anything like Lansing. Lansing! She still missed him desperately. On more than one occasion, she had attempted to phone him in New Jersey but hung up when the operator said the line was ringing. Julia was nineteen years old and wondered if she would remain this miserable for the rest of her life. Perhaps the man in the library might prove interesting. If only for an hour.

"May I help you?" asked Julia, trying her best to impersonate Hyacinth as she floated into the library,

"How could you help any more than you have done already? To take such a dull, uneventful morning and transform it into the Eighth Day of Creation is a minor miracle. Are you Flavia or Julia?"

"Julia. It's actually Ethne Julia. Mummy named us for the heroines of her favorite books. But no one could pronounce Ethne, so I've always been Julia."

"Well, Miss Julia, you represent the most magnificent blend of both your parents. Oh-ho! You inherited Ozzie's eyebrows. Most captivating on a woman."

"Who are you?" Julia was quite taken with the mysterious stranger and his enchanting Austrian accent.

"Jurgen Schiller."

Julia pointed her index finger at him and proudly pronounced: "Rupert of Hentzau!" Schiller looked around to see if anyone was behind him. "No!" She dashed over to the wall, removed a framed photograph from the wall of two young men engaged in a deadly sword fight and showed it to the Austrian. "That *is* you, isn't it? With Daddy. I grew up with that photo emblazoned in my memory. Daddy said you were a wonderful actor. Why did you give it up?"

"Because there was something more important in life than ego and curtain calls. A bloodthirsty beast is wandering through Europe bringing the civilized world to its knees. If it is not stopped, it will devour the world."

"Do you mean Hitler?" Julia shared an ignorance of world affairs on a par with her sister. "Are things that unpleasant in Europe?"

"Dear child, do you not read the newspapers?"

"Not very much. Unless my picture's in them. Does that sound utterly dreadful?"

"Not if one lives in Fairyland. But where do you think you'll perform when the Nazis conquer England?"

"That can't possibly happen."

"Oh, it would have quite easily if Edward had remained on the throne. The newly made Duke of Windsor is very fond of the *Führer* and has an intense dislike of the Jews. He is a born Nazi. The *Führer* has made it clear that he will restore the tragic lover to the throne. Look what has happened so far. Austria has fallen. Czechoslovakia. The Nazi Party rules Danzig in the Polish Corridor. They are begging the *Führer* to liberate them. If Danzig falls, Hitler will take all of Poland next. He will march further west and conquer France without a struggle. And only the Channel will stand between him and England. His new partner, the Emperor of Japan, has already conquered much of China. Only two oceans protect the United States from invasion. But the omnipotent Japanese and German navies will solve that problem. Why is it that people in this country have chosen to bury their heads in the sand? While I run around like Chicken Little telling people the sky is falling to no avail."

"You've certainly made a convert of me," said a starry-eyed Julia, who was hopelessly besotted with Jurgen Schiller.

IGNORANCE IS BLISS

Flavia and Julia had gone to the beach early to avoid the Saturday traffic and taken the Packard without telling their mother. Sir Osmond and Charleston had taken the Rolls-Royce and gone shopping for a new automobile to replace the disgraced MG. This left Lady Radford with neither vehicle nor chauffeur to drive her to her appointment. She was about to ring for a taxi when she remembered that Ito had spent the night in the pool house.

The poor Japanese boy had been a complete wreck since his father's celebrated visit five months earlier. The Admiral had literally beaten his son into what he thought was submission. But his father's physical brutality had only increased Ito's resolve. He would not spy for Japan, nor would he betray the Radfords. He could maintain this resolve for several weeks until a letter would arrive from his father demanding detailed reports of Ito's intelligence gathering. How many naval installations had he visited? How many gun emplacements had the Americans erected along the Pacific coast? What ports had the best and worst security? Ito would curl up in a ball on the floor for the next two days clutching his head between his hands to vainly attempt drowning out the sound of the detonator ticking away loudly inside it.

The letter he received from the Admiral on the previous day was the worst yet. Hashimuro accused his son of disloyalty not only to the Emperor but to the memory of his mother. Ito seriously considered taking his own life. Not by *seppuku*, the Japanese ritual of suicide by disembowelment, but by driving his beloved Model-T off a cliff. Perhaps the ocean would eventually carry the vehicle back to Japan with his remains. No! Ito refused to torture himself like this anymore. He would go and visit *Izanami*. She would know what to do.

After several hours of compassionate coaxing on Hyacinth's part, Ito finally verbalized what was tearing him apart. The shame of divided loyalty was too much to endure. Just before midnight and after several glasses of brandy, the Admiral's son poured his heart out to his beloved Lady Radford. He concluded with a plaintive wail: "How can I write the dishonorable reports that my father demands?"

"Must they be true?" asked Hyacinth, cutting through to the core of the problem.

"What do you mean?"

"Couldn't you fabricate them? Make up a whole series of reports that seem authentic but have no military value whatsoever."

"Would he believe me?"

"Try writing one and see what happens. Use a great many serial numbers. SJ4734Z. Verisimilitude is essential."

The idea caused Ito to giggle at first, then the volume of his laughter increased. To play such a prank on his ferocious father struck him as the funniest thing in the world. When he finally decided to take his leave, it was obvious to Hyacinth that the Admiral's inebriated son was in no condition to drive back to Little Tokyo. She suggested he sleep on a cot in the pool house. The next morning, Lady Radford roused her protégé from a deep sleep and asked him to drive her to Martin Kohlinger's house just north of the Sunset Strip. They rode together in silence for several minutes until Ito finally asked:

"How would Barbara Stanwyck feel if she knew what my father was really like?"

"Why would she need to know?"

Ito grunted in a manner much like the Admiral often did and resumed his silence as he steered the Model-T east on Sunset towards Doheny. When he finally brought the ancient vehicle to a stop across the street from the house on Cory Avenue, Hyacinth began collecting her bolts of fabric from the back seat. She was about to cross the street when her eye was caught by a familiar figure moving swiftly along the side of the house.

"Good morning, Chet!"

Lowenthal looked up and saw Hyacinth making her way towards him. He hurried across the manicured lawn to intercept her before she got to the front door.

"You don't want to go in there, Lady Radford."

"But I have an appointment with Mr. Kohlinger's fiancée. She wants the house redone. Feels it lacks the feminine touch."

Lowenthal gently took hold of his neighbor's arm and steered her back down the walkway. "Where is your car?"

"Ito drove me." She nodded towards the Model-T across the street.

"What's he doing?"

"Waiting for me. He volunteered to be my chauffeur."

Lowenthal walked over to the Model-T and leaned on the door. "Hello, Ito. Lady Radford won't require your services any further today. I'll take her home."

Ito nodded, waved goodbye to a befuddled Hyacinth, and headed down the hill towards Sunset.

"I don't understand," said Lady Radford. "Why can't I go inside?" Lowenthal looked around to see if anyone was watching them. An Oldsmobile sped by but didn't stop. The lawyer took the bolts of fabric from Lady Radford and walked her briskly toward his Lincoln Zephyr.

They drove for two blocks in silence as Hyacinth studied Lowenthal's intense face. Finally, she asked: "Has something happened?"

"You'll read about it soon enough."

"I'd like to know now."

"Martin Kohlinger and his fiancée are dead."

"Violet?"

"You knew her?"

"She was a new client," said Hyacinth. "Looked quite different from when we first met."

"Where was that?"

"*The Dawn Patrol* premiere. She was Alec's date that evening. A bit flashy and provincial. Clearly, she'd had some tutoring in the interim. Affected a grand aura. One hardly recognized her. Moving up in the world can do that, I suppose. How did they die?"

"Looks like they were murdered."

"What were you doing there?" asked Hyacinth.

"I was developing a screenplay with Marty. Saturday's my day off. We were supposed to work together on the script. The front door was unlocked."

"Have you notified the police?"

"Not yet. I was on my way to do so when I saw you."

"Why didn't you use the telephone in the house?"

"It's a crime scene," said Lowenthal. "I didn't want to disturb it."

"And you shooed me away because…?"

"It's potentially a juicy scandal, Lady Radford. Your presence— however innocent— could prove embarrassing to you and your husband. And Flavia."

"Oh, Chet! I'm so sorry about you and Flavia. Sir Osmond and I both hoped…. We're very fond of you. Perhaps you two will work it out."

Lowenthal greatly doubted the possibility of a reconciliation. If the rumors were true about Flavia and Bugsy Siegel cavorting in Palm Springs, she had already moved on. He prayed that the Pirate Queen wouldn't come to a violent end due to the proximity of her trigger-happy suitor. Even if it wasn't true that she had taken up with Siegel, there would always be the problem of Lowenthal's mysterious disappearances. The lawyer couldn't tell her about his double life smuggling Jewish refugees across the border into California.

* * *

Lady Radford returned to Best of Times, trying to lose herself in work. But her mind continually returned to Lowenthal's lame excuse about not telephoning the police. Unquestionably, he knew something about the murders— she didn't believe for a moment that he'd actually committed them— that he didn't want to reflect on himself. Why would someone want to murder poor Martin? Or Violet?

That afternoon the front door burst open. Julia and Flavia dashed into the house shrieking at the top of their lungs. Willi leaned over the upstairs railing and in a loud whisper said: "The baby is sleeping."

"Have you heard the news?" asked Julia breathlessly. "Martin Kohlinger has been murdered."

"We heard it on the radio at the beach," said Flavia, lighting up a Lucky Strike while nervously pacing about the sitting room. "One couldn't just lie there in the sun after that. I knew them both."

"Not well," said Hyacinth, a little too emphatically.

"What do you mean, Mummy?" Flavia wondered if her mother knew about her dalliances with Violet. Or the rumors she'd recently heard about Eddie Goulding's home movies featuring the girl with the half-moon scar and her missing brother.

"There is a probability that the police will be making inquiries. We needn't say more than is necessary."

Charleston steered the Rolls-Royce up onto the driveway an hour later followed by Sir Osmond behind the wheel of a new green, two-seater Aston-Martin Bertelli. The actor-knight was very proud of the bargain price he had paid for the British import. He stressed the word 'British' to convey to the women of the house that no possible comment or use of the word 'impractical' would be allowed to sully the air.

No one paid the slightest attention to Radford's new automobile. All anyone could talk about was the murder. Hyacinth asked her husband to come upstairs and look at the baby. Instead of the nursery, she steered him into their bedroom and shut the door.

"There is a possibility that the police may come here," said Hyacinth.

 "What makes you think that?"

"Martin Kohlinger was my client. Alec knew Violet Purdy. You met her, as well."

"Where? When?"

"*The Dawn Patrol*. She was Alec's date that evening."

"Oh, yes. The pretty blonde. I rather liked her."

"And I was at Martin's house this morning."

"What!?!"

"He had hired me to redecorate the house for his new bride. Chet was there and whisked me away immediately. Didn't want us involved in the scandal."

"Chet…?" Radford gestured vaguely across the street. "That was very kind of him. What was he doing there?"

"Not quite sure. But I may have made a mistake in leaving the scene of the crime. What if one of the neighbors saw me? Or described Ito's funny old car."

"What was Ito doing there?"

"He gave me a lift. All the vehicles had disappeared by the time of my appoint— "

"That boy came all the way from Little Tokyo to drive you down to Sunset? Hell's bells!"

"Nooo! Ito was sleeping in the pool house."

Radford lifted his arms in surrender and walked towards the bathroom. "I don't want to hear another word. Ignorance is bliss."

JOAN CRAWFORD STAG MOVIE

Lieutenant Patrick Lafleur, chief of detectives for the Beverly Hills Police Department, had been known as "Frenchie" since he was in grade school. As his family had lived in America since 1820, the nickname was more than a little annoying. Lafleur could neither read nor write French and had no interest in learning. His mother's people were Irish, and they were the ones, with whom the red-haired, strapping, 40-year-old police lieutenant identified. It was in that grand tradition of Celtic scrappers that he had defended his non-existent French heritage when people made fun of his name and his manhood. The price for that false pride was several broken noses that ruined his once admirable profile.

By four o'clock in the afternoon, Lafleur was extremely annoyed. The police lieutenant disliked outside interference with his investigations. Particularly in high-profile cases involving Hollywood types.

The station had received an anonymous phone call at eleven o'clock that morning reporting foul play at a house on Cory Avenue. The address was at a trisection of various jurisdictions: Beverly Hills, Los Angeles, and the Sheriff's department. When Lafleur arrived at the bungalow, it was clear that Beverly Hills and Los Angeles had lost seniority over the case.

"You're too late, Frenchie," said Lloyd Pennyman, his opposite number with the LAPD. Pennyman looked more like a basset hound than any other human on the planet had a right to.

"Too late for what?"

"Double homicide."

"Big names?" Lafleur figured not considering the size of the house and its proximity to the Strip.

"Kraut director out at Warners. Strictly B-movies."

"And the other one?"

"His fiancée. American. Late 20s. Something familiar looking about her," said Pennyman.

"Maybe she's an actress, Lloyd. Got a name?"

"Violet Purdy." Lafleur turned pale upon hearing the name. "Did you know her, Frenchie?"

"Can't be the same one." Lafleur felt he'd been kicked in the chest by one of Bing Crosby's horses. "Not engaged to this guy. Lemme see."

"Uh-uh. FBI's in there. They're calling the shots."

"Bullshit! This happened on my piece of the map."

"They'll only throw you out," warned Pennyman.

"Who's the G-Man in charge?"

"Floyd Hightower."

"The drunken Indian?" A smile broke out on Lafleur's face. "Word is he used to get loaded at FBI bachelor parties where they'd show confiscated stag reels. Supposedly Hightower would get so drunk and so excited, he'd jack off."

"That's not a story I suggest you repeating again," said Pennyman. "And not in front of Special Agent Hightower. Or you'll end up pounding a beat."

"There is no beat in Beverly Hills, Lloyd. Everybody drives. Wish me luck!" Lafleur knocked at the bedroom door and walked in.

"What do you want?" Hightower asked in his Oklahoma growl. "Get outta here."

Lafleur had reached the bed and was staring down at the two bodies. Kohlinger's eyes were popping out of their sockets. Probably the result of the garrote around his neck. His hillock of a stomach was matted with blood. A swastika had been carved on the dead Austrian's large belly. Violet had been dispatched in a less grotesque manner. It had been a few years since Lafleur had last seen her, but -no question about it- she was the Violet Purdy he'd arrested. And with whom he subsequently embarked on a torrid affair. Lafleur spun around and assumed another persona.

"Agent Hightower? This is an honor, sir. Your reputation has preceded you in the annals of— "

"What the hell's your name?" growled Hightower.

"Lieutenant Patrick Lafleur. Beverly Hills Police Department."

"Yeah. Well nice meetin' you, Lafleur. Now, I gotta go back to work."

"Oh! Of course, excuse me." Lafleur walked over to the door, then turned around and said conspiratorially: "I've got the Joan Crawford stag movie."

"What?" Hightower was certain he hadn't heard right.

"From before she was famous. Louis B. Mayer's been dishing out a king's ransom for years to suppress any copies. She apparently gives great head."

"Why are you telling me this?" Hightower's growl had turned into a rumble.

"You're a stag movie guy from way back. Thought you might like to see my collection." Lafleur leaned in close to Hightower and spoke in a stage whisper: "Don't tell anybody but I jack off watching them."

"What do you want?" asked Hightower in a totally neutral voice.

"Partnership. Freedom to pursue this case in tandem. Or as separate plates twirling round on sticks. Who breaks first?"

"I got to think about this. Call you later."

When the phone rang on Lafleur's desk a few minutes after four, he picked up the receiver with his fingers crossed.

"You're on it." Hightower obviously didn't waste time with greetings or social niceties.

"Great," answered Lafleur. "I'll check in with you from time to time and see how you're progressing."

"Got a little rider here, Lafleur. You cannot discuss with the press or anyone what Kohlinger looked like when we found him. Especially his stomach."

"You mean the swastika?"

"Don't even say it!" Hightower was issuing an order. "This comes straight from Washington. The big guy himself. This country is neutral. We have no interest in European quarrels. And we're not here to rescue Jews. They can take care of themselves. They got enough money."

"That mean you never had a *bar-mitzvah*?" asked Lafleur. "Cause with that nose, you could easily be— "

"Don't piss me off!" Hightower growled in his best forty-miles-of-bad-road voice. "I got a low threshold."

"Sure thing. When would you like to have a Joan Crawford night? I've got a really nice projector. Bell & Howell."

BLIND MUSKETEERS

Eunice was having her own Quiet Time at home in the garden of her cottage on Doheny Drive. She needed to erase everything from her mind except the problem at hand. What to do with the valuable knowledge she had acquired that morning? It had only been a fleeting glance from behind the wheel of her Oldsmobile, but Eunice had seen her sister-in-law led away from a house on Cory Avenue by a handsome young man. That same house was all over the front pages of the morning papers.

DIRECTOR AND FIANCEE FOUND MURDERED

There was no mention of Hyacinth in any of the newspapers or the radio reports. Eunice hated the word blackmail and all it represented. What she had in mind was 'redistribution of wealth'. One was merely taking money from people who had far too much and were loath to share it. Particularly one's relatives, even if they were merely in-laws. Knowledge is power, thought Eunice. Power always gets the best seats and all the money.

She would need help affecting this redistribution. Bijou would know what to do. It was Bijou Destino, who had introduced her to Moral Rearmament and the teachings of Dr. Buchman. Bijou was a statuesque woman with an impossible Italian dialect. Eunice suspected that Bijou might have been on the game back in Naples before settling in America. Considering Long Beach was a port city, Bijou might still be covering the waterfront.

"Did I waken you?" asked Eunice, staring once again at the front page of the morning newspaper, while she held the telephone receiver to her mouth.

"Are you kidding? I got two men in my bed. Why you don't laugh, Units?" Bijou's accent was as thick as a block of Pecorino. No matter how hard she tried, she always called her red-haired English friend 'Units'.

"I have a problem."

"*Si*. Your husband is a crook."

"No, no. This has nothing to do with Jasper." Eunice related what she had seen on Cory Avenue while driving home the previous morning.

"What you want?" asked Bijou. "A new car? Diamond ring?"

"Don't joke, Bijou."

"Is not a joke, Units. They got money, you relatives. They can pay and you can go wild. Get yourself a boyfriend, maybe. Treat you better than that *sadico* you married."

"I can't blackmail them."

"Of course not. I do that and we split fifty-fifty."

"How would you go about…?"

"That's no you business, Units. Just dream about Capri. And a young boy. You deserve it."

"Isn't this contrary to what Dr. Buchman preaches?" A part of Eunice had hoped that Bijou would dissuade her from this course of action. She never dreamt the feisty Italian would take over the scheme.

"We got three of the fives C's," said Bijou. "Confidence, Conviction and Continuance. Hey, Units! Maybe we make enough money, we start our own religion. *Ciao*!" Bijou replaced the receiver on the telephone. She debated how much of this conversation she should include in her weekly report to OVRA, Mussolini's secret police in Rome.

* * *

Lafleur heard dogs barking loudly on the other side of the door. He checked the safety on his gun and prayed he wouldn't have to use it. The lieutenant had been viciously attacked by a dog when he was a kid in Glendale. Canines had been a problem for him ever since. Unless they were Chihuahuas or Yorkies. The door was opened by a beautiful chestnut-haired woman in the shortest shorts Lafleur had ever seen. As if they'd run out of material and said to hell with it. She also had an incredible pair of legs. Not to mention arms strong enough to grab the collars of those Great Danes and keep them from lunging at his throat.

"Shall I lock them up?" asked Flavia.

"Before I do." Lafleur flashed his police badge. "Lt. Patrick Lafleur."

"Bonjour, Monsieur Lafleur. C'est un grand plaisir de faire votre connaissance."

"I don't speak French. Mostly Irish on my mother's side."

"Quel dommage! Are you with the Los Angeles constabulary? Or Beverly Hills?"

"Does it make a difference?"

"Oh, indeed, Lieutenant. Beverly Hills police are so well bred. You look frightfully uncomfortable. Why don't I lock the boys up in the laundry room?" Lafleur watched her walk away in those maddening short shorts and exhaled for the longest time. This was going to be a difficult interview.

At that moment, Sir Osmond emerged from the cellar and stared with curiosity at Lafleur standing in the hallway.

"Does anyone know you're here?" asked Radford.

"The young woman. She's locking up the dogs."

"Dark hair or blond?"

"Dark."

"Has she been gone long? Are you some sort of salesman?" Lafleur raised his police badge. "Ah! One rather expected you might call. Please, come into the library. Would you like some coffee? Willi!"

Five minutes later Radford and Lafleur were seated across from each other in wing-backed chairs sipping their coffee.

"If you've come to ask me about Martin Kohlinger," said Radford, "I didn't know him all that well. Only met him twice. At a fund-raiser and in this house for a party."

"Would the fund-raiser have been the Hollywood Anti-Nazi Dinner at the Ambassador? Back in October."

"Yes, I believe it was."

"What about Violet Purdy?"

"Poor girl. Met her briefly at a film premiere. She was my son's date."

"They were quite close," said Lafleur.

"Were they?"

Flavia popped into the library, flashing her most devastating smile at Lafleur. "I wondered where you disappeared to. Has Daddy been entertaining you?"

"How well did you know Violet Purdy?"

"Barely."

"Not what the powder room attendant at the Trocadero told me." Lafleur removed a small notepad and read from it. "According to Esther Jefferson, you, Miss Purdy, and a Consuela Gonzalez were like 'the three blind mice'. I think she meant musketeers."

"Are there blind musketeers?" asked Flavia, who was keenly interested in the strapping Lafleur.

The police detective turned to Radford: "Would you mind giving me a moment alone with your daughter?"

"There are two attorneys living across the street," said the actor-knight. "Should I invite them over?"

"Only if they want a great cup of coffee. Don't worry. Sir Osmond. I'm not here to arrest anyone."

"Would you like a refill?" asked Radford, as he was about to leave.

"Let me get back to you on that." Sir Osmond left the library. Lafleur turned his attention back to Flavia. "You knew Violet was a hooker, right? Didn't really want to talk about it in front of your father."

"It's an honorable profession. Which Vi had abandoned some months ago."

"I'm not here to judge her."

"How refreshing! A man with an open mind."

"Where's your brother?" asked Lafleur.

"Nobody knows."

"Think he might have killed her?"

"Don't be rude!"

Lafleur burst out laughing: "Lady, that's a first. Accused of bad manners for doing my job. Do you know about the movie they did together?"

"What studio?"

"You're lovely to look at, Miss Radford. Under a totally different set of circumstances, I'd invite you to lunch down in Laguna. But don't dick me around. Okay? They appeared in one of Edmund Goulding's private 'art films' which has been floating around town for some time."

"Pornographic? Have you seen it?"

Lafleur nodded. "It's pretty raw."

"Please don't tell my parents about this," pleaded Flavia. "They'd be shattered."

"Did you socialize with Violet other than encounters at nightclubs?"

"Not really," replied Flavia, unable to meet the lieutenant's gaze. "Other than the *Dawn Patrol* premiere. I had no idea they knew each other till then."

Lafleur knew she was lying. He'd already sorted through Violet's private papers and discovered the prostitute's diary. Repeated references to a female lover she called Limey. Lafleur had known from his time with her that Violet swung both ways. The thought of it turned him on. Now that he realized Flavia was the mysterious Limey, he knew he was in serious trouble.

As if reading Lafleur's mind, Flavia asked: "When would you like to go to Laguna?"

PERFECT FORM

Hugh Harcourt was astonishing himself that Sunday morning on the cricket pitch. His energy seemed boundless, and he'd brought in an amazing number of runs. All because of Toby. He truly loved the little cigarette girl and had resolved that morning to finally ask Gwen for a divorce. He passed Radford clutching his bat and running in the opposite direction. Harcourt put the tip of his bat in the crease and resolved to stay put. In less than a second, however, he decided to be audacious and go for one more run. Spectators on either side of the pitch applauded his derring-do enthusiastically. A look of boyish exhilaration swept across Harcourt's florid face. How he did love applause!

"What the hell!" said an astonished Harcourt as his legs suddenly stopped moving.

"Come on, Hughie!" Radford called out to his friend as he passed him. "Don't want to be dismissed."

Harcourt saw Radford pass him by before his legs turned to rubber and he collapsed to the ground. As Harcourt fell, he barely whispered: "Toby".

Cricketers on both teams swarmed towards his fallen body *en masse*.

"Stand back!" ordered Aubrey breaking through the throng. "Let the man breathe." The old Carthusian discovered Radford cross-legged on the grass, cradling Harcourt's head in his lap. "Shall I telephone for an ambulance, Ozzie?"

"Too late," said Radford, fighting back tears. "He's gone."

Basil Rathbone squeezed his way in next and asked: "Do we count the last run?"

"Not sure," replied Aubrey. "No precedent."

"Who do we call first?" asked Niven.

"Explain yourself, boy."

Niven blushed and remained speechless. He had assumed the veteran actor knew about Harcourt's mistress. Niven had no desire to shatter Aubrey's image of his favorite batsman.

"Well, speak up, boy!"

It was Radford who finally broke the silence while continuing to cradle Harcourt's head in his lap: "For all intents and purposes, Hughie had two wives. One was a former actress, whom we all know. The other was a little cigarette girl, to whom he had given his heart. Why did I ever think he'd changed? When we were in Australia, Hughie would seduce girls using my name. God knows how many children he left behind Down Under! Who's going to phone the women?"

Aubrey cleared his throat and made a Solomonic decision: "Ozzie, as you were Harcourt's oldest friend, it's best you deal with the widow. Niven, being of the younger generation, the… er, cigarette girl is your responsibility. Hugh was Church of England, wasn't he?"

Radford nodded. "Gwen sings in the choir at St. Mary of the Angels. In Los Feliz."

"Know it well," said Aubrey approvingly. "Wonderful acoustics. I shall make arrangements forthwith."

* * *

Hugh Harcourt died on a Sunday. His funeral was held four days later, the last day of August. The church was packed with the cricket team and other members of the Raj. Hyacinth and Sir Osmond sat in the front row comforting a stoic Gwen clad in black and wearing a veil. Vic Pomfrett and his drunken wife Sybil sat on the other side of the grieving widow.

Aubrey stood at the pulpit addressing the congregation: "The British colony is devastated by this, the tragic and unscheduled demise of one of its members."

Flynn turned to Niven seated five rows behind him and whispered an incredulous: "Unscheduled? Can one really make an appointment to die?"

Niven tried to suppress his laughter behind a cough, but failed miserably and began giggling uncontrollably. Flynn clapped a hand over his friend's mouth. He then did a double take when he saw a delicious bit of crumpet seated alone and weeping in the back row.

"Who's that?" asked the aroused Tasmanian Devil.

"Toby Winslow. Harcourt's mistress."

"Poor kid needs comforting," said Flynn. "Will you be alright on your own, sport?"

Niven nodded enthusiastically and began giggling again.

Flynn moved purposefully up the aisle. He was almost at the back row when he saw a familiar looking man slide into the pew next to the sobbing Toby. It was that bloody gangster from the Radfords' party. Flynn did an abrupt turn and headed back down the aisle.

Chester Lowenthal had arrived late and was right behind Flynn looking for somewhere to sit. There was a seat in the third row if the woman seated there could manage to slide over a bit.

"Excuse me," whispered Lowenthal. The woman looked up at him with a stern look.

"Are you following me?" asked Flavia

"Not at all," replied an embarrassed Lowenthal.

Flavia smiled: "Cockfosters! Still don't know when I'm pulling your leg." She patted the spot next to her. Lowenthal sat down. Flavia took the lawyer's hand and squeezed it.

* * *

Lafleur sat in an unmarked police car across the street from the church trying to figure out the complicated relationship between the mourners and his two victims. Violet Purdy had been the occasional lover of Flavia Radford and sex partner— at least on screen— of Alec Radford. Alec had also been the lover of Leni Riefenstahl, who was reputed to be Adolf Hitler's mistress. According to Hightower, Alec also set off the explosion at Warner Brothers and had been smuggled onto the lot by the late Martin Kohlinger, who had been engaged to Violet Purdy. One circle.

Then there was Toby Winslow, who had been escorted to the church by Bugsy Siegel. Siegel's right-hand man, Mickey Cohen, had recently abducted a black drug dealer named Temple Brown (whose brother Charleston was the chauffeur for Sir Osmond Radford) and his partner, Jasper Radford (who was Sir Osmond's brother). Esther Jefferson, who had worked at the Trocadero with Toby Winslow, confided to Lafleur that the Brooklyn-born cigarette girl had been carrying on with the deceased Hugh Harcourt, who was the best friend of Osmond Radford. Another circle.

And there was the weekend at the Dunes Club where Harcourt and Toby had registered under fake names. Bugsy Siegel had also been there briefly with— hold on to your hats— Flavia Radford. A smaller circle.

Who were the suspects, wondered Lafleur? Best bet was Alec Radford, a Nazi sympathizer, whose (maybe) girlfriend had been stolen away by Kohlinger. That could explain the swastika carved on the dead director's stomach, which Hightower had forbidden him to discuss. Only problem was Alec Radford had fled to Mexico with no proof that he had ever returned.

What about Flavia? Lafleur didn't want to go there. Totally unprofessional to have romantic thoughts about a potential suspect. What motive would Flavia have had for killing Violet? Jealousy? She didn't seem the type. And why carve a swastika on Kohlinger's stomach?

The homicide detective's reverie was interrupted by the mourners filing out of the church: Edmund Goulding, who had shot the stag movie Violet had performed in. Could he be the murderer? Maybe Violet had been black-mailing him; Bugsy Siegel with his arm wrapped around a sobbing Toby Winslow. Lafleur's heart began to race. Flavia stepped out of the church into the sunlight, more beautiful than ever. Who was the guy whose arm she was clutching? Lafleur knew him from the courthouse. Divorce lawyer. What was his name? Lowenberg? No, Lowenthal. Lafleur's old LAPD boss, Frank Doherty, worked as an investigator for him. He'd call Doherty when he got back to Beverly Hills and take him for a drink.

*   *   *

Following the internment at Forest Lawn, Gwen invited a select few to her house on Locksley Place for drinks. Hyacinth had gone ahead with the Widow Harcourt to help prepare for the mourners' arrival. She had also pressed Willi and Boggs into service. Aubrey asked Radford if he might ride along with him to the Harcourts.

"Terrible, terrible tragedy," said Aubrey, driving west along Franklin Avenue. "Could be the ruination of the Cricket Club. Hard to replace a bowler like Harcourt."

"Perhaps this isn't the best time to discuss it, Aubrey. We just laid the man in the ground."

"Yes, yes, yes. Not insensitive, you know. But life does go on. One must look to the future. Damned inconsiderate of Harcourt to leave us like that." Aubrey stopped speaking abruptly and snapped his head round like an Irish wolfhound on the scent. "What the devil was that? Mr. Brown, did you hear a gunshot?"

"No, General." Charleston always referred to Aubrey as 'the General' because of the many military roles he'd played in the movies. The veteran actor never complained about the appellation. "We got ourselves a flat tire." The chauffeur pulled the Rolls-Royce over to the side of the curb and opened the trunk.

"Need any help?" asked Radford. He climbed out of the back seat with Aubrey following him a beat later.

"No, sir. Everything's under control." Charleston removed the jack and was wrestling with the spare tire when he noticed a mangy Indian rubber ball wedged inside it. He grabbed hold of the ball and hurled it down the street.

Aubrey's mouth dropped open as if he'd just witnessed a miracle. "Did you see that, Ozzie?"

"See what, old boy?"

"What Mr. Jones just did."

"He removed the spare from the boot."

"No, no, no, Ozzie. Didn't you see his arm? The man has perfect form. He's a born bowler. Do you realize what this means? We have nothing to fear about our future. Mr. Brown! Might I have a word with you?"

* * *

Half an hour later, the mourners were exchanging their favorite Hugh Harcourt anecdotes. Except for Victor Pomfrett, who was attempting to spread the gospel of non-intervention.

"Why doesn't Churchill simply admit to being a warmonger and be done with it?" asked Pomfrett. "Clear to anyone the man's in cahoots with all the armaments dealers— Jews every one of them. War! What did it get us last time except for a stronger Germany twenty years later?"

Boggs thrust a plate of puffed pastries into Pomfrett's face. The weasel-faced actor shook his head and took another sip of whisky.

"Yes, yes, yes," said Aubrey. "But tell me, Pomfrett. Don't you think this chap Hitler's a bit tetched in the head?"

"Why?" asked Pomfrett. "Because he's a vegetarian. Or because he doesn't play cricket?"

Pomfrett laughed aloud at what he thought was a display of wit. Aubrey trumpeted a harrumph and went off to join the Radfords, who were standing together by the fireplace chatting with Gwen.

"Strange fellow, that Pomfrett," said Aubrey. "Don't believe he went to a public school. How are you holding up, Gwen? Terrible loss."

"It comes and goes in waves," replied Gwen. "I wake in the morning thinking Hugh's slipped out of bed to make me a cup of tea. But that's never going to happen again." She turned away from Aubrey and asked Hyacinth: "Would you mind awfully if I stole your husband for a minute?"

"As long as you need him," said Hyacinth.

Radford followed Gwen through the French doors and outside to the garden. He was not prepared for the question she asked him.

"Did you know about the cigarette girl?" asked Gwen.

"Cigarette girl?" Radford's face was a blank slate.

"You're such a great actor, Osmond. Foolish of me to even ask you."

"What are your plans, Gwen?"

"Plans? Plans? Who had plans? I always thought I'd grow old with the silly bugger and the char lady would find us dead one morning holding hands in front of the fireplace. I'll tell you one thing, Ozzie. I don't want to go back to England. I can't. There's nothing there for me."

"Don't try to make any decisions now, Gwen."

"But what will I do if I stay here? Hugh never wanted me to work. I was a bloody good actress once. Would it be difficult to start again? Out here?"

"On stage?" asked Radford.

"Don't be daft! There's no theatre in Los Angeles. But there's plenty of work for all the other English girls in films. Don't look at me like that, Ozzie. Think I'm too old?"

"Not at all."

"Liar. Sweet, sweet liar." Gwen grabbed hold of Radford's arm and squeezed it. "I'm scared to death, Ozzie. What am I going to do? Hugh took care of everything. I can't even drive a motorcar." She squeezed the actor-knight's arm tighter. "Mmm. Quite fit, aren't you? Ever wonder what might have happened if you hadn't stood me up that night in Manchester?"

Radford stepped back from her grasp and asked: "How are your finances?"

"No idea. That was Hugh's domain, as well. It was all that bloody bastard's domain."

Hyacinth stepped into the garden and called out to her husband. "Sorry to interrupt, but your brother is here."

"Jasper?" Radford had never been quite so happy to hear his scapegrace brother's name. He kissed Gwen quickly on the cheek, followed Hyacinth into the house and out the front door.

Jasper was waiting in the walkway with a cigarette dangling from his lips. "Ozzie! A lifesaver, as always. Can you spare a fiver?" The older Radford pointed to a taxi waiting in the middle of the street. "Put on the wrong trousers. Haven't got a *sou*."

"What happened to the Oldsmobile?"

"The wretched *gendarmerie* has taken away my driver's license. DUI, they call it. Bloody nonsense!"

"I'll take care of the taxi," sighed Radford. "You take care of Gwen."

"Ah, yes!" Jasper's eyes lit up. "The grieving widow."

LET SLIP THE DOGS OF WAR

T he morning air was brisk, and the shire engulfed in fog. The two women were glad to be bundled up in tweeds. Their shotguns were aimed towards the ground as they stepped gingerly to avoid tripping on any exposed roots. A man with a deerstalker cap walked towards them with a no-nonsense look on his face.

"Please, try and keep up. Your lagging behind reflects badly on the aspirations of other women."

"Sorry, Jasper," said Hyacinth. "It's jolly difficult seeing through the fog."

"All the more reason to stay close," said her brother-in-law, who pinched her cheek and promptly disappeared into the mist.

"Honeychile, you have been mashed" said Florabelle, in a very posh, British accent tone she had mysteriously acquired. "That odious creature was a masher."

"Nonsense," said Hyacinth. "He's my husband's older brother."

"They are the worst kind. I had occasion to take a skillet to my brother-in-law. He wore a patch over his eye for a month."

"Florabelle, you are ferocious."

"One has to be when hunting big game."

"Pheasant can hardly be classified as big game."

"Keep your voice down, honeychile." Florabelle's voice became a deadly whisper. "Check your gun."

"What is it?"

"Don't move," said Florabelle.

"You're frightening me."

"Can't you hear it?"

Hyacinth saw it before she heard it. Red eyes were glowing through the mist. Then it appeared like a minotaur with tusks.

"Kill it!" said Florabelle. "Go on! Kill it!"

"I can't!"

"It will kill you, if you don't."

"It's against my beliefs."

Jasper had returned by this time with Hugh Harcourt.

"Just shoot, Hy. It won't respect you otherwise."

"Hugh! Are you alive?"

"Please, don't tell Gwen."

"Is someone going to kill that beast or not?" asked Jasper.

"But it's half-man!" protested Hyacinth.

"Anyone we know?" asked Florabelle.

The creature raised his human hands and removed the bull's head from his torso.

"Hello, Mother." Alec stood before her in a Nazi uniform. "You're not going to shoot me, are you?"

"I'm not going to kill anyone," said Hyacinth.

"Good." Alec removed a shiny Luger from his leather holster and shot Florabelle between the eyes.

Hyacinth screamed and sat bolt upright in the fourposter. She turned to her husband's side of the bed, but he wasn't there. Lady Radford began to panic. Was this part of the dream or was she awake? The bedside clock read 4:15. Where was he? Footsteps could be heard on the stairs. Moments later Sir Osmond was standing over the bed.

"Did you scream?" asked the actor-knight. She nodded her head unable to speak. "Did you see something outside?"

Hyacinth shook her head, patted his side of the bed, and finally spoke:

"Please, get in."

Radford removed his dressing gown and slid into the bed next to his wife. There was a look of fear on her face that he had never seen before.

"Where were you?" asked Hyacinth.

"Felt a bit peckish. Went down to the kitchen." Radford felt like a cad lying so blatantly to his wife. Alas, there would only be more such lies in the coming months. The Germans had invaded Poland two days earlier. Sir Osmond had been visiting his secret room in the cellar for the past two nights in expectation of a communique from Dickie. He had just received what he had been dreading. Two words: War Declared.

He couldn't tell Hyacinth. She would have to wait for the news later that day like the rest of California. One more item on the list of things he couldn't share with his beloved wife. He had kept her in the dark over Alec's involvement in the ill-fated Warner sabotage and his subsequent flight to Mexico. Going further back, he had never told her the truth about Willi and why he had hired her so quickly.

"Promise me," said Hyacinth, affectionately stroking her husband's face, "If there is another war, you won't leave me again. I couldn't bear it."

"Fear not, my darling" replied Radford drawing his wife closer to him. "His Majesty's forces have no need of a 51-year-old former matinee idol."

Hyacinth kissed him on the lips and said: "You're still *my* matinee idol."

"Are there any more of those to be had?" Radford brought his lips towards hers.

Hyacinth abruptly propped herself up on one arm. "What will happen to Ito? Japan and Germany have formed an alliance. Will he be arrested?"

"We're not in England, Hy. America is neutral. For now." Radford wanted to tell her everything but knew he couldn't. He had signed the Official Secrets Act. He was now part of the war that would unfold at daybreak.

"Will Alec have to serve?"

"Which side?"

Hyacinth stared in annoyance for a moment then burst out laughing: "Is nothing sacred to you, husband?"

"You. Our daughters. And my son and heir, whom I pray will come to his senses before it's too late."

The twin Dromios began howling pitifully outside the bedroom door.

"They'll wake the baby! Let them in, Ozzie."

"It's a dangerous precedent."

"Go on."

Radford walked over to the bedroom door and opened it. He stared down at the Great Danes, who hung their heads in shame and wouldn't meet their master's gaze. Did they know that war had already been declared? Dogs had telepathic powers. The actor-knight was convinced of that. He pointed to the throw rug at the end of the bed. The twin Dromios walked over to it, their toenails clicking on the hardwood floor. Radford turned back wondering if Hyacinth was pleased about the dogs. She was fast asleep. He was wide awake. A moment later, tandem snoring could be heard on the throw rug.

"Cry havoc and let slip the dogs of war." Not exactly the sort of dogs Shakespeare had imagined. The war in Europe that had just commenced would be beyond anyone's imagination. Radford stared up at the darkened sky

and waited till a star shone through. Remembering such moments as a child in Kent, Osmond Radford prayed that his family would be safe in the coming conflict.

How This Book Came To Be Written

His name was Charles Bennett. He had written a play in 1928 called *Blackmail*, which eventually became Great Britain's first talkie directed by a young man named Alfred Hitchcock. Bennett and Hitchcock were born eleven days apart in August 1899. They got along famously and worked together on several subsequent films *including The Man Who Knew Too Much, The 39 Steps, Secret Agent*, and *Sabotage*. When David Selznick brought Hitchcock to Hollywood in 1939, the producer asked the director what writers he should import. Hitch recommended Bennett, who took the next boat over. He worked on *Foreign Correspondent* with his old chum and was nominated for an Oscar. Throughout the 1940s he was Cecil B. DeMille's in-house writer and served the same function for Irwin Allen in the 1950s.

I met Charles Bennett in 1974 at an event celebrating British Cinema. He was chatting with the actress Anna Lee, whom Bennett never ceased to claim he'd discovered, and her husband, Robert Nathan, the author of my favorite novel, *Portrait of Jennie*. Ms. Lee was known as 'the Queen of the Quota Quickies' because of the numerous English B-movies in which she appeared. She and her first husband, director Robert Stevenson, followed Bennett to California where they all became members of the Hollywood Raj. (Bennett was the head of the Beverly Hills Cavalry.)

When the Nathans discovered that we were neighbors, I became a regular visitor to their home where I bonded with Charles Bennett. Anna Lee drafted me into service to assist with an event she was coordinating to save the White Cliffs of Dover from would-be land developers. Over a period of months, I found myself surrounded by numerous British expatriates, who regaled me with tales of the Hollywood Raj.

I lost track of Charles Bennett over the next decade until a man named Jones Harris, the son of Ruth Gordon and Jed Harris, pitched me the notion of a play set in Hollywood during World War II. My thoughts turned to Charles Bennett and the octogenarian author welcomed me like the Prodigal Son to his home in Coldwater Canyon. About an hour into our conversation, the oft-repeated rumor of Errol Flynn being a spy arose. Bennett said it wasn't true and casually mentioned that he, in fact, had been a spy for the British Secret Service in Hollywood. Hitchcock's former collaborator held me spellbound for the next hour with his vivid reminiscences of wartime Hollywood.

Several years after Bennett's death, I attempted to interest Vanity Fair in an article about the secret life of this once famous screenwriter. I contacted my friend, Julian Fellowes, to find out how I could access Charles Bennett's British government files. Vanity Fair never responded to my pitch. I gave up the attempt to reveal my old friend's secret and allowed my imagination to take over. Why not take the idea of a spy in Golden Age Hollywood and turn it into a TV series? Change the hero from a screenwriter to a former matinee idol facing a mid-life crisis, who is coerced into spying by the British Secret Service. Hmmm.

Not long afterwards, I was having lunch with Holly Palance, to whom Julian Fellowes had introduced me a few years earlier. I told her my idea for the series, which I called *Hollywood Raj*. I described it to her as *Downton Abbey* set in 1930s Beverly Hills.

Holly insisted I start writing immediately. I wrote a bible for the series. Julian Fellowes submitted it to Gareth Neame, who had produced *Downton*. I subsequently spent the next two years in development hell.

While waiting for contracts to be concluded, I began writing the novel of *Hollywood Raj*, the first of a series in the proposed Radford Saga.

There are so many people I have to thank: Nicole & Brian Cox, Emma & Julian Fellowes, Gwen & Ian McShane, Robin & Bryan Cranston, Lisa & Michael Lindsay-Hogg, the late Ed Asner, the late Norman Lloyd, Rachelle & Ed Begley Jr., Bob Wallace, the late Ken Welsh, Serena Dessen, Elliott Gould, Julie Garfield, Dabney Coleman, Linda & Neil Dickson, Shawn & Brent Huff, Fred Melamed, Sondi & Pete Sepenuk, Maurice Lipsedge, Michael Swan, Sue & Colin Fox, Kelly & Loren Lester, Marjorie & T.J. Elliott, Nicholas Meyer, Rosie Shuster, Tedde Moore, Liz & Ross Benjamin,

Paula & Richard Benjamin, Drew Bell, Mike Shara, Michele Scarabelli, Carolyn Seymour, Jared Harris, Danny Huston, and Greyson Early.

Special thanks to Sarah Roger and Brian Cutler for making the book available again; Emile Riley Abdelnour, my older brother, who introduced me to my first Raj member; the late Macey Dennis, my oldest brother, who introduced me to books and movies when I was very young.

Finally, the incomparable Ulrika Vingsbo, who in her constant search for new challenges in life, became a publisher and made *Hollywood Raj* her first book for the Vingsbo Press. *Tack*, my darling Ulrika.